MODELS AND CITIZENS

Andrew Sweet

ISBN: 978-0-578-33680-0

Thank you to my wonderful wife, Hollee, for tolerating my writing compulsion.

For beta-reading and editing, thanks to Becky Lipinski, Lesley Raquet, Sally Lopez, and Leila Garrett.

Additional thanks to the Auburn Writing and Critique Group ~ Justin, Donna, Jolene, Aisn ~

Caduceus image by Pulmonological / CC BY-SA (https:// creativecommons.org/licenses/by-sa/3.0)

Prologue

The Orphan Program

A declining birth rate over the previous thirty years had impacted the global economy disastrously. Economists realized too late that year-over-year growth atrophied without an actual growing population. The global response had been to heavily promote childbirth. Each nation attempted to out-breed the others, although no one said this out loud. In the United States, this led to a period of don't-ask, don't-tell adoption and abandonment. The Childhood Investment for Lost Descendants (ChILD) legislation enacted by Congress on May 5, 2150 as a national imperative included the Orphan Program. Any unwanted child could be dropped at an orphanage, to a commitment of half of a percent of total GDP. Negotiations with most private grade schools, boarding schools, and colleges to create a school-to-enterprise pipeline, which propelled many abandoned children toward becoming captains of industry.

The plan worked to some degree. The birth rate in the United States began to stop its decline. But there was the unintentional side effect that many poverty stricken families began to abandon their children into the Orphan Program as the general social welfare programs in America continued to be choked for funds during the economic squeeze.

The Madison Rule

By 2153, global industry innovated its way to another solution. First in China, and eventually in other countries, cloning began to take hold. Children were created in factories, and from there, streamed directly into similar orphan programs in many countries. The birth rate finally increased in Germany, England, then Russia. China's birth rate soared above the rest. All eyes were on the United States, whose religious fundamentalist background had crippled what little existed of their cloning infrastructure. Predominantly northern states adopted cloning programs, which combined with the orphanage programs, added to the positive birth rate, making cloning competitive.

After a multi-year climate destruction event known as Equilibrium split the nation into two halves, creating a desert from most of the mid-west, even the fundamentalist southern states eyed cloning as a recovery strategy. Breakthroughs in League City created a 'Silicon Valley' of cloning in Texas. The Cloning Revolution was in full swing.

In 2157, Regious Madison, proposed a law in Louisiana that if clones were created by a company there, then they were the property of that company, and not actual United States citizens, having not been born, but manufactured. Once proposed, a national discussion emerged, and the national opinion on cloning soured. The term 'clone' was used in such a negative way, that those proponents of cloning shifted to calling clones 'models' instead. In February of the same year, cloning companies began marking their clones with bar-codes on the inside of their wrists, a practice that became widely adopted.

The industry, faced with the prospect of becoming obsolete

in a society which had begun to resent clones generally, supported the Madison Rule in Congress in February of 2164, where it passed both houses with an overwhelming majority vote.

Once the status of clones became enforced by law, the industry expanded. Instead of depending on government compensation for helping resolve the population crisis, clones were purchased for manual labor, and high-risk work, the result being that though the population did rise faster in the United States, the majority of the rise was in what equated to slave labor, which overall drove down wages for everyone else, leading to high unemployment everywhere else.

This fueled the re-branding of several hate organizations, swinging from supporting racial superiority to supporting birthright superiority. One of these organizations was HPM, or the Human Pride Movement, which took the extreme stance that cloning was anathema to God and as such, cloning should be stopped completely.

1

The College Graduate

Tuesday May 17, 2185

Harper concentrated on the crash of the waves as she pushed back in her magnetic-suspension rocker, nudging the ground with the tips of her toes. Straight, black hair, inherited from her mother, fell across her bare shoulders. She closed her hazel eyes and focused on the sound of her breathing, then counted with the waves. Each one relaxed her more and more. Thick, wet air blanketed her skin. She eased into serenity.

"Harper's just outside, Matthew."

Loud, harsh whispers interrupted her meditation. Her eyes opened to the sound.

"I know, Aayushi. Dammit, this is important."

"What do you want? I'm sorry? Absolutely not."

"I expected you to be faithful."

"I expected you not to hit Harper or me. And be sober every once in a while. I guess we're both disappointed."

Harper's micro-mood stabilizer implant struggled to reign in her spiking emotions. Her heart accelerated, fighting back against the increase of melatonin. The moist air formed into a dank cocoon around her as her body sweat mingled with the humidity. She existed in a sealed balloon, and each breath reduced her limited, precious oxygen. The stabilizer notched up, making her a detached observer as her heart now slowed. The world around her became brighter and happier-looking. An artificial spike in endorphins took the edge off, but she wanted her edge. The stabilizer flipped into emergency mode and the artificial high overpowered her ability to concentrate until her mother's voice punched through.

"You're never here, Matthew. When you are here, you're drunk and violent. I've been waiting for thirty years on you."

"I own a restaurant. I gotta go talk to people, keep them entertained, keep paying on this house somehow."

"You own a dive. And the 'people' you talk to there aren't people, Matthew. They're HPM."

The mention of HPM caught Harper's attention. The Human Pride Movement tortured and killed models. The group had more weapons stockpiled than the Texas Rangers. She'd seen them at his bar, with their three-bar tattoos. Even through the haze she could envision the drunken patron telling her how they indicate "God, blood, and country - and no damn clones".

"They're not wrong, Aayushi. We're being replaced!"

"You only think that when you're drinking, Matt. How many have you had? It's not even noon yet."

"Don't you dare change the subject! How could you cheat on me with one of those shills?"

"Models, Matthew, not shills."

Harper visualized her mother flipping her head back and forth with her perpetual black ponytail following the laws of the pendulum. Her mother. Cheating. The idea was laughable. Still, she would have congratulated the woman if she'd gotten the news in confidence.

"How could you cheat with one of ...them?!"

Harper heard the raw hurt in her father's voice. She couldn't stop smiling, still on her endorphin ride, but the goodness had gone out of it. The summer would be another prolonged running battle. She couldn't remember why she had expected an idyllic summer break before she started on her doctorate, or work, or whatever her future held. The spike ebbed just enough for her to understand how sad that idea was. Voices rose again and cut through her concentration.

"One of them? Listen to yourself. He's around, and you're not."

"I'll show you, bitch."

Harper's smile vanished. The stabilizer couldn't keep up. With willpower that she didn't realize she could muster, she forced herself to focus on the situation. Endorphins fought against her, telling her that everything was fine, and she should relax. She struggled to maintain focus and with slow, deliberate thoughts. Harper mustered up the hope that her mother could resolve the situation soon. Harper recognized the wavering in his voice as the tone he took on just before violence erupted.

With all of her conscious effort, she stopped the rocker and held her breath, working up the nerve to intervene. Each noise that escaped through the walls caused an involuntary seizing in her chest.

"What are you going to do? Shoot him? You don't even know where he lives."

"I'll find him. He'll come into Jarro sooner or later, and I'll be there."

There was a good chance the argument would wind down now that he talked about Jarro. Once he got the idea in his head, he'd be on his way there a few minutes later to get plastered drunk. Then one of them, she or her mother, would go get him. The unmistakable high-pitched whine of his proton rifle charging told her that this wasn't going to end that way. Harper sprang from the chair, stumbling as the friction-less seat slid backward faster than she'd anticipated.

She ran to the back door and the voices get louder as she approached. Harper swung the heavy door open, and her eyes fell to her father. He stood with his back to her beside the living room couch. Her mother stood just beyond him, eyes wide with terror.

"Matthew, calm down and put that thing away. Think – your daughter - "

"How could you do this?! How could you cheat on me with one of them? I'm going to find him, and I'm going to kill him. You'll see – "

Harper made eye contact with her mother, though her father's back prevented her from seeing where the gun pointed. Her mother's frantic eyes shot wider. The woman shook her head violently side-to-side and mouthed the words 'go' without sound.

Harper heard the whispering sound of a proton rifle discharge. Then the air pressure changed a millisecond before a sharp retort shook the entire house. A hole appeared in the right side of her mother's face. Her mother looked stunned for half a second before she slumped forward to the floor, knocking the weapon from her father's hands as she fell. Harper tried to scream, but the most she could muster was a wheezy gargling noise as her stabilizer stopped working altogether. A panic attack closed off her airways.

Her father turned toward Harper when she made the sound. He didn't seem to see her as he picked the gun up from where it lay on the floor and placed the barrel under his chin. She clasped her hands over her mouth as he charged it again. As he pulled the trigger, he seemed to recognize her, and tears welled up and streamed from the corners of his eyes. Recognition wasn't enough to change his mind. One more bang, and he collapsed into a pile on the floor in front of her.

Silence.

Harper stood in the porch doorway, unable to move any part of her body. She felt a sunburn forming on the back of her neck. A warm breeze kissed her skin, encouraging her to relax. The sun primed her Vitamin-D pumps. Her mind flashed the images again and again. First, her mother's recognition of her, followed by that sickening look of surprise. Then the hopeless, tormented stare from her father. Two lives gone in less than a minute.

By the time the police arrived, her neck was on fire, and she struggled not to pass out. An officer in the League City Police Department's dark-blue uniform walked across the living room toward her, side-stepping the bodies. His curly black hair and healthy, confident smile reminded her of a classroom assistant who had asked her on a date once. That boy was built like a linebacker, whereas the officer had the build of a soccer player. He seemed nice.

He waved his hand in front of her face and mouthed what looked like her name. He stepped so close that she could smell his aftershave lotion. The man seemed to be yelling something she could not quite make out. The tenseness of her body dissipated enough for her to take a step backward away from the advancing officer, which stopped his screaming and made him smile instead. So she took another step and then another. The man turned her by the shoulders to face the porch where the wooden staircase led to the sandy beach. They circled the house to where several police cars and an ambulance huddled together. In silence, Harper ascended into the back of the ambulance. It seemed like something she should do. When she finished, the policeman stopped moving his mouth, so she guessed she'd done the right thing.

Sometime later, a paramedic slopped sunscreen and aloe onto her burned neck and muttered something else she couldn't understand. She heard words, but they wouldn't reconcile themselves into concepts. Harper laid her body down on a mat in the center of the van and closed her eyes.

2

The Cloned Man

Friday, May 20, 2185

Ordell Bentley watched the Houston Aegis play against the Seattle AirCrawlers. Rain materialized above the display area and fell in thin streaks of static flickers, as four mechs and three drones on each team formed up at opposite ends of the field. Forward drones on both teams seemed confused and lost whenever the hovering goal hoop came close enough for them to score. For Houston, a combination of the rain and cold temperatures kept the team from scoring. Southern drones, optimized for the hot, dry climate, often failed in the dense rain. Seattle drones, heavier and slower because of the weatherproofing, performed better. Mechs labored in combat below the air dance, occasionally taking pot-shots at the opposing team's drones.

Ordell strained to make out the truck-sized mechs, reduced to the size of sheet rock anchors, as they moved across the flat surface. Their holograms collided and then distorted on impact, only to flicker back into focus a moment later in another position. The dancing images brought to mind the only in-person Zephyr game he'd ever experienced - barely a year ago.

A photograph on the mantle captured that game. He looked up at the flickering image positioned on the mantle, which showed him grinning as a drone zipped by in the background. Beside that was another picture of him and the dark-haired woman who had accompanied him, back when she was still too nervous to be called his girlfriend. He stared at the picture, tracing the lines of her face in his mind. Ordell always found it difficult to believe that such a wonderful woman could be his. Of course, like everything else a model possessed, she couldn't be entirely his.

Her lips were the shade of the Rose Red glossy external paint - a color he'd used to restore pseudo-Victorian homes outside of League City. Like the homes, her down-turned eyes were haunted by an air of sadness and loss in their beauty.

The game faded into the background. Ordell reached out for the picture and his hands closed on the frame. The bar code tattooed across his wrist brought a grimace to his face as his bushy brows furrowed up. His teeth clenched shut in the reflection suspended above her warm smile. Ordell let go of the frame and turned away from the mantle, bumping the table. On impact, the dilapidated holovision skipped channels from sports to news.

"...babies. We have to have more babies. That's the only way to make sure that we don't go completely extinct."

A familiar voice expounded on procreation's benefits in the usual way. Ordell glanced back towards the holovision to see Gregory Ramsey's head rotate in a circle. The man's mouth never stopped moving.

"The only way to keep natural-born citizens in control of

11

this country is to out-produce. You have the most critical role. Have babies, lots of them. One point three million clones are produced every year to meet demand, and it's only going to increase. You think those clones won't take your jobs? You think the sterilization works?

"Look, I don't hate clones. Clones work for me in my home. That doesn't mean that I want more clones in America than God-fearing Americans. And why should I be ashamed of that?"

A panning effect swiped Gregory's floating head from view and replaced it with the head of a woman. She stared forward with piercing blue eyes beneath close-cropped blonde hair.

"Mr. Ramsey, what would you say to professional women like me, who don't have any desire for children?"

"You must know my answer to that. I would say that maybe it's time you started thinking about the decline of humanity. There's no reason you can't be successful and do your part to keep humans from going extinct. Look at the Orphanage Program. Professional women can pop out babies too. As long as they're natural-born, the federal government will take care of them, no questions asked. Nine months and back to your life. It's just that simple."

Ordell couldn't see what the anchor thought of that, as the camera had panned back over to Mr. Ramsey and stayed there until he answered the next question. Ordell suspected that he could have guessed what kinds of faces the fiery news host made off-camera though.

"Lots of people - the majority - disagree with you. Women generally don't like your recommendation to 'have more babies' to solve an economic problem. Do you have any new ideas?"

"Well, in the meantime, why don't we add some teeth to the Madison rule? Where are the penalties for companies who fail to sterilize their clones, or mark them properly? What about the Sanctuary States, which don't report escaped clones at all to the federal government? What about the 'underground railroad'? It's past time we do something about the terrorists who fail to take the law seriously. And frankly, maybe the law doesn't go far enough."

"I think you're referring to the 'Freedom Underground'. A political organization. Why are you so obsessed with them?"

"It's time to call them what they are, Janet. Terrorists, plain and simple. They steal from God-Fearing Americans and funnel clones to Sanctuary States. What happens after that? Nobody knows. I tell you what I think, they're organizing, and before long, everyone will be telling me how smart I was to see this coming."

The woman's head came back on, with a look on her face that betrayed her contempt for the man before she seemed to realize that the cameras were on her, and plastered back on her thin smile.

"Thank you, Mr. Ramsey. We'll call you back if that happens."

"Mark my words, Janet. But it's been a pleasure to be on your show."

Only after Gregory finished did Ordell realize that he'd been unable to turn his head away for the entire interview. This man could capture the attention of the very people upon whom he heaped hate. What must he be doing to those "God-fearing Americans" he talked about? Frustration mounted in him as he considered just how little control he had of his life, while people like Gregory Ramsey kept trying to take more.

Lights flashed through his window as a car pulled into his apartment complex. He peeked out between the curtain and a corner of the window to see who pulled up.

The parking lot appeared mostly the same as it had the day before. On its far edge sat the only volantrae he'd ever seen in Tribeca. Like everything else in the community, it lacked major pieces. A tan cover hid the model name and distorted its shape so he couldn't tell what make or model it was. He could tell it used to be self-piloting by the slight bump up in the center of the hood, which operated its sensors. He doubted it would ever fly again though.

A long black luxury car with chrome on everything that would take it marred the "scenic" view. It looked expensive by a ten thousand dollar chrome job. He could tell that it couldn't fly like the Falcon it imitated. It lacked the necessary boosters, and the volantrae with distributed ion engines didn't come with wheels.

When Mark Ruby stepped free of the car, his red hair popping out against a backdrop of gray twilight, Ordell knew who the he was there for.

Even as he rationalized that Mark's presence might have been unrelated to his own, his body tensed up to run. When an angry looking friend emerged from the vehicle as well, Ordell knew they weren't there for the famous Second Avenue prostitutes. May and Juliet, purveyors of the oldest profession, would be lonely tonight. Both of these men were HPM sympathizers, and both of them were friends of Matthew Rawls, who happened to be married to the woman in his photograph.

"Come out here, shill!"

Mark positioned himself center in front of Ordell's apartment door, removing all doubt. Ordell pulled away from the velvet orange print curtain and ducked down to hide his silhouette. As heavy as it was, it still permitted a surprising amount of light through.

He fled to the back of the house, stopping only to pick up his go-bag. When Ordell pulled the bag up from its hiding place, he felt his shirt snag on an old wound. He reached up to his chest and touched a scar hiding under his shirt. He would not becoming a red line on someone's expense account.

Black duffel bag in hand, he needed only to make his exit. The best thing about his apartment was that it backed to a paved alleyway, and then to the trees. The second best was that it was on the first floor. All he had to do to escape was pop out the useless Climate Control unit and crawl through the opening. If he had the time to put it back, it would look like he hadn't even been at home. He could do it in about five minutes altogether - time Ordell suspected he didn't have.

He shoved the machine out with a loud crash and dove through. As he did, his foot caught on the window ledge, and he swung head-first downward toward the ground. He got an immediate mouthful of gravel and, judging by the pain and metallic taste in his mouth, lost a tooth or two. He had also skinned both palms in the process. Blood dripped from open wounds to the ground at his feet, but he ignored it and looked instead toward his car.

But there was no car there. An excellent place to hide a car, the alley behind the hotel was a lousy place to keep an eye on one. He cursed under his breath.

On foot, he re-evaluated his escape plan. To the east lay the beach. He could follow the sand around to the main road if he wanted. The road was drier. Once there, he only had to make it down the country road to Seven-Corners, where he would find himself with a small chance of blending back into anonymity. But men of hate were not the same as men of ignorance. Mark would notice his absence and the missing climate control unit. They would block the lone country road leaving the infected wound of a community. To the west, there lay the possibility he might not come back out with every piece of himself intact. The blossoming swampland had all of the real swamp accommodations, including cotton-mouth snakes and alligators.

Ordell loosened gravel wedged between his teeth and his

gums. He spit out a mouthful into a bloody splash on the pavement. With his tongue, he confirmed that the dive had cost him a tooth, but at least it was in the back where nobody would notice. Half of the bar code tattoo on his wrist no longer existed. He'd often wondered how hard it would be to get rid of that tattoo – apparently not very hard if he didn't mind the pain and did it quickly. It steadily throbbed now, though.

There was no more time to inventory the damage he'd unwittingly imposed on himself. He gathered up his black bag, spit out another mouth-full of blood, and headed into the nascent swamp, the decision made.

3

Friends of Humanity

Friday, May 20, 2185

The thin hospital gown rubbed against her bare shoulders every time she moved. Even the simple act of breathing created pain where the papery cloth shifted over her skin. Clicks and beeps from various machines confirmed that her hearing was restored. Harper swallowed when a faint scraping noise sounded nearby, yet her eyes refused to open. Someone else was in the room with her. She remained as still as possible while she listened intently. The sound continued with starts and stops; each time slightly closer than the last. Her heart pounded as she lay shrouded in darkness.

"Hi, Harper," said a distant, masculine voice.

Her eyelids finally parted, revealing a hazy sea of greens no more useful to her perception than the preceding black. Harper bolted upright and swung her legs around toward the sound, straining to make out anything at all within the writhing mass of shapes. An opaque turquoise blob materialized before her. Harper held her breath, unsure whether to trust the voice as real among her spurious hallucinations. The man's voice again penetrated the acoustic ensemble surrounding her.

"Harper, can you hear me?"

Thick overtones, dense and deep, caused her imagination to fill in what her eyes could not. Her mental image of the man strongly resembled the hero from the cover of a romance novel she'd finished only a few days prior. She pulled the thin bedsheet up to cover her exposed knees, nodded and stared at the wall behind him without making eye contact.

"Good. I'm Doctor William Jefferson. How do you feel?"

Slightly less nervous at the testament that he was a doctor, Harper shrugged as nonchalantly as she could. The crackling, swooshing sound a proton rifle charge interrupted her movement. A thunderous clap of discharging power followed and she tensed her body for the inevitable impact of the proton beam. Then, as quickly as the new sounds dominated her consciousness, they faded away, only to be replaced by her father's voice.

"Not with one of them!"

Images poured through her mind faster than she could interpret them. Each supplanted the one before it with frightening rapidity. The blue and white flame-shaped release of the proton rifle faded, leaving behind her mother's damaged face. After the flash, Harper stood alone, and the surreal scene evaporated into a hospital room where an older man with kind eyes stared, fixated on her well-being. She felt dampness on her cheeks where rivulets of tears had formed.

"I'm f-fine."

"You can talk to me, Harper. I'm a social worker and your assigned psychologist. Whatever you say to me is privileged," the man told her.

"I'm still fine," she protested meekly.

"You've been through a lot. Do you remember anything? I was told--"

The man paused for a few seconds as she heard fingers slide across the smooth surface of a pinamu as he searched for something.

"--that you don't remember anything from yesterday?"

She wished with all of her heart that that was still true. But as she sat only half-listening, her mind busily collated her mental flashes into cohesive memories.

"Didn't."

"What was that?"

"I didn't remember. I do now. Some."

"What do you remember?"

Still not entirely sure what was real or not from her memories, she slowly regained confidence as more time passed. Harper told the man about the series of images she had seen, and that she now believed they were memories reforming.

As she awaited his response, she took the man in with her restored vision. White hair sprouted from his head and reached skyward, framing a narrow face with deep, inset brown eyes visible through thick eyeglass lenses. A hot pink tie contrasted against a checkered shirt beneath a smoking jacket with elbow patches. Everything about the man supported his social worker demeanor, down to worn shoes and argyle socks.

"What do *you* think?" she asked.

"Oh," he stammered, pushing his glasses back up on his face quickly before collapsing his hand back down to his lap. Then he choked out a cough before he continued.

"Uh… you had quite a bad experience, Harper," he told her without making eye contact. "A bad experience which may be causing some dissociation. You'll remember more with time."

He rose to his feet. The man's glasses slid further down his nose, but this time he didn't correct them. He gazed intensely at Harper over the tops instead.

"Do you have anyone you'd like me to call for you?"

She answered his unexpected question honestly by swinging her head slowly from side to side. Her eyes welled up again.

"Here," he told her, advancing in her direction with hand outstretched. Before she could think about it, her hand had left her side to intercept the flat data-coin, about an inch in diameter, which he pushed toward her.

"It's someone who can help if you decide you need it."

"Th-thank you," she said, wrapping her hand around the object so tightly that her knuckles turned white.

"Call anytime. You are important. You matter."

The sound of his footsteps faded as he departed. She breathed a deep sigh of relief when the door clicked into place behind him, then lowered the coin down onto the arm of her bed.

The door swung back open automatically a few seconds later to admit a robot that resembled a hovering end table. Upon its back was a glass of orange juice and something that may have been eggs and toast at one time but had degenerated into a crispy pile of browns. The bot settled beside the bed and, once stable, raised the 'meal' to Harper's level. She could only stomach the orange juice, which she drained in a single draught before placing the empty glass back on the tray.

"I'm finished," she told the bot, which then flashed a green light acknowledging her before it lifted back off and returned the way it had approached.

She took the next few moments to examine the room with her now functioning eyes. A host of machines loomed around her bed on the opposite side from her legs. As she looked more closely, she could see that they were interconnected parts of a single humming wall of vibrating electronics. She followed the wall upward and discovered that it curved over the top of the bed, so high that she hadn't noticed before. The wall and ceiling wrapped around the bunk, complete with an awning that looked as though it could connect with the floor for privacy. The crowded space reminded her vaguely of her dorm room from college, down to the faux privacy provided by temporary partitioning.

Three light raps interrupted her observations. Without a pause, the door swung open to admit a man with a thin brown mustache who would only have come up to her nose at standing height. He scampered to replace the social worker on the narrow orange seat made of molded plastic.

"Detective Jasper," he said, without looking at her directly. She gleaned it was an introduction, even though his mannerisms were agnostic as to whether he was Detective Jasper, or if he expected her to be. She absently placed the cylindrical communicator on the bed beside her as she waited for the man to elaborate on his presence. The officer's brown eyes paused at the communicator before finally swinging towards her face. Still, he said nothing as he stared unblinking at her.

"Somebody was already here," she whispered to him guiltily, not sure why she felt that she had to explain.

"I can see that. How long have you associated with Friends of Humanity?" He nodded his forehead toward the data-coin on the table. She hadn't noticed the symbol stamped on the face looked - a lowercase 'h' with an extended left leg. Harper visualized the 'h' transforming into an 'f' for Friends of Humanity.

"The psychologist left that."

He let out an exaggerated sigh and paused for a long time as air slowly hissed through his lips and nasal passages, reminding Harper of deflating an inner-tube.

"Well, I guess there's no kind way to do this."

The officer paused again and shifted uncomfortably. As he did, his worn brown suit revealed a small hole near his ankle. It was clear he didn't make a lot of money enforcing the law.

"Your father was a member of a radical group called the Human Pride Movement. Did you know that?"

She assumed that he already knew the answer to the question before he'd asked it, so she didn't lie. HPM frequented her father's pub since she could remember. He'd sold to them the same as he'd sold to the police and the local politicians, at first. Over time, as Equilibrium approached and the oceans rose and grasslands shriveled, the police had stopped coming, then the politicians, so that eventually the only people to frequent her father's bar were HPM. It didn't surprise her that he'd become a member. She didn't know, but nodded anyway.

"Did you know that Friends of Humanity is a charitable foundation that funnels money into HPM?"

Harper pulled the robe tighter around herself as the room temperature dropped precipitously. Icy shivers reverberated through her body and her breath stopped. Neurons fired as she connected the concepts in her mind – HPM was keeping an eye on her.

"That data-coin you have is one of theirs. And — well, Friends of Humanity are paying for his funeral. Do you know anything about that?"

Silently, she indicated that she didn't have any idea. The man's response was to pull out a data-coin of his own, dirty and bent as though he'd worn the thing through a car accident. He leaned his face very close to hers and stared directly into her welling eyes.

"Don't call them. Don't accept them as visitors. If you see them again, call me."

He patted his chest to show her his communicator affixed

there outside his coat jacket lapel. She accepted the data-coin from his hand and lay it next to the other.

"He said he was a doctor..."

"He may have been a doctor, but not your doctor. Or...."

The man paused thoughtfully and reached for a pinamu screen hanging from her bed stand. He examined it for a moment, then returned it.

"What did he look like?"

"White hair. Older, like you. Thick eyeglasses."

"Name?"

"William ... Jefferson?"

"The Senator from Georgia?"

She hadn't made that connection, but she did know that the man she'd met probably wasn't the politician three terms into a government career.

"Not that William Jefferson," she protested.

"Doesn't matter. No psych-anything has been to see you today. If he gave you that data-coin, he's Friends of Humanity."

Then, as her anxiety ratcheted up more, his voice and demeanor broke with compassion. She tensed in expectation of an endorphin spike, but nothing happened. Her hand shot up behind her head, and she winced as she touched a bandage on her neck.

"They had to remove it," the detective said. "The thing overloaded and shorted out. I'm sure the doc will tell you about it."

His tone softened then.

"Look, don't worry about Friends. I'll have officers watching the door for you. They won't let anybody else get in here who's not supposed to."

On cue, the door opened behind him, and two men in uniforms entered. One was a short, stocky man with no neck and an orange-reddish sunburn covering half of his face. The other had dark curly hair and an effortless grin, with a chocolate complexion.

"Officers Aaron Hecht and Idris Agemba. They'll take care of you while you're here."

With that, he pivoted quickly by placing the point of his toe behind the heel of his scuffed black shoes and spinning around on the linoleum flooring. Despite his disheveled appearance, the move was swift and sharp. He gave the impression of clicking into place when he ended the movement and addressed the officers.

"Nobody except the doctor and nurses. Everyone coming in here shows valid ID."

They nodded in silent unison and stood as he continued to stare well beyond the point of it being awkward. One turned to leave the room, and the other followed closely behind. The door swung to a close, so she shifted her gaze back to Detective Jasper, who returned an empathetic yet slightly annoyed look before following the pair from the room.

Harper struggled not to ruminate. She pushed down memories as quickly as they surfaced, yet somehow not fast enough. The memories sewed themselves together despite her efforts. Finally, she saw everything in full graphic detail. Her heart raced, and she froze in place, breathing in rapid, shallow breaths as a panic attack began swirling in her chest. She skipped a breath, then another. The seconds trickled past and congealed into minutes before she could steady her breathing. She stared numbly at the wall as nurses came and went. They tried to talk to her, but conversation was risky, given her lack of emotional control. So she waited.

Sunday, May 22, 2185

Two days passed before she was finally cleared to go. As predicted, the doctor told her about the removal of the stabilizer. She would get it back after an 'appropriate period of mourning.' There was some concern that she might short it out again. The device was designed to handle everyday anxiety peaks, not extremes like a murder-suicide.

A nurse stepped through the door and into the room. "Hi, Harper, dear." The woman addressed Harper as a child although the woman couldn't have been much older. Her skin was the shade of vanilla ice cream, and dark chocolate hair topped her head. A half-sleeve of tattoos resembling a Japanese ocean mural covered her left arm. A skinny dragon wrapped itself around her bicep and ended with a thick face breathing a short burst of fire near her elbow. Her name tag read 'Rachel.'

"Today's the day! How do you feel?"

Harper didn't answer, which seemed expected as Rachel continued without waiting for a reply.

"Well, we kept you as long as we could."

Harper only looked downward without responding.

"Are you okay, dear?"

"Yeah," Harper lied, getting to her feet. "It's fine."

The nurse picked up Harpers' clothes from a surface on the far side of the equipment and handed them to her with kindness in her eyes. Harper's bare feet collected little grains of sand as she carried her clothing into the bathroom for privacy, where she quickly changed before making her way back towards the bed. She slipped on dark-brown hospital flats, which someone had placed underneath the edge of the bed before she felt she was ready to address Rachel.

"Do you have my purse?" Harper asked, on the off chance that one of her rescuers had had the foresight to grab it.

"Purse?" Rachel asked. Then she shook her head, indicating that she hadn't. Harper's eyes flitted across the room, and for a moment, she met Rachel's, who looked away almost immediately. But it wasn't quick enough to prevent Harper from seeing the thin lines on the corners of each of her eyes. Rachel only *seemed* Harper's age from afar, but those lines gave it away. Rachel was at least five years older, if not ten.

"Love, go to the nurses' station. Do you remember how to get there?"

"To the right?"

The nurse bobbed her head quickly and then proceeded with the work of clearing the room.

When she passed through the door, she saw that only one of the officers stood guard still. Harper wondered if he would follow her back to her home, or even if he would continue to guard the room after she was gone. He smiled at her and stepped forward as she emerged.

"Harper, hey," he grinned at her as if they were old friends.

"Officer Agemba," she greeted him courteously and nodded, but didn't smile.

He held out something to her, and she grabbed for it before she knew what it was. Her hands closed on a small pendant, just the size of a charm from the bracelets she'd liked to wear as a child. She held it up to see what it was in the light. It was translucent green with gold trim. Ridges on the back of it gave it away as yet another data-coin. This one showed the HPM three-bars logo emblazoned into its surface. Behind the pendant, she could see Idris' grinning white teeth.

"You have friends everywhere, Harper," he told her, as the smile morphed from a grin into a thin, knowing smile.

Her numbness subsided, rapidly replaced by fear.

"Friends, Harper. Everybody needs friends. Can I get you a ride?"

She nodded in silence, not knowing what else to do. She clasped her hand around the object, terrified to return it yet afraid to keep it. She walked away from him with rushed steps as she shoved the pendant into her pocket. Behind her, she heard him fish for his communicator in his uniform pockets and begin to talk into it.

"Yep. Harper Rawls. That Harper. How soon can you get here..."

The message was clear – Human Pride Movement had people everywhere. They could be her friends, or they could be her enemies, but she couldn't get rid of them.

Half an hour later, she arrived at home. The driver flashed her a hand sign when she exited the overused volantrae and didn't charge her for the ride. She let herself in through the front door and latched it behind her.

They know where I live.

When she crossed over the doorway, she no longer felt at home. The prudent beige walls seemed foreign and strange, not like the walls she remembered from her childhood. Her eyes hit the mantel and then drifted down to the two rust-colored spots on the floor. The two stains had soaked into the carpet, and neither looked like the last remnants of lost lives. She circumvented them as best she could, and then fled to her bedroom.

Harper's body heaved violently from sobbing. She jettisoned the brown sandals and fell into her pillow. She fought against tears because she wasn't sure she would ever stop crying once she started. Shudder after shudder went through her as she screamed. Dry convulsions rocked her body and her eyes threatened again to disgorge their contents down the sides of her face. She let tears out in rivers.

Harper had a backup to the stabilizer, in the form of little round pills that she used to take before the implant. She fished through the nightstand, retrieved her pill compact, surprised that there were any of the bead-shaped tablets left, and dropped two into her mouth. When they finally started working, she remembered how poor a substitute they were. Exhaustion swept over her, and took over her anxiety.

Harper focused what little she retained of her willpower on slowing her writhing body. Then she dug into her past, looking for signs that she missed - hints that she might have somehow prevented the tragedy. Her father had always been an oppressive, angry man for as long as she'd known him. He wielded insults like daggers and fists like, well, fists. But the proton rifle was a level of violence of which she would not have ever thought him capable.

Thursday, May 26, 2185

Four days passed with Harper confined to the safety of her childhood room. Ancient stuffed animals stared at her from various perches, along with their wall-poster accomplices. Beyond the door and into the hallway, death lurked. A gnawing feeling grew in her stomach as her steady diet of pills took its toll. She ran out that morning.

Stop being such a victim, she told herself, angry at her helplessness.

Armed with self-admonishment, Harper pulled herself slowly up from the bed. She smoothed the wrinkles in her stained sundress, though they immediately returned as soon as her hand passed over them. The act made her feel a little more in control.

Step by step, she staggered down the hallway with unsure footing, feeling along the sides when she could, rendered incapable of walking by the heavy emotional burden. Family pictures suspended from the walls, untruthful testaments to a happiness that never really was.

She made it to the kitchen before her rally subsided. Then she melted against the stove and slid down to the floor in a ball. The kitchen cabinet on the island across from where she landed hung slightly ajar, broken like everything else her father touched. Through the opening, she could see a bottle of whiskey stash, though she couldn't quite make out the label in the dark recesses. She crawled across the floor and pulled the cabinet the rest of the way open.

She stared at the bottle for a while. It reminded her of her father's glassy-eyed stare when he couldn't walk and patrons walked him out of the bar, then called her mother. Patrons like Greg Reed always seemed to have time to leer on those occasions when Harper's fourteen-year-old self helped to fetch him. The pedophile groomer took her virginity the next year. Her childhood was stained with clumsy hands that smelled like fermented cabbage plucking at unripe body parts. Silent consent was one of the rewards reaped from her fear of embarrassing her overbearing patriarch.

She popped the cork out.

"The good stuff has a cork."

Her father's voice came from nowhere - maybe another hallucination. Harper studied the bottle, took a deep whiff, and smelled the combination of whiskey and old tobacco. Nobody else she knew could even afford the 'bad' tobacco from Louisiana. Her father always could, even when complaining about stolen jobs. HPM paid well.

She bit back rage as she pulled the bottle to her lips and drew a short sip and inhaled at the same time. Her nose burned in protest when the searing fluid threatened to come back up. But the first drink stayed down, so she took another. There seemed nothing spectacular about the sensation, except perhaps, the nausea building in the pit of her otherwise empty stomach.

Harper took one more swig. This time, she nailed it perfectly. She held her breath in until the liquid was deep in the back of her throat, then forced it down, exhaling instead of inhaling.

She still hurt. After a few more, she didn't. Her parents, her college degree, the marred memory of her own home – all of these vanished. She sat dumbly, vaguely aware that she should be in pain, and that only moments before, she could barely walk from the jagged emotional knife in her heart. Harper's thoughts cleared and once again subjected themselves to her control, or at least, she felt that they did, which might have been good enough. She leaned back against the refrigerator door and felt her shoulders loosen.

Harper knew that the reprieve was temporary. As soon as she stopped drinking, reality would come back again and re-assert itself violently into her life. But that thought was as momentary as her alcohol-induced peace, and she found herself slipping slowly into the deepest sleep she'd had in days.

She awoke in the same uncomfortable position on the kitchen floor. The bottle was half-empty, and she was thankful to have the remainder. As she struggled to her feet, this time it was a physical pain that crippled her, and her brain screamed out as dim light assaulted her eyes. Her sole reprieve was that the windows were still tinted nearly black, as they were the day of the shooting.

Harper filled a glass with cold water from the tap before remembering that the tap water came out salty this close to the invading ocean. Equilibrium had outpaced the water treatment system. She dumped the brine into the sink and tried her luck crossing the kitchen floor. Harper screamed when she stubbed her right big toe on the half-full bottle.

The refrigerator saved her. With its built-in desalination unit, Harper filled the glass with clean, cold water. The vice-like pressure in her head and the bitter taste in her thirsty mouth subsided with a long swallow. Then until she felt hungry. Minutes later she was mid-way through making a peanut butter and jelly sandwich when she heard a sound from the living room. She turned to face the source of the noise, but found only silence. Harper became acutely aware of the overpowering aroma of death - an acrid amplification of rusted iron drenched in simple syrup.

As she listened, her jellied slice of bread slid face-first to the ground. The silence stifled her. Harper collapsed to the linoleum, gasping so hard that her sides complained with short stabs of pain.

A steady throb in her foot reminded her of the bottle she had kicked earlier, so she groped around until she found it again. She managed the cork and took three big swigs, the final lasting twice as long as the first. That feeling of numbness she sought came on in seconds. She hugged the whiskey to her chest and welcomed the upcoming stupor.

That's when she heard rapping on her front door. Harper staggered her way toward it, dragging her toes across the cold linoleum and over rough carpet. When she opened the door, she stared up at the largest man she had ever seen. A second later, he collapsed before her like a demolished building.

4

Awkward Conversations

Thursday, May 26, 2185

Ordell awoke in pain. His eyes burned and watered, blurring everything he tried to take in. He slid his tongue across his parched lips. The square corners of a window gradually came into focus. The soft cushions beneath him were not the ground upon which he had fallen. His first thought was of Aayushi.

His heart quickened as he realized that he'd made it to his lover's house. Something shuffled beyond his field of vision so he strained to gain a better view. His lover stared back at him with wild eyes from an oversized armchair. Not Aayushi. The eyes were undeniably hers, but the lips, thin and pale, contrasted the lush red from his memories. His mind denied the difference, until it clicked who the impostor was.

"Harper?"

"Who are you?"

"Ordell Bentley. Where's your mother?"

Her face contorted as flashes of anger and confusion swept across it.

"I'm too late," he muttered, more to himself than to the silent girl opposite him.

"Almost a week now," she slurred, staring off into the distance at something he couldn't see.

All of the air sucked from his lungs at once. Sickness gathered in his stomach. A week meant that the afternoon he spent shouting at tepid zephyr playing, his lover had already passed from the earth. And the lie continued as he struggled through the swamplands and nearly drowned in the murky depths of a hidden river. That Aayushi's daughter looked just like her was a cruel joke. It made him want to reach across and take her hand. It made him want to console her and tell her everything would be okay - not to worry. But he would have been talking to Aayushi, and this child wasn't Aayushi, no matter how her hazel eyes and coal-black hair tempted his senses. He didn't know how to soothe her. And so he stared too.

Harper sat without words still before him. Her eyes swung from discolored patches of carpet up to the cluttered mantel. At the end of her gaze sat a picture of the man Aayushi used to love enough to marry. The man looked innocuous in the bright sunlight, holding a bass on a line and grinning with a battle's success well won. Boundless anger lurked beneath that amiable smile. Harper's eyes shifted back to Ordell, so piercing that he felt every thought laid bare.

"Are you a model?"

His body tensed at the question. Two types of people asked this: those who would follow it up with some vulgarity about shills, or those who feigned empathy with shallow regard. Few concerned themselves to learn what it meant to be a noncitizen in the United States. Ordell wondered then whether Harper held her father's beliefs or her mother's. He answered by way of nodding his head. He then flashed his scarred tattoo, answering the next question people ask before she could insult him with it: can I see your tattoo?

She revealed nothing more of herself or her intentions. Ordell distinguished the smell of alcohol, mingled with vomit, sweat, and urine. Part of him wanted to ask how long she had been there alone. Another part wanted to scream and cry, and plead for Aayushi's return. That part of him insisted on being alone with his pain. But the indentured class's skill was to subjugate emotion - and his reflex, the same. So instead, he made conversation.

"Are you okay?" he asked. It was a stupid question and he tried to recover. "I mean, of course not, but is there someone to help you?"

"Nobody can help me," she retorted, an unprovoked anger clouding her sunken eyes. They resumed their dance around the room. She pulled one of her sleek tanned hands toward her mouth, only to set it back down again. He watched her do this three times, her face evolving with each movement. The first mask coldly uncaring, to the point of aggressive dismissal. An intermediate look panned across so quickly that he couldn't interpret it, and that was book-ended by something he placed as mistrust or apathy.

"Why were you with her?"

Ordell thought about the question. That night that he drank too much at Jarro in the hostile company. Ordell's keys went missing that windy evening, maybe for his safety, or more likely for the entertainment of the barflies who collectively hated shills. It was a shit car, so he didn't have to worry about people stealing it. Aayushi, too gorgeous and kind, and he, too drunk to walk, and the two of them somehow leaving together anyway.

Words fled from him as he attempted to form them. He sat up and pulled himself forward on the edge of the cushion, resigned to return to Emergent Biotechnology, who by now had noticed him missing. Better for him, and for her, to avoid obsessing over what neither could fix.

"I'm sorry for your loss," he muttered as he pushed himself to rise. Still unable to support his body, he sank back down into the beige cushions, exhausted from the effort.

Harper didn't respond. Her bony fingers drummed on the chair's arm. A few seconds later, she rose and padded barefoot across the living room toward the kitchen, filled a glass, and brought it back to him. The smell of the room became even more overpowering as she approached. He then understood that *she* was the source of the odor that hung so heavily in the air. He accepted the glass anyway.

"Nothing's clean," she half-apologized while avoiding eye contact. Harper re-positioned herself back into the chair. She seemed more composed. Her stillness cued him to drink down the questionable liquid, which may have been water. He couldn't be sure how it tasted because the musty smell seemed to saturate everything. Still, he felt energy restored throughout his body as he drained the cup of its contents.

"Harper," he began, "your mother was kind to me when others weren't."

She turned away from him as though she didn't want to hear. He kept talking anyway, and told her everything he could think of about what their relationship had been to him. At times he had to pause to correct the wavering in his voice when he invoked memories of Aayushi. Ordell lacked the gift of oratory, but he continued to spin words, if not for her benefit then for his own.

During the first few minutes of his explanation, Harper nodded and occasionally glanced back towards him. When Harper turned to the window, she let out a stream of laughter which escalated from a slight chuckle into a harsh cackle.

She leaned forward in the direction she stared while her

face scrunched into a look of stabbing pain. She lurched sideways and almost fell backward into the kitchen in a physiological response to something he couldn't understand. Ordell tried to catch her, only to realize that he still hadn't fully regained mastery of his muscles and fell back to the couch again. She tumbled down, missed the chair, and landed backward on the floor. Her sundress flew up and revealed the thick, white cotton underwear beneath.

The cackle morphed into the free, wild laugh of an insane person. She rolled over on the floor with her head cocked back, screeching laughter at him. Oblivious bliss stamped into her features.

The laugh broke the tension. Ordell erupted into nervous reciprocal laughter. Harper responded with an intensity that continued to grow until eventually, the two screamed violent laughter in unison. Ordell forced himself to stop.

"Why are you laughing?" He muttered while trying to stifle his response, conscious of betraying his lover's memory with an offensive celebration.

"So...that whole time you were talking, I was thinking about where I can get another drink."

The grin provoked by his laughter fell into a thin frown. The fickle, transient emotion forged of awkwardness and cathartic response faded. At the same time, the death of his lover still hung in the air. Harper's grin remained fixed in place.

"You're horrible at explaining things. You go on forever," Harper continued.

Pained that she didn't reflect his empathy, Ordell attempted an immature response that he was far too old to wield.

"Maybe you're bad at listening."

"Don't feel bad, Ordell. I kind of like you for that. If you're this bad at explaining, you've got to be telling the truth."

After a short pause, she continued.

"Why were *you* laughing?"

Ordell shrugged his shoulders and scrunched his nose, then changed the subject.

"It's ripe in here."

Her eyes clouded and Ordell regretted his callous words. She continued to smile, but now in a more strained way that told him his attack penetrated. Harper pulled herself back up from the floor and pressed her dress flat with open fingers as if trying to recapture whatever remained of her dignity.

He struggled to sit up. The pain in his left cheek spiked as he closed and opened his mouth involuntarily.

"I could use a drink too."

Ordell offered a shared drink as an olive branch. She blinked once and then leaned slightly forward, eyebrows furrowed.

"What happened to you? You knocked, and then by the time I got to the door, you'd passed out. I could barely pull you inside."

She looked at him askance. She seemed to be trying to make sense of him but failing. Before he could answer, she continued without waiting.

"It's been a pretty shitty week, Ordell. I'm taking a shower; then I need to get out of here. Help yourself to whatever you want."

She generally waved toward the house in mock invitation, as though there were anything worth wanting other than Aayushi. The gesture reminded him of his lover, as she'd often walked towards the bathroom with her head held high and with an elegant stride. Aayushi did that when she'd just gotten the last word in a fight. Harper was as poised and graceful as Aayushi had ever been, even in her soiled dress and bare feet - save a slight stumble into the hallway wall.

He pulled his thick hands over his dense eyebrows and

down across the right side of his sweaty face. The stagnant air irritated his lungs, but he managed every breath he needed to recover from the bout of laughter. He strained ribs with every inhale. The mottled side of his face throbbed.

Harper's absence gave Ordell unwanted time to think. He sometimes felt that he was only a complicated robot made of flesh and blood. If he looked too far within, he feared seeing the machinations at work. He wondered if normal humans felt more deeply than models like him, as the fliers distributed around his work-site always claimed. He questioned if models fell in love.

Aayushi talked him down when he got like this. When he allowed himself to get sucked into the stereotypes he'd heard since he was barely free of his second birth ten years earlier.

Shills had no feelings. They were robots. They couldn't love. They had no honor and didn't know respect. Therefore, they were unworthy of consideration or agency. Shills were little more than animals.

It was too late to push back the thoughts, and this time, there was no Aayushi to stem the tide. He closed his eyes and tried to think of other things, but only Aayushi came to mind. When he opened them again, Harper stood before him in straight jeans and a blue halter top. Her freshly cleaned hair was pulled back into a thick ponytail, more clearly revealing her weary, makeup-free eyes and face.

"Are you coming?" No smile graced her lips.

Ordell tested his strength first by lifting one leg, then the other. He swung them back to the ground and pulled himself to his feet, finally able to stand. The idea of spending more time in that dank, foul-smelling house turned his stomach, so he followed her through the open door and out into the haze of descending twilight beyond. The lock engaged automatically behind him as he cleared the doorway. No sooner had she approached the curb than a self-piloting volantrae arrived, and the door opened.

"Jarro, please," she ordered, then slid over to make room for him to squeeze his massive frame onto the seat beside her.

5

Jarro

Thursday, May 26, 2185

Jarro was close enough to walk to, given enough evening sun. Harper had walked it before when she had to. The proximity meant that it was faster for the volantrae to take the paved earthbound road than to merge into the skyway. Gnarled oak trees flashed outside of Harper's window as the vehicle made its way down the two-lane farm road that connected their private drive to her father's obsession. Squeezed in beside her sat a giant with his teeth chattering with every bump and a singular focus on the road ahead. They had both been cast into cruel circumstances in which neither had volunteered to participate.

The volantrae dropped them off in an abandoned parking lot behind the one-time-ironic shack of a bar. She remembered it as a source of fear, but the place had lost its power with her father's death. Now, it was only a tin-lined building with enough alcohol in it to level a small town in the right circumstances. She owned it now. Or if not now, then soon. The idea turned her stomach.

Harper made her way in through the back door, where two security sentries scanned her for her biosignature. Once verified, they backed away to let her past, and Ordell followed unchallenged as she navigated through an abandoned kitchen with pots and glasses hanging from the low ceiling. She heard pots jangle behind her as Ordell failed in his attempts to dodge the suspended cookware.

The two emerged through bat-wing doors that separated the kitchen from the bar. Ordell lowered his massive frame onto the first bar stool he reached, while Harper remained behind the counter. She shuffled behind the counter, looking for glasses below. Then she remembered the martini glasses were with the pots, dangling from a rack over her head. Harper pulled one down and placed it on the bar before clutching at the mahogany edges, slamming her eyes closed as her insides tumbled into devastation. She turned toward Ordell, and their eyes met, hers full of tears and his full of pain. He turned away first, and she sunk back into thought and rummaged through liquor bottles without seeing what they were.

"This is where you met my mother?"

"I guess...," Ordell responded in a deep guttural voice, and stared past her into the kitchen. Harper waited in silence, tilting her head.

"We didn't mean to fall in love," Ordell finally spoke. "It just happened."

"Love," she repeated, taking her time with the word. Drawing it out gave it a mocking tone and she clipped the word off, turning the soft 'v' into an 'f'. She turned the term over in her mind to tease out its meaning. Instead of insight, she caught a mental flash of her mother mouthing the word 'go'. Harper shook her head to clear the image and turned away from Ordell to find the glass she'd taken down seconds before.

She filled her glass half-full of a green apple liqueur. Harper grabbed another from the rack and filled this one as well, which she placed in front of him while he continued.

"Your mother talked about you. A lot. She was very proud."

Harper brushed her hand across her face to hide the glare she knew was there. Intertwined victims or not, this man's familiarity with her mother still grated her.

"No. Maybe… but it doesn't matter. She's not here, is she?"

"I … I thought you wanted to talk," he said.

She forced her eyes up to his, but couldn't hold them. Glancing down again, she raised her martini glass and swallowed the entire drink at once.

"It's not your fault," she admitted. "I'm not even sure why we're here. I can't be home right now. I don't want company, but here you are."

"I'm not company," he protested. "I'm...nobody, I guess. Your mother –"

He trailed off, his voice wavering. Harper poured herself another drink while she waited for him to decide whether or not to continue. When he didn't, she shared her own experience.

"You know in those old holovids, the soldier crawls through the trench, knowing that any minute if he raises his head, he might take a bullet. Maybe even if he doesn't? That was every day in our house."

Ordell's huge hand closed around the martini glass, and the entire thing disappeared inside of his fist.

"Aayushi told me some, but she didn't like to talk about it."

Harper paused, remembering the feeling with far too much clarity.

"She took a lot of the abuse."

She didn't tell him that once a month, her father came

home later than usual, or drunker than usual, or both. He accepted nothing but an impossible level of perfection from her mother. Everything had to be in place as he expected it to be. Although he never bothered to share *when* he was coming home, his food had to be warm and what he felt like eating. Harper had to be finished with schoolwork and in bed. When she let herself think about all the times she had been brandished, suspended between two struggling titans, she could see the roots of her perpetual anxiety forming.

"She couldn't leave. She wanted to, she told me so," Ordell said in a hushed voice.

"I know. When I left for college, Mom told me that she would be right behind me. But every time I asked her, the answer was always 'soon.'"

When Harper said 'every time,' she made it sound as though she constantly nagged her mother to leave. In fact, 'every time' was precisely twice, once when she left for college, and once more when she returned for Christmas a year later. She and her mother shared the same crucial weakness. Knowing the right thing to do, and doing it, were different things—yet another thing to spur guilt.

Harper sipped at a fresh Appletini without further comment. Ordell stared into the kitchen, with a look of pity in his deep, dark eyes, hidden beneath overpowering eyebrows that made his brown irises seem black. A reddish hue layered over his tan complexion - the kind of mixture working in the sun produced. She searched his features for signs of cloning. No indication that she could make out prompted her to believe he lacked human parents. His blotchy cheeks indicated a preference for drinking heavily, which differed little from the other Jarro clientele. She would never have been able to pick him out of a crowd and say 'that one – he's the model.'

"Tell me about being a model. For real this time."

Ordell rubbed the back of his massive hand down the left, then right, sides of his face wiping away tears that weren't there. He gathered himself together to speak, then gave up with a dismissive shrug, before he finally began.

"Everything about it is normal for me. I don't have parents, but I guess you know that."

She nodded.

"We have two births. The first one they trained me until around I guess thirteen or fourteen. Then we go back into this - it's hard to describe - hibernation chamber, I guess? We stay there until they find a job for us."

"How long?"

"Depends on the market. I came out about ten years ago to do construction jobs."

"What if there is no job?"

"Then you end up an 'unclaimed resource.' You get recycled."

"Recycled?"

"Killed. Then melted with biological agents into proteins to be re-used."

Harper shuddered. Since her father had hated models, she always walked a careful line between ignorance of modeling and acquiescence to her father's opinions. The behavior had become so ingrained that she had skillfully avoided learning anything useful about the topic, a difficult task for a bioengineering major. She stuck to the biology, and steered clear of the politics or the manufacturing process.

"Will they miss you...when you don't come back?"

"Miss me? Probably."

She watched him finally take a taste of his drink. His mouth shriveled into a tight circle, but he didn't complain, behavior that cleanly differentiated him from other barflies she'd known. He might have been more of a Scotch man after all, or perhaps whiskey. These were her father's favorites, anyway. She reached back behind the bar to produce a bottle of whiskey.

"Didn't figure you for a liqueur drinker anyway," she told him, casual and relaxed, like a real bartender.

"Beer is more of my thing."

She put the Scotch away and pulled a pint glass from beneath the serving area. She then poured a foamy glass of import from the tap, which he accepted graciously, swallowing half in one effortless swig. She marveled at how much a non-drinker like her had picked up about bartending. Probably par for the course when one's father owns a dive.

For hours, the two of them talked. Harper asked more questions about modeling, and Ordell answered most of them. She'd lost the appetite to tackle deeper issues, and he seemed equally uninterested. Harper kept both of their glasses full and the topics superficial as the evening progressed.

By the time another cab arrived to deliver them back to her home, the morning sun had broached the horizon. She nodded in and out of consciousness during the short drive home. Afterward, alone in her room, sunlight already peeked in through closed curtains. Drunken peace washed over her as she lay among the soft down blankets. She wondered how much the apple liqueur contributed to her tranquility. Ordell's calming demeanor and deliberate, patient way of talking had grown on her. Some of her peace originated with him.

Drowsy, she heard clanking as one of the family pictures in the hallway fell to the floor. A scrambling, scratching noise accompanied several of what she guessed were Ordell's attempts to re-hang whichever image fell. She smiled at the idea of him clumsily wandering the hallway. Ordell made her feel safer, even if he was pacing loudly and occasionally running into walls. She reflected beneath her heavy eyelids that it might have only been the trust drunks place in other drunks that created such a feeling of kinship. She let herself have it anyway. She needed more than the constant emotional trial of her parents' deaths and her loneliness.

Friday, May 27, 2185

Harper finally rose at noon the next day. Ordell greeted her with perfectly timed pancakes. She threw a smile toward him as she took her seat and accepted the plate he slid across the kitchen counter in her direction. The aroma replaced the pungent smells of the day before. Immaculate counters greeted her. Even the floor, where she had lain near-comatose before his arrival, had been scrubbed and revealed its original hideous polished orange luster.

"Did you sleep?" she asked him.

"A bit," he replied, smiling gently at her beneath sleepy eyes, "but it's strange not being at home."

Harper almost felt normal, save the throbbing headache from a hangover, as she sat with a stack of hot pancakes before her, covered in syrup and whipped cream. The feeling couldn't last. Ten minutes later, she struggled again to fight off the emotional pain of her loss. Having tasted respite and something like normalcy, she believed now that she could overcome.

After breakfast, or lunch possibly, she wasn't sure, Harper cleared the dishes and waited while Ordell ate the rest of his sandwich. When he finally finished, she nodded in his direction.

"What now, Ordell?" She asked.

"Back to Emergent Biotechnology."

"And to those men who were trying to kill you?"

"They're not Emergent. Those men were a couple of the site

workers we share the contract with."

"Won't they still try to kill you?"

"Probably," he shrugged. "What's the difference? Aayushi's gone."

He hid his emotions behind his monotone and body language. Ordell only seemed a little tired. Despite everything, she couldn't match his words with his affect. His endless energy seeped into her and made her want to be better.

"Don't go."

She waited for his reaction, but he only shrugged again.

"There's about as much point in not going as there is going. Emergent will send someone looking if I stay here, and the result will be the same either way."

"If you're going to die anyway, can't you stay here with me? You saw what condition I was in yesterday. I need someone…"

She trailed off at the thought that she admitted being so dysfunctional that it necessitated a chaperone, but she couldn't deny the truth. Harper instinctively reached her hand to the back of her neck and slid it over a healing bump, once her emotional stabilizer. She wanted that back, too. Barring that, something in Ordell set her at ease. The second choice, sure, but the only real one. No doctor would re-install an emotional stabilizer this close to her trauma. Even the high-end stabilizers that could handle extreme emotions still had the potential to become addicting.

"You don't need me. I'm barely keeping it together."

He turned his face to hers, and she saw the eyebrows knitted up together, frozen in sadness. His eyes glistened with tears that she guessed he would never cry. Her heart broke at the realization that what drove his actions that morning, the cleaning and the pancakes, was the same need for distraction that made her shudder at the thought of being alone.

"Ordell, you make me feel safe. This house - it's so big and empty. I can't take the emptiness. Can you please stay?"

He looked away.

"I guess it doesn't matter," he told her. "Maybe I'll stay today. Tomorrow's as good a day to leave as any."

6

Aayushi's Ghost

Friday, May 27, 2185

Ordell lay on the couch again that night. Left alone, he curled himself into a ball and sought out Aayushi's scent in the couch pillows. It was there, buried deep, and when he found it, he whimpered into the back cushion, his massive body shaking with convulsions. He buried his head in between the pads to conceal the sounds of his lament. He grieved uninhibited for several hours before he fell into a brief uncomfortable sleep.

Saturday, May 28, 2185

The following day, Ordell constrained himself to the tiny kitchen rather than encounter the stains in the living room. He seated himself at the table in the dining area and looked around. The refrigerator still kept the few fresh foods Aayushi loved. If he opened it, he knew he would find cherries inside in the small compartment near the bottom. Replicated cherries had a tinny taste that Aayushi hated. That was probably because she wasn't any good at using the device. He smiled as he remembered Aayushi's horrible attempts at meal preparation. He could smell the aroma of burnt toast, a spectacular feat in a replicator.

"What are you thinking?" Harper asked as she stepped into the kitchen from the hallway.

"Just thinking about Aayushi," he replied.

Harper took one of the two other chairs at the table, and rested her chin on the backs of her hands as she looked at him. "Do you want to share?"

He smiled at her.

"I've never known someone so horrible at using technology."

Harper grinned a thin smile in return.

"My mother was *horrible* at food, replicator or not. She couldn't even make sandwiches."

"How does someone not know how to do that? Even models know that basic survival skill."

"She wasn't always from here. We weren't, I guess."

"She followed your father from New York?"

"She did. My grandfather, Bodhi - he was dead set against it. When she left, he cut her out of her inheritance."

He pondered for a second, poring over his memories of her.

"She never mentioned that part of it."

"My grandfather owned a chain of high-end restaurants. My father used to be a chef - did you know that? That's how he met my mom. She used to say he had such great plans for Jarro, back before the ocean took over. It was going to be fine dining. Some nights, when he was out, we would dress up in her fancy dresses and pretend..."

Her eyes teared up as she trailed off. Ordell's eyes misted

and his face felt hot. He reached out to touch her hand.

"I miss her too."

"Ordell, sometimes I imagine she's here. Like when I'm in my room, I can hear her telling me to put my clothes away. Stupid things like that."

Ordell smiled at her. "It's eleven."

"What does that mean?"

"That means in New York, it's brunch time. Do you have anything to drink?"

"In this house? You've never lived with an alcoholic, have you? That was the last of the whiskey before you got here."

He thought for a moment.

"Do you mind if I use the replicator? I want to try something," he told her. "Do you have glasses that will work with it?"

"Those mugs."

She pointed to a cabinet.

"Okay, one second."

He scooted away from the table and picked up two mugs from the cabinet she'd indicated. These he walked over to the replicator and placed into designated slots inside. Then he rapidly typed in fifteen digits that gained him override mode. He scrunched his eyes together, trying to remember the code he wanted. He visualized his Didactics suite. Langley used his technical prowess to hijack replicator functions all the time.

Ordell recalled the numbers, and punched them in. In three beeps, the replicator whirred and he slammed the door shut as it began filling the cups with a brownish liquid. Then he pulled the cups out and slid one over to Harper. She sniffed and scrunched her nose up.

"What *is* this?"

"We call it skree. In Didactics, we didn't get money, so we couldn't go out on the town for drinks. Langely figured out how to rig the replicator to produce liquor. It's not very good, but I feel like we could use a drink."

Harper raised the glass to her lips, and took a swig. Ordell could tell by the way her lips puckered that she got the full skree experience. He followed suit, then realized that he'd forgotten how truly bad the liquor was. When he recovered, he raised his coffee mug and smiled at Harper, admiring her likeness to Aayushi.

"To your mother," he stated, "a wonderful woman who changed my life."

Harper's eyes teared up. Ordell felt tension melting from the air as she smiled.

"To mom, the most wonderful mother I could have had."

She paused while she took a smaller sip than the first, lesson well learned. Then she looked up at him.

"I complained a lot yesterday," she said, "but I've always been amazed at how she could get up the next day, and get to work, no matter how bad things got."

"She said you were stronger than she was."

Harper shook her head.

"I couldn't handle it. By twelve, I was a wreck, and had to get a mood stabilizer implant to make it through the day. She handled it though. Day after day, getting done what needed to get done, regardless of how abusive he was or the humiliation he put her through."

Ordell nodded.

"Me too. She told me about the early days of her fairytale-like wedding, and the rapid degeneration when the climate shifted. Did you know that she never really blamed anyone - not even him? She said it was Equilibrium that did it. The ocean moved in and killed that tree in your yard just the same way it killed her marriage."

"She was too forgiving."

"That I'll drink to. I've been undeserving many times."

"Me too," she said, and got that faraway look that Harper sometimes got when she examined her past. He lifted his mug, and she clinked her mug to it, then they brought the drinks to their lips at the same time.

"Can I ask you something? Why do you think your mother never left him? I've asked her to leave over and over, but she never would."

"She is - was - sentimental. You probably got that. My guess is that even while she was with you, she hoped that her marriage could be saved. You'd think after these years that she would figure out that he wasn't going to change. You would be underestimating my mother's faith in people to think that, though."

Harper raised her mug this time.

"To Mom, seeking the humanity in everyone."

He felt a lump form in his throat, as he took a sip. She shifted her gaze to him.

"To you, Ordell. I don't know what happened between you, but I like to think you brought her some happiness. I've never met anyone quite like you before."

He took another sip and then smiled.

"This stuff is horrible."

"It's very bad. Tomorrow I'll make a run to Jarro. All that liquor is just sitting around. If we're going to drink, we should at least drink something palatable."

They spent the rest of that morning and afternoon sipping on skree, reminiscing about Aayushi, and wading through good memories while avoiding bad ones.

Sunday, May 29, 2185

"Warning light?" Ordell pondered the flashing light on the replicator on Sunday morning.

"It's the low protein light. Just need to get some more."

Harper seemed to fixate on the orange spot, pulsating gently.

"Where do we go to do that?"

"There's an appliance shop a few miles from here. It's in-and-out, so shouldn't take too long."

"Okay."

Ordell said nothing else and found himself sucked in by the light as well. It was entrancing in its regular appearance and disappearance. His mind strayed to the matter of his status as escapee. Emergent Biotechnology would be moving to get him back.

"I have to leave soon."

She swiveled her head over from the lamp to meet his face.

"Where will you go?"

"Canada, I guess."

"Across the desert?"

The desert stretched northward across Colorado, Kansas, and the Dakotas. Equilibrium had ruined the midwest as certainly as it had provided the rebuilding jobs that Ordell found himself tied to for most of his short life.

"Maybe."

"I've got some money," Harper mentioned. "I think a thousand altogether. Do you think that would help?"

Even if it could, Ordell wouldn't take the last of Harper's money when she had a home to pay for, and a bar too.

"Not really. I haven't run the numbers yet, but I'm guessing a lot more than that. A car alone would be at least two-hundred thousand dollars. Not to mention food for the trip, and model-friendly places to stay."

"Are you willing to wait?" Harper asked, raising one eyebrow.

"Wait for them to find me?"

"No, Ordell. I can get a job and we can save some money. A good lab position would be about a hundred thousand a month. Work for a few months, save a few dollars. Then we can send you off in style."

He smiled at that.

"In style? I'd settle for just not getting caught."

"More money would with help that too."

Through her actions, he recognized Aayushi's hands. What else could he do but accept?

Thursday, June 2, 2185

Watching Harper recover strengthened him, and she bounced back fast. She insisted on getting to some sort of routine, even though he told her she should take more time to grieve. Harper blatantly refused his suggestion. They needed the money. The replicator was on its last protein pack, and it was time for her to look for a job. The part about the replicator was right enough, and models didn't have money, so he stopped arguing. He hadn't realized that she'd already lined up interviews for Thursday afternoon.

After she left, unlike every day prior, he didn't make an excuse to avoid returning to Emergent. He reclined in Aayushi's living room listening to a storm begin outside. Thunder crashed in rolls as the rain fell. Having burned through any obvious chores, Ordell turned to ruminations of the past. He remembered a time before Aayushi when he'd first been allowed to venture out unsupervised.

Saturday, January 1, 2180

A hopeful, younger version of Ordell frequented the non-fiction section in the tiny Memorial Library near Tribeca. Narrow, cave-like hallways filled the interior of a building the size of a double-wide trailer home. Ordell arrived after the workday closed, physically exhausted from slinging sheetrock. He craved more from life. Through the precious few tomes in the library, he found sustenance for his curiosity. A sharp rattle attracted his attention, drawing him toward the sound and out of his book. A young boy hid nearby in the tiny children's' section, little more than a rack of games next to a holovision which streamed cartoons nonstop.

"What's that?" The boy's tiny finger pointed at the bar code tattooed across Ordell's left wrist.

The child couldn't have been more than seven and made the youthful mistake of drawing attention to a sensitive topic. Before Ordell could respond, an emaciated woman clawed a desperate, clutching hand into the boy's shoulder and pulled him back. She glared at Ordell as she clasped the boy tightly into her embrace and whispered something in the boy's ear.

He thought nothing of it as he watched the two walk away. People became rude or frightened, or both in the company of models. Even the evil eye the woman served him back over her shoulder only proved the situation's normalcy. He turned his attention back to reading.

"Ordell," came a voice he recognized as that of the aging librarian. He glanced up to see the thin, bookish man with a walking cane clack closer to him over dilapidated plywood floors.

"Hi, Holden, what's up?"

"You've got to leave," the man said again, his voice trailing off into a sigh that shook his frail body.

Just past the man, Ordell met the eyes of the woman who had walked off with the boy. Her piercing gaze cut through him as understanding dawned. He was no longer welcome in his sanctuary. He nodded absently to Holden, but never took his eyes off of her.

"So," he asked the man, "I shouldn't come back?"

Holden twisted his graying head from side to side, again a

movement which continued through his body and down a cane that wobbled so fiercely Ordell thought he might fall. Like a good model, Ordell did what he was told, without fuss. None of his body language or features revealed the betrayal he felt as Holden, who he'd had several conversations with, dismissed him without a fight.

Thursday, June 2, 2185

Many years later, Holden died a natural death in his bed. Someone had posted an obituary in the League City Times. Ordell's original fondness for the man had waned by then and metastasized into hatred. The man had deceived him, feigning friendship, and offered no support when he needed it. The storm seemed to wax with Ordell's rising anger. The rumination was unhealthy, so he turned on the holovid for distraction.

"Ordell Bentley," he called out, wondering if anyone had noticed his absence yet. Two announcers appeared in the holovision matrix.

"Two hundred thousand dollars, folks. That's the biggest reward since Jeremy Lido of Prescient two years ago," said the male newscaster briskly, "and he was a scientist."

"If you think about it, Joseph, it makes sense to go with bigger rewards. Weren't we talking about the rise in escaped models lately?"

"It's true, Kath," Joseph replied, "there's been a fifteen percent increase in the last two years, consistent with the increase in legal cases by models seeking their freedom."

"So they need to get these models back, quickly," Kath continued, with brown hair swinging across her disembodied face, briefly obscuring her perpetual newscaster grin.

"That's right. Hey League City, this could be your chance. Somewhere out there are two hundred thousand dollars, waiting to be found in the name of Ordell Bentley."

"What do we know so far, Joseph?"

"Only that he fled Tribeca on May twentieth, so about two weeks ago now. He is considered dangerous, and police are looking for him. This is important, folks. Do not try to capture him. You can still get the reward by just letting the police or Emergent Biotechnology know where he is. They capture him; you get two hundred grand."

"Thanks, Joseph," the woman said as casually as though she were ordering pizza. "Next, was Equilibrium real, or just a hoax? Stay tuned!"

Ordell turned the holovision back off. That kind of money would put bounty-hunters on his trail. He wondered how long it might be before they showed up at Harper's house.

A crash sounded as something collided into the side of the house and made him jump. Ordell retreated to the master bedroom's relative quiet to await Harper's return, growing concerned for her safety as the storm raged. The power flickered out, enshrouding him in temporary darkness.

Thursday, February 2, 2175

The darkness reminded him of his second birth, trying to focus his eyes opened only to have them filled by the thick, viscous fluid in the modeling chamber. The compartment was a night sky devoid of galaxies or any heavenly objects. The first emotion Ordell felt was the loneliness as his consciousness slowly awoke.

"Ordell Bentley, construction worker, identification 874233," a voice penetrated the fluid clogging his ears, "come forward."

The idea that he possibly could move formed in his mind. He had the will but lacked the ability since he couldn't remember exactly how to move his body parts in coordination. Not to be denied, the chamber popped open and ejected Ordell toward the clean, rubberized floor. Immediately a poly-foam blanket covered his body. Even with that, he still felt icy and frigid. He began to shake as he struggled to wipe away the liquid that clung to his frame. It was a violent way to come into the world. He entered the chamber a skinny child of thirteen, and he emerged as a massive yet uncoordinated man.

Thursday, June 2, 2185

It had taken him years to learn to walk correctly, and he still swaggered more than he walked. He'd spent too long in the chamber to learn to do it properly. But that was all past now. Preoccupation with the past wasted energy.

A flash of lightning illuminated the room, imprinting his lover's dresser into his vision before it plunged him back into darkness. Intimate and personal items hid in those drawers, tucked away from most prying eyes. Knowing that these items of hers existed crippled him with longing. He lay his head into her pillow and took a deep breath in, letting the smell of her wash over him. Some day soon she would be gone, and the pillow would only smell like him, sweat and musk.

Another clang sounded against the wall outside, which he recognized as the sound of a troublesome branch he'd meant to cut back. Ordell rolled over and planted his feet on the ground. He buried his head between his hands and waited for the storm to pass.

"Ordell?"

He must have imagined it. Somehow, darkness shimmered, and he heard the voice again.

"Ordell? What are you doing here?"

"Aayushi? Is that you?" he half-whispered.

"Yes, of course, it is."

He strained his eyes, but only the darkness looked back.

"I don't know what to do, Aayushi," he told her.

"We were on borrowed time anyway, odd one," he heard her reply. "I've told you many times."

The pet name was something that she'd come up with on their fourth date when she first saw his velvet Elvis curtains. She'd whispered it to him, as she ran her fingers across Elvis's face, changing it from pale to slightly orange as the velvet remembered her touch. It was a name he hadn't realized he missed.

"Will you... come back to me? Your daughter is here; I'm here. We need you."

Her laughter echoed as the storm surged again. This time a snapping noise came from outside, like a twig breaking, and Ordell suspected there might be someone out in the shower. He listened for a little longer after her laugh died, but no other sound followed.

"I'm not in this world anymore, and there's no way back. This is as much as I can do."

"Tell me what to do then, Aayushi. You always knew."

"You're asking a dead person for advice," she warned him, "and if I had good advice to give, I think you know that I would still be with you."

He felt as though she toyed with him. He was intimate enough with Aayushi to honestly express his anger.

"What good is it for you to come here, when you have no advice, and I can't even see you?!" he shouted into the darkness. He saw a gentle golden shimmer light up the dresser in response.

"I came to thank you, odd one," she told him, "for taking care of my Harper. She was very close to hurting herself. Thank you. And I came to warn you."

"Warn me?"

"You're on borrowed time," her voice faded into a sad whisper. "It seems like borrowed time is all you ever have."

"What do you mean?"

"Leave, Ordell," she said firmly. "It's time to go, isn't it?"

"Where? How?"

He imagined her sad eyes downcast and her head shaking in the returned silence.

"I don't know. Asking the dead for advice again, Ordell. All I can see is what I can see."

Ordell thought on this, and on the fact that it was nonsensical to believe that his dead lover haunted the room. The humanity in her voice evidenced her being there, cloaked in darkness. Still, the possibility existed that someone cruelly egged him on. The thought made him flick on the red belly of an antique lamp on the nightstand, emanating a rose glow. He lifted his head toward where the voice of the interloper originated and gasped.

There, with a teal sari draped over her shoulder like royalty, stood his lover. The storm waxed again. As it did, her hair spread behind her into a halo of tiny black tendrils. She smiled remorsefully and began to fade.

"I love you, odd one," she told him.

He struggled against tears as he watched her fade away. Then he felt a sense of peace, her gift to him. Perhaps death wasn't the end, and maybe, someday, he would again hold his love in his arms. Or, his cynical nature told him, his mind slipped away from grief. The decision rested with him, which version of reality to accept, and he decided then that her ghost had been real. Believing that, he also had to believe in the inauspicious future she predicted.

The weather outside raged up again in a final surge demonstrating its power before there were silence and only the dripping of the trees to tell that it had ever been. As it waned, he heard footsteps disappearing into the nearby forest. Two hundred thousand dollars was a strong incentive to brave the lightning and wind and dangerous flying branches. He bolted to the window in time to see a flash of white between the trees. Whoever it was disappeared into the night.

Aayushi was right - borrowed time.

7

Failed Interviews

Thursday, June 2, 2185

The storm subsided as Harper arrived at the foot of her driveway. Thunder that had nearly shocked her off of the highway became a distant rumble, and only wet streets remained. She inhaled deeply as she pulled in, and took three seconds to check her make-up in the mirror. None of the frustration of a day of failed interviews showed on her face. She had kept the tears at bay for the entire drive.

A job wasn't essential, she told herself, it was only a part of the plan. They could wait a day or a week. With this thought, she firmed up the quiver in her lips. Ordell would ask what's wrong if she went in as a devastating wreck, and she didn't want to talk about it. She gathered her shoes and listened for the click of the door as it recognized her biometric signature and unlatched. Then she nudged it softly open to reveal an empty living room.

Harper sighed with relief and tossed her shoes in a pile on

the floor of the foyer. She checked the time. A wall-clock told her it was just after seven. She tested her breath for the remaining smells of the two drinks she'd consumed as part of her personal pity-party, then popped in an extra breath. The door swung shut behind her and the lock clicked back into place. No other sounds reached her ears. Ordell was asleep.

In stockinged feet, Harper tip-toed past the couch, only to step without thinking onto the brown bloodstain. Her stomach dropped and fought back the urge to vomit. Harper pulled up her foot and stepped around the stain, then continued down the hall.

The day had chipped away at her. Harper fished a hidden candle from a drawer in her room, along with her robe, and a lighter. Then she snuck back across the hallway to the shared bathroom. After pushing the door open, a pile of Ordell's clothing on the floor caught her attention. She smiled as she moved them to the side, despite the annoyance. Five minutes later, she submerged herself into a bath with the soft glow of the tea-light trying feebly to illuminate the room. A long sigh escaped as she sank below the water's surface up to her chin, letting the warmth coat her body, and the soft soap bubbles lift away her day. Tomorrow would be better.

Her thoughts turned to Ordell. The extent to which he had fallen for her mother had become more clear as the weeks passed. He didn't talk about it much, but every day he sulked more than the day before. None of her words of encouragement improved things. It was as though his spirit drained away slowly. He'd been sleeping later too, sometimes well into the afternoon. She felt as though she were losing him when she'd only just gotten used to him being there.

Harper forced her thoughts away from him and back to tomorrow. The sense of failure faded with the bubbles. She hadn't time for it anyway, with another interview coming up in the morning. Just for the night, she would have to be selfish. Harper closed her eyes and cleared her thoughts.

She slept soundly that evening. The silence left in the wake of the storm, and the steady drip of water as the trees rid themselves of the its evidence, lulled her to sleep.

Friday, June 3, 2185

Sunlight woke Harper from her slumber. When she pulled herself from her bed and went through her morning routine, she found herself alone. By eight, she started to wonder about Ordell, but not enough to risk waking him. He had the right to sleep in if he wanted, however concerned she might be. Harper scratched out a quick note telling him that she had more interviews that day. She mentioned nothing about the previous day's failure since he already had enough to worry about. Harper dressed, then packed up her things and left, leaving her simple note for Ordell on the kitchen counter.

When she arrived for her interview, the location turned out to be a tiny unfinished laboratory in a strip mall. Piles of discarded plastic tarps littered the parking lot. She picked her way through the mounds toward the door, above which were emblazoned the words "Toussaint Labs" in seven inch tall letters. Harper paused as her skin flushed at the prospect of yet another failure. She wanted to turn away and go back home, but the idea of Ordell wasting away as a slave for Emergent Biotechnology made her queasy. She swallowed and stepped through the door.

On the other side was a spacious foyer, where a short woman with sandy-blonde hair greeted Harper with a smile. She smiled in return before noticing a man in a lab coat approach from the far wall. She smiled at him too. So far, so good - smiles all around.

"Welcome," the man addressed Harper as she pulled the door closed behind her.

"Dr. Toussaint? I'm here to interview for the job of Biology Lab Administrator."

"You're in the right place. Pleased to make your acquaintance. This is Ms. Marche, my business partner."

Not Doctor, she noticed. Harper reached out to shake hands with Ms. Marche. The woman's smile reached her eyes, and somehow even extended into her handshake. The woman had a strong, firm grip.

"Great," Ms. Marche said. "Things will be picking up very soon. Come this way?"

Ms. Marche turned and strode across the foyer and through a door, and Harper followed. On the other side was a long hallway. Harper trailed behind, and Ms. Marche slowed then drifted to her side. A moment later, they were in the privacy of an empty conference room. Ms. Marche and Dr. Toussaint sat to one side of a short white table cluttered with chairs. Harper took her seat across from them.

"Welcome to our lab," Dr. Toussaint said. "It's not much yet. But it will be. Just a little construction left to go. Tell us a little about yourself. Harper, right?"

Harper nodded and smoothed out her business-casual blue slacks, and then pushed her round personal identification data-coin across the table with the tips of her fingers. The surface of the table lit up as the coin slid across, bringing up her school and work history.

"I have a baccalaureate degree in bioengineering and have completed several research projects."

"Wet lab? Or dry lab?" asked Ms. Marche.

"Both," Harper responded quickly. Several of her school experiments had required mixing chemicals and processing real DNA instead of simulating them, but she'd had a fair amount of that as well.

"This is a biology lab. The actual job doesn't have much to do with the research, directly. But I'm excited to have you apply," Ms. Marche told her. "Your background will make it so much easier to explain what we're doing to investors."

"Can you tell me a little more about the job?"

"Absolutely," Dr. Toussaint began, as he met her eyes with his own. "We're researching modeling - pretty high-profile. We have major donors who like to visit sometimes, and we need to plan for those visits to ensure that we're ready for them. If donors show up unannounced, we need someone to greet them. That's where you come in."

"As I said, the bio-engineering degree isn't directly applicable," Ms. Marche continued. "But it will be good to have someone who can explain the research. I think it speaks volumes if our coordinator talks the talk."

Harper felt her pulse slow, and the tenseness in her mind ease. This part of the interview sounded as though it was going well so far.

"How do you feel about modeling, Harper?" Dr. Toussaint asked.

Her mind placed the question in the immediate context of her parents' deaths, which had been on every news vid in Texas. The sensational story of a double-murder involving a model was irresistible to cover. In this context, the innocent-seeming question took on an antagonism that conflicted with Dr. Toussaint's and Ms. Marche's kindness so far. Harper's mind built other questions from it: Are you an infiltrator? We read about your father's FoH and HPM ties – why are you trying to work in the same field your father hated? Are you secretly harboring a model in your house and breaking about fifteen laws?

She shrugged the ideas away as best she could, and swallowed.

"It's the future if we do it right," she said, "and I think we can."

"No moral hang-ups?"

"None," she replied. "It's the perfect response to a declining population. It's a gift, at a time when we desperately needed it. I want to be a part of that."

"Good. The problem with modeling is that it's controversial. We get people applying who are secretly working for HPM. We had some vandalism just after we bought the place earlier this year."

Silence fell across them then as Dr. Toussaint and Ms. Marche both seemed to ponder her resume without talking about it out loud. Then Dr. Toussaint tilted his head. Harper recognized the pose as that of someone receiving a call via an implant - one of her instructors had one. Harper waited patiently and smiled at Ms. Marche, who responded in kind.

"Sorry, I have to take this call," Dr. Toussaint whispered. Then he leaned forward in his chair and extended his hand for a departing handshake.

Ms. Marche addressed her as Dr. Toussaint left the room.

"You get used to it," she said. "Are you willing to work for us, faults and all?"

"Absolutely," Harper responded.

"Can you start tomorrow? I've been filling the gap, but Torrent - uh, Dr. Toussaint - seems to forget that I have my own research and can't sit at a desk all day."

The woman reached down to the table and tapped twice. An offer letter popped up on the screen, which Harper briefly read through, and then confirmed it with a touch. Ms. Marche slid the image in the display toward the data-coin, giving her an official copy.

"Welcome aboard, Harper," Ms. Marche told her.

"Thank you, Ms. Marche."

"We're colleagues now. Call me Railynn."

Harper couldn't help but smile at that.

"Okay - Railynn."

* * *

Finally home, Harper's heart jumped when she saw Ordell leaning industriously over the kitchen table. She made her way across the entryway, her sore calves throbbing. They needed a hot bath - this time, a celebratory one.

Ordell glanced up from the tabletop.

"Ordell, wanna hear some good news?" she asked.

He pulled his hand up to rub the back of his neck, then turned his to face her her. He swiped away something she didn't see.

"I got the job! I start Monday, so we..."

Before she could finish, he raced to her and scooped her up in his arms in a giant bear hug. Then he placed her gently back down. A wide grin wholly replaced his focused concentration.

"That's good news. A new job calls for a celebration!"

His change in mood caught her off guard, but she smiled anyway and went with it. Ecstatic, over-the-top Ordell was better than sullen Ordell.

"Yes! What do we have to celebrate with?"

"Peanut butter and jam, toast, and, um, dehydrated milk."

"Really?"

She checked the refrigerator and then the pantry. She pounded some keys on the replicator, but it only flashed the words "Low Protein – Dried Foods Only." All were as unfortunately empty as she remembered them. They were down to dried pasta and what remained of canned fruits and jams – another reason a job was more than just a convenience.

"Macaroni and cheese?"

"Al dente," he said with a boyish smile she hadn't seen in days.

Harper left Ordell alone to start on dinner while she spent fifteen minutes to run a quick bath and soak her tired, aching legs. She then quickly dried and dressed before making her way back down to the kitchen. She hummed quietly to herself as Ordell strained the pasta and added cheese to it, and then helped set the table. After dinner, they bused the table and set up for several celebratory rounds of a holographic board game where they took turns trying to kill a gentleman who had wronged their characters in the past.

As they played, Harper watched her friend study the cards with his face wrinkled into a focused frown. Friend, maybe. Good friend, or great friend? She pondered the question. Perhaps best friend? It felt right, and it wasn't as though he had much competition for the job. Harper smiled and let the joy of the day fill her. She moved her pawn to the Dining Room, where the antagonist's automated pawn flickered.

"I kill him with a hammer," she said quietly, tapping the digital display in front of her.

8

Freedom Underground

Monday, June 6, 2185

Refusing to face the morning, Ordell traced the lines of Aayushi's face in his mind. He pondered the uselessness of the secrets they had shared between them - like how the word 'chocolate' always made her think of chocolate bricks laced with Ghost Pepper spices. She had once forced Ordell to try the unfortunate experience. He could sometimes still feel the burn on his tongue. But he had shared too - like the fact that he never really felt clean without the irritation of an instant sanitization laser over his skin. She'd laughed a laugh that filled the room when he told her that.

The sound of Harper's shower cutting off distracted him from his thoughts. Ordell jumped out of his bed and threw on a shirt and pants from a nearby pile. He'd have to hurry to catch her before she left for her new job. Harper's first day in the working world deserved a sendoff. A little emotional support would help start her day right. After a quick check-in in the mirror, he stepped into the hallway.

"Good morning, Ordell," Harper greeted him as she crossed the hall in her robe.

He drew up a smile. "Are you ready for your big day?"

"I think so," she replied with a grin.

"You'll do great."

She disappeared into her room. Much of her mother shone out of her when she smiled. Sometimes it made him long for Aayushi. With a dull ache in his chest, he took his normal place at the kitchen table.

The two-dimensional display sprang to life, showing the last thing he had investigated the night before. He took a few minutes to resume his newfound obsession - searching for an unencumbered path north - as he waited for Harper to join him. Three interstate highways left Texas heading toward Canada, I-35, I-40, and I-30, all of which went through checkpoints at the Texas border. The five skyways, S-17, S-6, S-89, S-2, and S-20, had fewer checkpoints, but nearly all funneled through three blockades at the Canadian border. They would have to figure out how to get past those checkpoints if they stayed on the main roads or tried to book flights. Ordell pulled up a different map of the United States transportation system. He followed each line again, disappointed as each dead-ended at a red square, indicating a checkpoint or a funnel.

The sound of Harper's shoes drew his attention, and he swiped the screen to hide his efforts. He didn't want her to worry about his upcoming trip. She had enough stressors in her life.

"Can you show me?" She asked.

He wanted to say no, having nothing new to report - but she seemed earnest.

"I guess."

He pulled the map back up as she retrieved a mug of coffee

from the replicator and came to look over his shoulder.

"What about there?"

She pointed to the Mississippi River, flowing to the Great Lakes.

"Got to take I-10 or I-20 to get there, and both have checkpoints in Louisiana."

He glanced at her as he said it, catching her eyebrows furrowing up in concern.

"Look there," she said, pointing to a thin, unmarked line that led from just above Amarillo and snaked across Oklahoma into Nebraska before transitioning to a dotted line that continued through the Dakota's.

"Old I-29." He'd already considered that approach—desert sand and hopelessness. "When the climate shifted and the midwest turned into a desert, construction stopped. From what I've read, there are no businesses, and barely any towns."

Ordell spared her the rest of what he had found. People called I-29 by another name since Equilibrium – the Trail of Death. In places, it was so hot that tires on moving cars exploded, and automobiles sank down into the tacky asphalt. Starting the day with hopelessness wouldn't do her any good.

"Still, might work," he said, feigning hope he didn't feel. Then he smiled. "Let's eat. You don't want to be hungry your first day!"

She played along with his positivity. With brave faces, they went through the motions of breakfast.

After a quick hug goodbye, he sat back down to look into the problem some more until he registered a scratching sound outside the kitchen window. He glanced up towards the noise in time to see a shadow flit across and disappear.

Ordell pushed away from the table and stood, careful to keep his eyes on the glass. Nothing else moved. He made his way to the front door and pushed it open just wide enough for him to slide through sideways. Birds chirped in the background, and insects hummed, followed by the occasional gust of wind making the Aspens chuckle. When he arrived at the window, he saw nothing but dust and broken branches from the big storm a couple of nights before. He tiptoed closer and breathed a sigh of relief. Whatever he'd heard, he didn't see anything outside.

As he turned away, a hint of unnatural color drew his eye. A purple thumbtack-sized piece of fabric jutted out from the corner of the window frame. He pinched it carefully with his hands, pulled it free, and examined it. The material was clean, synthetic, and dry. The rain hadn't soaked it through, unlike the still-damp wood in which it clung. The fabric was a recent deposit.

He spun to face the woods, but they were empty. He walked toward the edge of the porch and looked downward at the thin strip of dirt separating the house from the trees. There he saw a tread-less shoe-print.

He turned and went back inside. As he sat down, a memory jogged loose in his mind, from a time in Convocation. Cyrill had mentioned escape. Like the ancient slave trades, he spoke of an organization that helped models seeking freedom. They provided tattoo removals, biometric mapping and re-registration, and starting money in Canada. He struggled to remember the name hiding in the back of his mind. Underwood? Under – something.

"Freedom Underground," he said the words loud enough for the table's built-in microphone to detect. A flashing red light indicated that it switched from 2-D to 3-D display as the device connected to the Labyrinth. The screen whirled momentarily and pulled up a symbol of three links of a chain hovering before him, one whole link straddled by two broken ones.

So it did exist.

According to the site, activists established the organization forty years earlier as a legal defense fund for models. The signing of the Madison Rule into law in 2164 made any legal defense efforts obsolete since it explicitly deprived models of all rights from that point forward. After that, Freedom Underground morphed into a citizens' organization, lobbying to change the Madison Rule. He navigated a clunky interface that he was sure would have been much better fully immersed with a haptic suit than through a holographic computer, but he found the ansible address of a point-of-contact.

The truth fell short of the myth. Even the legal defense that Freedom Underground once provided had been discontinued. Ordell clenched his jaw and pushed away from the table. He slammed his fist into the top, causing the hologram to shimmer with static. He would have to find another way.

9

Revolutionary Research

Monday, June 6, 2185

Harper pulled into the parking lot of Toussaint Labs at precisely nine o'clock. Officially, the office wouldn't open for another thirty minutes. She waited anxiously, working up the nerve to enter. A slowly-building feeling of panic gave her ample incentive not to. Her fingers tightened against the steering wheel, and her stomach wound into a knot as she willed the anxiousness to pass. Harper forced herself to breathe through her limbic system, sucking air into her abdomen and blowing it out slowly. She missed her stabilizer.

There's nothing to worry about. It's just a job.

Her fingers slowly released, and the drum of heartbeats in her ears faded. When she felt steady enough, she entered through the glass doors. Her eyes widened to see her name on the wall with the words, "Welcome to the newest member of our family - Harper Rawls!" Each letter was as tall as she was. The sentence moved as a group across three walls of the room and then bounced back before settling over a tiny aluminum desk. A small box of chocolates sat in the seat as a pleasant final touch. Her anxiety melted away.

She heard a creak from behind as she sat down. Turning toward the sound, she saw Railynn Marche standing there.

"Good morning," Harper beamed. "Thank you for all of this."

"Of course," Railynn told her, "and I've put some supplies in there too. Your password is 'welcome harper,' but you can change it to whatever you want."

"Password?"

"For the desk. Oh, and the walls. You can do all of that from the desk display. It's all connected."

"Oh, okay. Is it normally this quiet?"

"At nine-twenty? Yeah, usually. Things don't start around here until ten or ten-thirty. But that gives us early birds time to work in peace. Would you like a tour?"

"Sure."

She followed Railynn past the desk through the rightmost of two doors against the far wall.

"This is my side of the lab," Railynn explained. "The other door leads to Dr. Toussaint's. He directs the lab, and I lead most of the research."

"So, you do the work?"

Railynn laughed.

"Exactly, but don't tell him I said that."

The hallway allowed six people to walk abreast. The walls emitted an ambient glow so soft that Harper couldn't tell from where the light originated.

They must have interviewed on Dr. Toussaint's side, because Railynn's side had no sign of the work-in-progress sections she'd seen before. The pair stopped outside of a room labeled the Replication Room.

"How much do you remember about the cloning process?"

"I remember that we start with an egg cell and replace the DNA with whatever it is we're trying to make a copy of."

"That's a start. Oh, no. I completely forgot to ask you if you want any coffee. Do you? We'll be in the break room in a minute, but we can go there first if you want some."

"No, I'm okay. But thank you."

"Okay, good. So before we can do that DNA swap, we have to have a bunch of egg cells. Since we can't legally get many human egg cells, we make our own. That means replicating, in this case, somatic cells. You might remember them as body cells, like skin cells. We reprogram them to think that they're egg cells."

"Yes, I remember. So replication is the process of getting those somatic cells to divide so that you have enough to reprogram?"

"Exactly. You do remember a lot of your bioengineering. In this case, team members donated somatic cells."

A little further down the hallway, they came upon another door. This one was marked "Production Lab."

"That one?"

"That's where we're going to transform the healthiest into egg cells. Less than a percent of those transforms will work."

"Because the 'transformation' is more of a suggestion."

"Yep. Skin cells want to stay skin cells, even if we try to convince them to be egg cells. Most will refuse. Even the ones that do change won't all be usable."

Just before the end of the hallway, another door emerged as they continued along the arc.

"Egg Lab is the last step," Railynn told her. "There are two parts. In the one part, our clone DNA replaces the egg DNA. In the other, the zygotes are grown into babies."

Her eyes glimmered with excitement as she talked, and she beckoned to Harper to join her peeking through a window in the door. Through the window was a chamber with another door on the far side. The surrounding wall was transparent, allowing Harper to see rows and columns of electrical outlets built into raised platforms.

"Imagine each of those outlets having a container holding a cloned fetus, and bringing them to gestation."

The more Railynn had talked, the more Harper remembered from her classes. Everything seemed the same from what she'd learned so far. There didn't seem to be anything to set the lab apart from any other cloning company.

"Railynn, what's different about this lab?"

"You mean, what set's us apart? That's exactly the question that our donors will ask - good for you. So what set's us apart is that we're not replacing all the DNA. Research experiments don't require that. We only need to control certain biological systems. To do that, we isolate the genetic component driving the system development, and hack that out to replace it with what we're studying."

"So, these aren't clones?"

"They are technically still clones, because of the resetting, and starting with somatic cells. But because all cells have the entire DNA of the person, we're leaving most of it intact, and using nanites to slice out the particular pieces we need to be changed."

"Nanites?"

Harper knew that there were natural ways of editing genes, using RIZRxm, for example. If other similar research was happening, it hadn't made it into her curriculum before she graduated.

"Yes, isn't it exciting! Dr. Toussaint's interface allows rapid development and precise base-pair matching—editing on the single base-pair level. Mass producers are still using molecular methods. You know how biological processes are."

"Messy." Harper agreed.

"Extremely. With nanites, we get more specificity and

nearly no accidental deletions. If this project succeeds, it will revolutionize the modeling industry. Models will be higher quality, more specifically attuned to the work for which they're produced. It will be a new age."

And cheaper. Railynn hadn't said that, but the subtext of fewer errors also meant cheaper. Better value for half the price, or some proportion. That meant that Ordell and his entire generation would become obsolete, along with those who came before. The next-generation models would be more muscular if needed, and dumber if required. In the legal and scientific fields, they would be smarter and more innovative. Sex industry workers would all have perfect proportions. What would happen to the entire existing generation of models? Stacks of burning Ordells flashed in her mind - the logical consequence of efficient commercial machinery ruthlessly purging the old.

At home, Harper resigned not to let her day show on her face. Barely into her new job, she already found herself uncomfortable. The fact that cloning was the major industry for bioengineers, especially in the League City area, was a motivator for getting a bioengineering degree in the first place. It couldn't be helped that her circumstances had changed, and the job she qualified for was in that industry. She took a deep breath and collected her things from the car. Moments later, Harper pushed open the front door of her house, and stifled a laugh.

Ordell clutched a tiny duster in his over-sized hand and leaned over the mantle as though he pondered what exactly to do with it. Harper flashed a smile at him as she entered, and he seemed to smile back, though he was also still meditative as he continued about his self-imposed chores. She wondered what his day must have been like, trapped inside of the walls of her childhood home. She would never have been able to do it. Maybe it was different for models, though. Or perhaps just for Ordell, she corrected herself, careful to excise him from the group in her mind. She pushed down any lingering thoughts to prevent herself from pitying him. He didn't deserve that, and he wasn't a prisoner anyway. He could leave whenever he wanted, though the idea of his possible departure caused her to shudder with fear.

"Hey, are you in there?" she whispered to him as he finished dusting the window.

"Sorry. Just thinking some things over."

"Do you want to share?"

"No, it's not important. How was your day?"

"Well, it was good actually. I have a desk, nameplate, and very strange co-workers."

She explained the rest, leaving out the thoughts bouncing through her head about what would become of the older models. Ordell nodded thoughtfully as he listened.

"Sounds interesting," he told her, his face set.

"Interesting? I guess. It was the only place that called me back, anyway."

His face muscles slacked as he smiled grimly.

"We do need the money."

Later that evening, in bed, she found that she couldn't sleep. She thought about the purge - that shift when the new generation of models replaced the old. Every time she closed her eyes, she saw the image of burning bodies stacked into a smoldering pile. Once, her stabilizer would have taken the edge off, and spiked her with melatonin to knock her out. Without it, she tossed and turned, and struggled to keep her mind controlled well enough for sleep to take her. As she finally did manage to sink into a slumber, she faintly registered the smell of burning flesh.

* * *

Tuesday, June 7, 2185

On Monday, personal and professional curiosity inspired her to spend her free time exploring more about the current cloning process. Her desktop screen connected to Lattice, the network optimized for scientific journals and data, instead of the Labyrinth immersive virtual network. Being the dominant global industry, finding research articles on cloning was quick. The complexity was in weeding out the bad ones, a skill she owed to her undergraduate education. Harper learned that all cloning processes required two stages. The first birth saw the clone come out of the cloning chamber as an actual child. The second birth occurred when the clone came out of stasis to get a job assignment.

Harper had an expert in the process at home, but she couldn't bring herself to ask Ordell about his past. The more she learned, the more she realized how difficult Ordell's life must have been. Unlike him, she had grown up with parents, at least one of whom loved and supported her. The idea of going through life entirely alone made her eyes water. She wondered how someone could go through that and come out as compassionate as Ordell. She pulled a tissue from her purse and dabbed at her damp eyes to avoid smearing her make-up.

"Are you okay?"

She hadn't heard Dr. Toussaint come out of his wing of the lab. One more dab cleared away the remains of a tear before she glanced toward the sound of his voice.

"Allergies?" she said, more as a question than an answer. Dr. Toussaint nodded, confirming that he would go along with her story, even though he knew she was upset about something more.

"If you need to take the day off because of... allergies... you can, Harper. We can handle it here for a day without you. Although you do make it hard and we probably won't be as efficient - so maybe not two days, okay?"

He smiled, and she returned the gesture.

"No, it'll pass. I'll take some allergy meds," Harper replied. "Thanks."

Life without a working stabilizer was a challenge.

Dr. Toussaint turned away, feet pounding so loudly as he left that she wondered how she had not heard him approaching. After a few minutes, she felt the threat of tears subside and took a deep breath. She swiped her desk's top to clear the research screen because she didn't think she could handle it at the moment. Then she checked the schedule - there was nothing on it for the day. She really could take off with almost zero impact. Harper was too diligent to take advantage, however.

She tried to pass her time counting the graduate students as they entered, but it was too late in the morning, so she got to five and then gave up as they swarmed through the foyer. Then she unlocked her desktop to look for a game or something to do, but all she found were office tools. The boredom of the empty room gave her far too much time to think. She pushed herself away from her desk, stood from her chair, and decided to walk the building. Fifteen minutes to wander would be enough to break up the monotony, she hoped.

10

Bad Memories

Tuesday, June 7, 2185

Ordell began the task of packing away the man who had murdered his lover. He pulled the first image down, and pushed the collapsing button on the back of the frame. It folded in on itself like an accordion, bringing the two ends together as the fine micrometer thick print rolled up into one side. He then dropped the scroll into a re-sealable metal container he'd found in the attic.

The next was shaped like an oval. He pulled it down and paused mid-way, examining it in his hand. Within, a youthful Harper smiled widely and held up a stuffed animal. She must have only been ten or so. Aayushi leaned casually against the man who would eventually kill her. The trio stood on the back porch, with the ocean gleaming blue in the background. At first glance, it was a happy family enjoying the sunshine. He thought that perhaps the animal, which vaguely resembled a porcupine, was a birthday gift of some sort. As he examined the photograph more closely, he could see that even at ten, Harper's smile hadn't made it to her eyes. Aayushi's even less so, with her deep, dark eyes surrounded by thick make-up. Ordell knew why she used concealer.

The dead way her eyes stared out of the photograph jogged a memory in him. That look of defeat and resignation to an empty life was something he'd seen before.

Convocation and Didactics training took place in New York State after his second birth. Phineas Lancaster, two other models with the last names of Bentley, and others he didn't know well, comprised his platoon and became his roommates for the entire year. He smiled as he recalled briefly how the sight of him, Lancaster, and the two Bentleys sent the polli scattering away on their infrequent forays into the city. People in the non-model world didn't often come across men as big as genetically enhanced construction workers.

Thursday, July 20, 2175

Lancaster and five other models followed Ordell to his first assignment near Atlanta. Initially, nervous anxiety kept them quiet, even among each other. The hard work kept them too exhausted to think. He and Lancaster shared the only two-person room there just by sheer luck. One day, Ordell noticed when Lancaster smiling. Since he never smiled, the change became the topic of conversation for a full day.

"What's the matter with you, Lance?" Ordell asked him in the late morning.

"I'm in love," came the gruff reply, ridiculous sounding in his raspy voice.

"Love?"

"Yep, love. I met a girl."

"As ugly as you are?"

The smile faltered but only briefly before it broke into a

wide laughing grin.

It wasn't love.

Looking back as he did, now through the eyes of a man who truly had loved, Ordell saw that what Lancaster suffered consisted of little more than a crush. Only twenty-years-old to Ordell's thirty-five, Lancaster could have caught a glimpse of the girl from afar and thought he was in love.

Ordell delved back into his memory.

Together, they heaved a stack of boards onto the back of a truck, then turned back toward the pile. Yellow gloves and bright orange construction vests complemented garishly bright safety uniforms.

"A girl? Here?" he asked, now thinking that Lancaster made it up. He couldn't imagine what sort of girl would frequent a construction site in the middle of a forest. The road leading in was a muddy, bumpy dirt one which only large trucks could pass safely. Ordell had so far not seen a single woman.

"Yeah, look," Lancaster told him, motioning over toward the only completed building nearby. Within that building, the site boss did his paperwork and went through contracts. On the verge of the doorway lingered a petite looking girl about Lancaster's age, who flashed a smile in their direction before she opened the door to let herself inside.

Later, months or weeks (time blurred together in Ordell's mind) there came a day when Lancaster missed roll call. The site boss predictably asked Ordell about his suite-mate.

"Food poisoning, sir," Ordell replied.

"Why don't you have it?"

"He had a bad piece of fish. I didn't eat any."

"Well, why didn't he tell me himself?"

"Sir, when I left him, he couldn't leave the bathroom. He could barely talk."

"You'll have to cover his work then," the site boss told him.

That would have been the end of it. The lie was reasonable and believable. Lancaster destroyed the story when he arrived on the site an hour later with a completely different lie about having gone into the forest to piss and getting lost.

The site boss questioned them together. One of them told the site boss about Lancaster's girlfriend, but Ordell could no longer remember which of them it was. Once he started talking about her, Lancaster couldn't stop waxing on the virtues of his mystery woman, as though love could conquer vitriol. He professed true, once in a lifetime, love.

Lancaster's gravely voice espoused her virtues, like the gold of her hair. He compared her to various flowers like daisies and white lilies. They both knew they were in for some punishment after that - a beating, or perhaps missed meals, more likely both. A single word magnified the cruelty of that punishment ten-fold.

Edelweiss.

The word came forward, raspy and dry, from Lancaster's lips. The noble white flower, a tiny plant that neither of them had ever seen since, dictated their fates. The site boss turned beet red at its mention. He sent Ordell away and called in the Overseer.

Tuesday, June 7, 2185

The look in Aayushi's eyes was the same one in Lancaster's, after he received such a beating that he never walked the same way again. The light, the joy, had wholly left him. To Ordell, only a hollowed-out shell of something that used to be Lancaster took over his life and responsibilities. There was no more talk of love after that.

For his part, Ordell received ten lashes with a laserwhip across the back, three of which were deep enough to leave him with scars that sometimes still caught on his clothes. His back itched and burned as the memory freshened his sensitivity to them.

Engrossed in his thoughts, he hadn't noticed Harper come. He jumped as the door slammed shut, and turned toward the sound to see her standing, motionlessly in the doorway, staring straight at him.

"I...don't know if ..." he began, but then decided he didn't know what to say. His memories had temporarily stolen his ability to think.

"It's your house too, Ordell," she told him. "I didn't know those pictures bothered you."

"Don't they bother *you*?" he asked, and then he regretted posing the question, but she answered anyway.

"They were never real, so I've always kind of ignored them."

Yet even through saying all of this, she didn't move. She stood, staring blankly at Ordell as if he wasn't there.

"Are you okay, Harper?"

She nodded, then shook her head.

"I'm just tired, I think," she told him as she finally stepped forward towards the bathroom. He could tell that she wasn't okay, but he also didn't want to pry during her moment of insecurity. He only watched as she walked to the bathroom and shut the door behind her. A few minutes later, she made her way past him in the other direction and back toward her bedroom.

"Good night, Ordell."

"You too."

The packing continued much faster than it began. Fifteen minutes later, he found himself out of images and still reeling with turmoil inside. Two days had passed since contacting Freedom Underground, and he'd heard nothing back. He began to wonder if reaching out had been a mistake. A few minutes of late-night holovision might be enough to help him unwind, he thought.

"Start holovid - show news," he said, and the holovid started up to show Gregory Ramsey's disembodied head, his face twisted into anger mid-rant.

"Sure, there are some good shills, I suppose," he all but screamed at whoever was interviewing him, "and there are good wolves too. Most of 'em will eat you given half a chance."

The man had been on more and more often. He dominated the airwaves now.

"Mr. Ramsey, are you comparing models to wolves?" a newscaster's voice chimed in.

"Look, I'm not saying they're animals, but what do you think they're like after coming out of storage? Especially this missing one – have you heard about it? Nineteen years in storage. Do you think a happy, well-adjusted human comes out of that? Just think ..."

"Turn off holovid."

Alone in the darkness, his mind wandered back to Lancaster, who should have been very close to twenty-six. He saw the same cruel look on Ramsey's face as he had on the site boss's.

Thursday, July 20, 2175

The connection between that furious look and the mention of the Edelweiss flower eluded Ordell at first. Much later, he overheard another Bentley talking to a Briggs.

"... seventy-one lashes, on maximum. Of course he's still in recovery. Can you believe he could be so dumb?" Bentley said.

"He was in love. What do you want?"

"Models can't love."

"You know what I mean, Bentley," Briggs replied, "he was

in love. Fuck all of the lies about what models can and can't do."

"Don't say that too loud."

Bentley looked around, and made quick eye contact with Ordell, who turned away and pretended he'd heard nothing. The conversation continued more quietly.

"All because of a flower. I heard that Edelweiss is the site-boss daughter's favorite flower."

"Who did you hear that from?"

"Clayton Briggs."

"Yeah, how would he know?"

"Really? You do know about the site-boss's daughter, don't you? Around all of these men - no birth control needed?"

Ordell stopped listening after that - enough models together always made up stories. It was enough to know that the girl who Lancaster had successfully wooed turned out to be the site boss's daughter. That had exacerbated Lancaster's punishment and rendered his back and the backs of his thighs a pulpy mess. He later found out that it was true - that evening, when he hadn't returned at all to camp, and arrived late for work the next day, she had been his accomplice. Ordell never discovered where they went or what they were doing, but he guessed it wasn't sexual, given that Lancaster had lived through his punishment. They may have been merely holding hands and searching for flowers in the woods. That thought wouldn't have surprised Ordell at all.

It didn't matter anymore anyway. Lancaster had fallen off of his radar years ago. All of it, like his Aayushi, was ancient history now.

11

The Hard Problem

Wednesday, June 8, 2185

Bored at work, Harper explored the building. Two open hallways flanked the circular lab, converging at Harper's desk. Having had the tour down Railynn's hallway, she decided that Dr. Toussaint's would be more interesting to see. She hadn't seen the corridor on his side since her interview. As she breached the entrance, she saw that the tarps had disappeared, and new walls stood where bare frames used to be. The path continued around the back of the lab until she recognized that it merged into Railynn's hall after all. The office was like a charm bracelet, where Harper's desk was the connector keeping the two halves together. The center of the bracelet was an open-aired courtyard, where young trees grew in freshly overturned soil.

There, she re-discovered Dr. Toussaint at a six-foot-long picnic table, studying something on its metallic-glass surface. She stared on as he tapped and swiped and sometimes made a hand gesture in the air while staring into space. Curiosity pulled her closer to him until she could see that he read through a paper displayed on the table's screen, probably from the data-coin near his hand.

"Dr. Toussaint?"

He snapped his head toward her with an intense frown. It melted into a smile a second later.

"Are you okay?" he asked. "Is there anything we can do to help?"

"Yes, I'm fine. Your schedule is clear for the afternoon."

She sat next to him to get a better vantage point of the screen and pointed to one of the sections he had underlined.

"Brain states consistent with experiencing objects?"

"The hard problem of consciousness."

The hard problem of consciousness had been called that for nearly two centuries. The term described the relationship between physical interactions and conscious understanding of those interactions—one of Harper's instructors had covered this in her philosophy elective. As monotonous as the instructor had been, she had learned at least this much from the class.

"What does modeling have to do with the hard problem?"

"We have a hard time studying consciousness because every human brain is different. With a hundred billion neurons, all uniquely placed, it's impossible to *see* consciousness. We can see the broad strokes, and guess at things, but what we need is to experiment with nearly identical brains. These papers all ultimately fail, because they are starting from the outside, trying to model the behavior of consciousness based on EEG or fMRI brain scans."

"I can see that. But why bother with the modeling? Can't you study, I guess, twins, or triplets?"

"What parents will allow me to put things into their kid's brain? I need something in there to help map things in real-time."

He tapped his temple for emphasis.

"Second, I need a lot of similar brains. Two isn't enough. Identical models to the degree that I would need, are way too expensive."

"Oh, I see," she muttered quietly, finally understanding. "You need cheap, similar models, and the modeling technology for that doesn't exist yet. So, create the technology, then you can have all of the models you need."

"Similar in brain development genotype," he replied. "Other things I really don't care about."

"Won't that hurt them?"

"What?"

"Monitoring their brains. Don't you have to cut them open to do that?"

"No, look," he said, and then turned his head slightly, and pointed to a tiny bump behind his left ear. It was the same ear he had leaned into during their interview when he'd answered a call. "Doesn't hurt after it heals."

"Comm implant?"

"Sort of. I started with a communicator implant, and added to it. With hundreds of similar enough brains, we can cross-correlate data and get at the elusive concept of consciousness."

"Did it hurt? Installing it I mean?"

"Only bad for a few minutes, then it's annoying more than painful. No more than a standard comm implant."

"May I look closer?"

She reached her hand forward and touched the side of his neck. In the condensing air, his skin was shiny and slick as her finger slid over it. The bump reminded her of when she got a splinter in her upper thigh. It worked itself out over time, but for months she had to deal with the unnatural feeling of a tiny quarter-inch long foreign body resting just beneath the surface of her skin.

"These papers are to firm up my conceptual understanding, and some of those state machines I feel like we can add to this mechanism or a similar one. By the time we're ready, this device – I call it the animus module - will interface with the brain on a neuronal level."

Harper got a flash just then of Ordell, emerging from his second birth, only to have a strange device drilled into his head. She turned away quickly before her face could betray her emotions, and reminded herself again that the job was only a job - a means to an end to get Ordell to Canada.

"Would you let the models decide for themselves whether or not to get it?"

The question surfaced before she could pull it back. She turned to the doctor, painfully aware that her eyes were still glassy from the thought of Ordell suffering. She felt that Dr. Toussaint finally looked at her and saw her instead of a sounding board.

"And wait twenty years?" he asked, and then his face flushed. He swiped the screen clear and stood from the bench.

"No, wait," she told him, fearful of losing her job. "I mean, how many could you need anyway? Make a lot, and then ask a few, and you could find many would agree."

It wasn't the apology and demureness that she had expected from herself, as someone who wanted to stay gainfully employed. The situation deteriorated quickly.

"I'll consider what you're saying, Harper," Dr. Toussaint told her coarsely, "but it's a very long time until we're even at the point where we need to make that decision."

Point taken. Harper was the administrative assistant and not the principal investigator. She should keep her opinions to herself.

* * *

Wednesday, July 13, 2185

Over the next few weeks, Harper caught Dr. Toussaint on many occasions standing aloof in the foyer and ignoring her as though she were invisible. He sometimes stared at her through the glass window in the door leading toward his office. When caught in the hallway, he greeted her the usual way, but his manner was distant and cool, which somehow seemed worse than if he had been rude. The combination ramped up her anxiety. She convinced herself that one day she would arrive to find her desk occupied with another less opinionated version of herself.

Had her job not been in potential jeopardy, she would have regarded his reaction to her as silly, perhaps grade-school, as she had only told him that his plan wasn't perfect. She wondered if she'd misjudged him as an educated and intelligent person who could tolerate criticism. He might have been a fragile, egocentric individual incapable of accepting his own flaws. She also wondered why she cared so much - there were other jobs.

Regardless, the stress followed her home, eating into her sleep. The evening of July 9th was worse than the others. In her dreams that night, a giant pink dragon breathed out something that looked like the Fruity-Os from her childhood but burned like acid on contact. She stayed ahead of the beast by leaping from rock to rock in a volcano filled with powdered milk as scalding hot as lava on contact but otherwise gave off a cold chill.

She bolted upright, wide awake.

For the next few minutes, she sat up in her midnight-black bedroom, terrified to reach for the light. Sweat seeped down her back and face, and her sheets were damp from the sweat she'd produced while fleeing the dragon. The cartoon-like dragon didn't warrant her waking physiological terror. She tried telling herself it was only a dream, but that terrified her more. She felt her breath quickening as she gasped for air.

"Or...delllll..." she managed to whisper through closing windpipes as the darkness began to swallow her up. This darkness was oncoming panic-attack induced unconsciousness; she knew from too much experience.

"Ordell!!!!" she managed to scream, clutching the blanket to her chest. The blackness swam before her, and she fell backward, gasping for breath.

She thought she heard the scrambling from her parents' old room, and a thud as something heavy collided with the wall in the hallway, followed by a curse. Then she hyperventilated and passed out.

Wednesday, July 14, 2185

Her room had changed from black into well-lit pink by the time she awoke. A rough hand stroked her hair back out of her face, and a damp cloth lay across her forehead. She could see Ordell's bushy eyebrows, twisted in fear, peeking out over his flat nose. She used what little energy she could muster to smile at him and convey that she was okay. Her mother used to take on his same role, only she would soak the cloth in chilled rosewater hydrated from concentrate so that when Harper awoke, she would smell the perfume.

"Harper, there's nothing to worry about," her mother used to tell her, stroking her hair in much the same way as the big man now did. Even though it usually wasn't true, it was still lovely to hear when she said it. This time she listened to a much deeper, much more anxious voice, less practiced at soothing the lingering effects of a nightmare. This voice wasn't telling her that things would be okay; it asked her instead.

"Harper, are you okay?"

"Yes, Ordell, I'm fine," she assured him, trading the smile

for the energy to speak. "It's just a panic attack, that's all."

"What's the matter?"

"Something at work. It's silly; you wouldn't understand."

"Share with me, Harper," he begged her. "I can listen."

So she did, though even as she told the story, she realized how silly everything sounded. Of course, her job wasn't in jeopardy. The idea that Dr. Toussaint would fire her for something so trivial seemed ridiculous with Ordell there, brushing her hair back across his lap. She struggled to sit upright and turned to him.

"Thank you for coming."

"It's what I can do, Harper, for all that you've done for me. For all that Aayushi did for me."

She sensed an opportunity, and though she was exhausted, she refused to let it slip away. The distant, moody Ordell was the other part of her anxiety problem, and she worried about him.

"Why have you been so moody lately?"

For almost a minute, the two sat in silence together as she awaited his response. When he sucked air into his barrel-like chest, she knew he would tell her.

"Aayushi," he whispered slowly. "She would want me to take care of you. She….would want me to treat you like my daughter. And I try, Harper, I do, but I don't know what it means. I'm a model, and having a child…. Still, I'm here, in this house, every day. You're taking care of me, and it should be the other way around."

"What?"

"I should leave. The reward keeps growing, and eventually, someone will think to come here. You're in danger because of me. I turn on the holo, and Ramsey's giving speeches, riling people up against models, especially highlighting the dangers of escapees. But here I am, hiding and afraid, god forbid, that someone, someday might walk through the door and catch me, or worse, hurt you. I can't stay, but I can't leave you here alone either. I guess I feel useless right now, and it's wearing on me."

"Ordell, I can take care of ...," she started to say "myself," but then thought better of it since he was in her room after a panic attack.

"Look, you do help me. Every day, it helps to have someone to talk to. But you should know, whatever you think of my mother, you're not my father. And I'm not a helpless little girl," then she smiled and threw up her hands.

"However much it looks like I am right now."

"That's not what I meant..."

"It is, of course," she interrupted, "but that's not what this thing between us is."

She paused, wondering again what precisely the thing was.

"We're friends, Ordell," she said. "As friends, we help each other when needed."

"Friends?" he asked, in a robotic way that made her want to laugh.

"Yeah, I think so. You don't owe me anything, and I don't owe you anything. We're just trying to get through this weirdly fucked-up situation together."

The furrows which had until then taken root between his thick eyebrows relaxed, and he smiled for the first time in weeks.

"It is pretty fucked-up," he repeated.

"Yes," she replied, feeling lightheaded as she the rest of her energy slowly depleted. She looked at the clock, dismayed to find that it was now nearly five. Even if she was able to fall back asleep and not dream about the pink dragon, what little sleep she got would probably work against her.

"I need to get ready," she said, carefully and deliberately, to make it clear that she wasn't rejecting him. She wondered at the commitment that he had to her mother and whether she might find someone who would have that same kind of commitment to her someday.

"Yeah, I'll go," he told her. "You sure you're okay?"

"I'm fine. It's just going to be a very long day."

The day stretched on. The afternoon passed excruciatingly slowly, and Harper found herself sneaking out just a few minutes early. Dr. Toussaint left at the same time, walking toward the same section of the parking lot. It became impossible to avoid him when she realized that his volantrae was only two spaces over from her beater of a car.

"Hey Harper," he called to her, in a pleasant tone. "How are you?"

"Uh-," she stammered, "Fine, I guess." She tapped her fingers against the window sill while waiting for her car's biometric scanner to figure out it was her and unlock the door.

"I've been thinking a lot about what you and I talked about," he continued. "Do you have a minute?"

She didn't want to take a minute to talk to him about anything, but he was the boss, and she would play along for at least as long as it took him to say whatever it was he thought he should.

"I've never considered what my research would do to the models. I mean, it's not risky. In a sense, I'm trialing it right now."

He tapped the bump behind his ear. The door unlocked, prompting Harper to pull it open.

"Ooookay," she replied, then started to lower herself into her seat.

"This is very awkward, Harper," he continued. "I'm impressed with you. What am I trying to say? You're smart, and you have empathy and can see things I miss."

"Oookay," she said again, starting to feel uncomfortable, but determined not to let it show.

"Would you like to grab some coffee sometime?"

"Coffee? Oh, sure," she responded. She was so tired that she could barely think straight, but she felt that he might have been inviting her on a date. Was that appropriate? She knew that it wasn't something that people did, date their supervisors in the corporate world, but was it more common in research labs? She didn't know. It was only coffee, and at least she wasn't getting fired.

"But it can't be now," she continued, "because I didn't sleep well, and I have to leave before I become a danger to others on the road."

With that, she ducked into her car before he had the opportunity to reply, and began the long drive home, her stomach churning out with something new to worry over.

Thursday, July 15, 2185

The next morning, Harper prepared breakfast by replicating something that resembled runny and monochromatic sunny-side up eggs. She sighed as she took the meal over to the table to sit, and realized that Ordell had gone to bed the night before without closing out of his Labyrinth session. In the two-dimensional rendering, she saw yet again a map of the United States, with highways marked in red lines. Several had x-marks through them where he'd scribbled on the screen in his finger. Old highway twenty-nine had a circle around it, with the word "maybe". A closer look at the line that made the road showed a gap between the half leaving Texas and the half heading into Canada. It was as if the road disappeared. But roads couldn't do that.

Harper swiped the session away as she placed her food down. The egg on the plate slid grotesquely from side to side, but she knew her skills with the replicator were limited, and it was the best egg she'd managed to make in a while. She cut the egg with the edge of her fork, and worked her way through the rubberized bottom layer before delivering it to her mouth. At least it tasted like eggs.

"You're up?" Ordell's voice caused her to lift her head and dribble a little egg onto her chin. She quickly wiped at the mess with her hand only to discover too late that she hadn't brought a napkin with her, and only succeeded in smearing it around. This made her laugh, and he quickly joined her.

The synchronous laughter made her think back to that first day they had met. It was a lifetime ago, and this time, when she stopped laughing, the warmth of Ordell's company persisted through her smile.

"I found a way," he said. "It's going to be rough, I think."

"I saw," she nodded, as he crossed the kitchen to use the replicator. He'd even shaved that morning, a good sign. "Old twenty-nine?"

"Yeah," he nodded. "It actually does make it all the way. The reason for the gap is that some bridges collapsed and deteriorated during the earthquakes in Equilibrium. Dirt roads connect to go around the holes though, from what I've been able to discover."

He punched some numbers into the replicator. It whirred up and made a slight clicking noise as it pumped the proteins in the right mixture to create whatever it was that he made. Just before the clicking stopped, he popped the door open prematurely, and pulled out two perfect over-easy eggs. She groaned at him.

"That machine loves you," she told him.

"I know. Did you ever figure out what to do about your problem?"

She clenched her jaw so hard that the muscles felt like they would tear. Then she forced her jaw to relax, and focused on

Ordell. In that moment, as he stood there with a smile plastered over his face, and such an optimistic grin about the future, she felt connected to him. And with that connection, surety washed over her, and she nodded.

"Yes. I think so."

Harper straightened her back and wiped away the last of the egg from her face before taking another bite. It wasn't a perfect egg, but it was her egg, and it was good enough.

"And?"

"He is a little old, but kind of cute - and the job is temporary anyway..."

At this, Ordell's smile widened, and she felt her breathing speed up as she smiled back, tight-lipped.

"So - no problem?"

"Only what to wear."

102

12

Seeking Freedom

Friday, July 16, 2185

Ordell punched numbers into the replicator. The machine was finicky today, and he waited just a hair too long. Burnt toast made a quick breakfast before he delved into the problems of the day. He found no messages from Freedom Underground on his communicator. As he began to place it down on the counter, the device vibrated in his hand, completely disrespecting the fact that his head hurt. He lifted it to answer but fumbled and dropped it to the floor. Scrambling, he leaned over to retrieve it, wincing as the pressure in his head increased with the additional blood flow.

"Harper?"

"Ordell," she whispered, "what should I do?"

But... what was Harper calling for? Wasn't she in her room. He squeezed his eyes shut as he thought through the previous day, then the morning.

She must be at work.

"About...."

"Dr. Toussaint. He just asked me to call him Torrent."

Puzzled, Ordell pondered his possible responses.

"What happened last night?" he asked.

"Wha - no! Nothing happened."

"A four-hour-long coffee date and nothing happened?"

"Well, hold on, I can't talk..."

She'd seemed focused and confident the day before. Today she was back to her anxiety-ridden self. The communication link stayed open as she gave someone instructions on how to navigate the facility. Then she spoke again.

"Nothing happened. Dropped me off like a gentleman. I *may* have indicated some interest in him. But we're at work, and first names doesn't seem like, well, like *him*. The only person who calls him Torrent is Railynn, and she's his partner."

"Everything is normal otherwise?"

"Yes, Ordell." Her voice took on a tinge of impatience.

"I would call him Torrent, then. I don't see what the problem is."

"Okay, thanks. Bye."

Ordell didn't understand how she could possibly see the ask as anything but a move in the right direction, assuming he knew at all what direction she planned to take that relationship. Before he could ask her anything else about it, she'd disconnected the communicator, and he found himself alone again.

Harper arrived home early, energized in a strange way that he hadn't seen before.

"Ordell, you'll never believe what happened today."

He doubted he wouldn't, but held his tongue.

"What happened?"

"Okay, so I had lunch with Torrent."

"Dr. Toussaint?"

"Yes, Torrent. Keep up."

Ordell nodded his head up and down.

"So we took kind of a long one. Just the two of us, and we went to Mad Monkey Dumplings downtown. It's on the second Strata in a little building that looks like it used to be a bank."

The excitement Harper revealed took his breath away. To see her so passionate filled his heart. He hadn't known that she could be capable of such intensity.

"The candles were low, and we may have had a moment. I think. Maybe not."

"Maybe not? I thought you like him."

"Dr. Toussaint's my boss. I can't really like him."

Ordell gritted his teeth together as images of Lancaster flooded into his mind. Aayushi's face took Lancaster's place, but he shook it away. Polli could have whatever relationships they wanted - Harper's future wasn't the same as his past. He tried on another smile.

"You can like whoever you want, Harper. I don't think there's much you can do about how you feel."

Ordell often wondered what he would have given not to have loved Aayushi. The woman's dark brown hair, framing her face, with sad eyes that always tried to be happy. His heart sank as her memory refused to leave. He'd been helplessly in her orbit, risk and all, only to have her ripped away from him. His memories of her had all become tinged with bitterness and anger. Still, Ordell would never trade their time together for safety - then or now.

"But be careful," he followed up. "Make sure he respects you. He has power over you, and it might only be a little fun to him. Is he interested?"

"I think so. Ordell, he's so easy to talk to. We were late getting back into the office after lunch because we just got carried away talking. Did I tell you he's an orphan? Just like me," she continued. "Only he's been alone since birth. Can you imagine…"

He saw the recognition in her eyes as she realized the loneliness of Ordell's situation.

"I'm sorry, Ordell. I didn't mean to…"

"There's no need to apologize," he said as he smiled. "I'm glad you found someone that seems pretty decent."

She beamed at this and shot him a grin.

"We're going out tonight. To the Firecracker Grill downtown. I came home early to change."

His stomach dropped as he began to understand how serious she felt and how quickly the relationship moved. Harper bolted down the hall into her bedroom, leaving him pondering their combined futures as she left. He couldn't shake the feeling that his ally and confidant had been hijacked. Worst, though, Ordell felt as though the gravity he'd brought into her life could crash her budding romance. Harper didn't need him anymore, and she seemed like she might be able to experience life, with relationships, and even friends.

An hour later, she gave him a brief hug as she passed on the way out the door. He listened wistfully as her car pulled down the drive.

Ordell used the food replicator to pump out something that resembled popcorn in shape but had less flavor. Even his skills with the device couldn't disguise the fact that he'd ordered the wrong set of proteins for it. The version he'd ordered for was the current market version, and this machine was nearly three years older. The difference produced some interesting side effects. One was a steak that tasted like a tomato. Green vegetables seemed okay, but that nearly everything else had an iron-like aftertaste.

He'd never had to consider the variety of proteins before. He used to eat breakfast, lunch, and dinner at the worksite. Usually, it was something gray for breakfast formed to resemble sausage and something that looked like a burrito for lunch. The best part of each workday had been after the showers when they would all sit in the big tent and eat actual real food instead of formed proteins. Often it was some bad cut of beef, such that they couldn't reasonably call it steak even though it looked that way. Something was still satisfying about gnawing on real meat drowning in a savory sauce.

Like every other night, he spent the evening watching holovid and eating his bland popcorn. No news this time, as he'd burnt out on it. Instead, he watched old documentaries of homes swallowed up by the ocean as climate-change Equilibrium approached. Tonight's was the battle of New Orleans. Despite federal, state, and parish warnings, the citizens filled sandbags in futility, attempting to stave off the encroaching Gulf of Mexico. It ended with thousands dead, and millions of dollars in property swallowed and now sitting on the ocean floor.

He wondered if it was an allegory for his life, his brief optimism diminished by memories of Aayushi and new-found isolation.

Saturday, July 17, 2185

The next morning he awoke on the couch, with a stiff neck and an ear that wouldn't pop, to find a note from Harper saying she left for work already. He pivoted his head over to the clock display on the wall to find that it was nine-o-clock already, well past when he had intended to rise. He groaned and slid his feet over the cushion toward the floor. He'd better get the day started.

His communicator lay on the ground nearby, knocked off

of the couch overnight. It flashed red at one end, a sign that someone had called. He assumed it had been Harper sometime during the night to let him know how late she would be. He pushed a button on its side. The device projected a face he didn't recognize against the far wall.

"Mr. Bentley, this is Joseph from Freedom Underground. We haven't forgotten about you. State scrutiny is high at the moment, and we need to be careful. If you can send us your location, we can send by a representative to get you started in the process. Reply to this message with your whereabouts."

Ordell sat up straight and stared at the face. This one looked vaguely like his old friend Lancaster.

Another model?

He entered Harper's address and sent without hesitation. At least he could be out of Harper's way. Then he stretched his arms and pulled himself from bed, ready to start the day.

13

Ethics Czar

Monday, July 19, 2185

Monday found Harper tucked behind her desk, picking at her cuticles while she waited. She took a deep breath, and tapped her fingertips against the top. She had fun with Torrent, but worried that she might have overshared. Each date, and she wasn't even sure they *were* dates, had been fun and relaxed. She'd enjoyed his company, and she thought he'd enjoyed hers. They were in some nebulous void between having a real relationship and being co-workers sharing drinks over happy hour. Harper smoothed out imaginary wrinkles in her slacks and straightened her back.

Torrent was different than she'd thought. The way he obsessed about her comments touched her. He seemed genuinely concerned about the plight of the models. That he hadn't considered them human without having had to be told concerned her, but Harper was willing to accept that it wasn't his fault. The scientific community invented cloning. Seeing models as only the result of an experiment was likely a natural progression. Besides, it wasn't too long ago that she harbored the same lack of understanding.

The door opened, and Harper's head shot up, seeking out Torrent's silhouette, but it wasn't him. Instead, she got a wide grin engulfed in blonde hair.

"Harper! I'm glad you're in. Got a lot of work today - if anybody's looking for me, can you tell them I can't be disturbed?"

"Sure! What's going on?"

"Prepping Egg Lab. I'm going to set up the egg chambers and need time to test."

"Oh … exciting!"

"I know! I'll see you around lunchtime. Maybe if you didn't bring yours…"

"Sure, I'd love to."

With that, Railynn popped around Harper and ducked through the door leading to her office, and Harper was alone again. Then she saw Torrent just beyond the glass doors. He paused for a few seconds before he made his way through and sent a fleeting smile at Harper that disappeared too quickly and he walked toward her. Not toward her, she reminded herself, but toward the door to his office just behind her. She put on a smile.

"Good morning, Dr. Toussaint."

He seemed flustered and didn't respond for a second.

"A-anything on the agenda?"

He asked the question without a smile and with a bit of a stutter. Harper, thankful for the excuse to look away, swiped her hand across the desk to pull up his schedule.

"Meetings at 3, 4, and 5. Also, there's a lunchtime meeting with Gallatin."

"Ah, yes, I forgot. Thank you, Harper."

"You're welcome, Dr. Toussaint," she said with a grin.

He didn't catch the joke, but ducked nervously around the desk and disappeared. She felt her face go flush with blood as three more people entered the room. There wasn't much time to recover, so she exhaled and put on another smile.

Just before lunch, Torrent poked his head out of the door to his hallway.

"Harper, do you have a minute?"

Startled, Harper nodded and pushed away from her desk. He hadn't made any effort to enter the foyer, so she assumed that she would need to follow him. She traced the familiar path town the hall and into his office. Harper sat at the same table where she had interviewed and noticed that the room had improved significantly. The walls reflected the ambient lighting as bright blue, but subdued enough not to be distracting. She took a seat, as he sat across from her, rubbing his temples with his fingers. She waited, but he seemed agitated and clamped his mouth shut.

"Harper…"

He gulped, and she felt her head grow hotter.

"I never got the opportunity to ask you to take on the role that I wanted."

That piqued her interest. She listened more intently, ready to decipher the next few sentences that Torrent uttered.

"What role?"

"Something like an Ethics Czar. Be an advocate for models here, to keep an eye on we're doing and make sure that we don't get so wrapped up in the research that we forget about the humanity of it."

He said this with an even keel and directness distinct from the rest of the conversation. Harper's heart sank at this return to stoicism. She both feared and hoped that he wanted to discuss the connection she thought they'd made.

"Could I think about it?"

"Sure. Take as much time as you need."

"Okay," she said and turned to leave.

"Harper, wait," he told her as she took her first step. "There's more."

She spun around to face him.

"About these evenings we've shared. I'm not sure we - as your boss -" he started. "Are we okay?"

His eyes implored her to return to 'normalcy' and to write their time together off as a fluke. She acquiesced by returning an innocent look that portrayed the face of someone who had no idea what he was saying.

"Okay? Yes, Dr. Toussaint, I believe we're fine."

That seemed to do the trick. Torrent let out a breath.

"You're going to be late for your lunch date," she spit the words at him.

Torrent morphed back into a disquieted mess, grabbed a few things from his desk, and flew past her through the door without making eye contact. She also had a lunch date to attend. Checking her emotions, she turned deliberately and exuded calmness as she exited his office alone.

Railynn met her in the hallway, a welcome distraction to her anxiety-ridden thoughts. Ten minutes later, Harper found herself divulging to Railynn over lunch at a nearby cafe.

"What the heck is an Ethics Czar?" Railynn asked, chewing a bite from her roast beef sandwich.

"I don't know," Harper responded, still irritated. "I guess I'm supposed to make sure that people think of models as humans and not an experiment?"

"I don't think you can make sure of something like that. You can't control what people think."

"You never know, Rai. Sometimes people listen."

"That's not what I'm saying. People may listen and nod along, but whether you change what's in their hearts is different. I don't know that you'll be able to move the needle there. *I* wouldn't want the job."

Railynn was right on that point. She wouldn't be able to change anyone's mind, and she wasn't sure why she should have to. It was Dr. Toussaint's lab, and if he wanted people to start acting like models were humans, he could tell them to work that way. There wasn't a substantial anti-modeling sentiment among them, or they wouldn't be part of the lab in the first place.

He could find another Ethics Czar. She had to go to Canada anyway.

Railynn continued over her thoughts.

"Of course, that job is more of an executive-level. And Torrent thinks you can do it or he wouldn't have asked. I guess you can look at it as a strange sort of promotion."

"Without a pay increase?"

Railynn laughed at that.

"Well, for now. Maybe that's the test - see if you can do it? He must see a problem that needs solving. I'll ask him about it."

"No, don't," Harper said. "It'll just be weird. I was only telling you as a friend."

She took a sip of her lemonade and then spat it back out into her glass, grimacing at the bitterness and lack of flavor. A waiter stopped by a moment later in response to her actions.

"Are you okay, ma'am?"

"This tastes horrible."

"It is Vita. I wondered why you ordered it. Usually, only shills drink that stuff."

"Shills?" She stared at the waiter's eyes until he looked away.

"Sorry, ma'am. Models, I mean. I'll get you another."

"Lemonade, please."

"Certainly."

The waiter trotted off as Railynn giggled in the background. Harper turned her head.

"What?"

"You," Railynn said. "You *are* an Ethics Czar. I'm not sure why I didn't see it before."

Harper considered what had just happened, and thought back to her initial conversation with Torrent. Her views had shifted, and she hadn't realized it was happening. Before, the word 'shill' wouldn't have bothered her at all. She wasn't sure, as a polli, that she'd have cared about involuntary experiments either, had it not been for Ordell. Harper thought about the word *polli* - what models called non-models. She'd never even heard of the word used before she met Ordell. She smiled at the thought.

"I guess I am, huh?"

"Yes. Are you going to eat those fries?" Railynn asked.

"Oh, no. Go for it."

Without worrying about Torrent's return, Harper spent the rest of the afternoon planning her approach to rising to the occasion of Ethics Czar. Her first order of business - change the name. She could only imagine how hard some of her upcoming conversations would be without the authoritarian title hanging over her head. Besides, the last self-proclaimed czar was in South Dakota, from when it tried to defect from the United States during the more challenging times of Equilibrium. Regardless of how Torrent had meant it, the name was likely to cause some friction.

Ethics Coordinator.

That one was too general. Harper expected to make sure everyone did the right thing. Maybe Torrent had already nailed the correct title.

Model Advocate.

She liked that. And, she thought Ordell might appreciate the position too. It was a tiny thing in the vast landscape of model affairs, but it was something.

14

Emergency Escape Plan

Monday, July 19, 2185

Something had felt off to Ordell ever since he gave Freedom Underground Harper's address. He found himself jumpier than usual, and he suspected the mystery visitor had returned three separate times. He would have been wiser to demand a neutral location for them to meet. Handing over his information felt like an unnecessary risk.

To be on the safe side, Ordell re-packed his go-bag. This time, he grabbed a couple of Matthew Rawl's old clothes too so that he would have more choices than t-shirts and jeans. Since Harper wasn't yet home from work, he had plenty of time to chart out an evacuation route.

Despite how weak he was when he'd arrived months earlier, Ordell remembered how he'd gotten through the woods. Retracing his route, he pushed through the front door and stepped into the driveway. A bush halfway down was where he'd come out of the woods. Beyond that, a trail hid tucked away. However, if anyone had come to try to capture him, they would likely have parked in the driveway - possibly with a partner As escape routes went, running toward danger was something he generally preferred to avoid.

He pushed back past the bush and into the woods. The trail was narrower than he'd remembered - more of a suggestion than a path. After the days in the dense jungle, it had probably seemed like a highway at the time. He examined the ground as beads of sweat dripped down into his eyes. The Texas heat was unbearable, especially someone his size. But he had to push on. He wiped the sweat away and looked closely at the trail. One end seemed to dead-end at the bush; the other end led back away from the house and toward the jungle.

Looking more closely, he saw that there was more trail going towards the house. The main route was probably a deer trail, where the continuation looked like some smaller animal - perhaps a fox. He had to push apart the upper brambles to see it clearly, and following it meant forcing his way through vines. He continued and the forest began to thin before him. The trail followed the house's rough contours and opened up near the far end of the house. Foliage there would be too thin, and would never be able to hide him. Somewhere along the side of the building, there had to be an exit.

The wrap-around porch stood just above his knees. Ordell placed one knee in the dirt as he knelt to examine the underside of the porch and smiled. He had assumed that this house, unlike other homes near League City, had walled in the foundation. Houses in this part of Texas usually stood on cinderblocks since there was no way to keep a basement from caving under the pressure of ever-shifting sands. A closer look told him that Harper's home was no different. Tin skirted the house, with the occasional vent opening. The solid-wall appearance was an illusion. The majority of the space was empty behind that thin wall.

He formed a plan. The vents in the master bathroom could drop him under the house. Then he could crawl to this point and push through into the woods. But would it be fast enough?

His arbitrary escape time had been five-minutes. He didn't have a reason, but he preferred his escapes to take less than five minutes from beginning to end. He needed to test it.

Ordell went back inside to the master bedroom. He pulled up the vent and groaned at how small of a hole it revealed. It would never work. He might be able to push through the tin wall from under the house, but he couldn't muscle his way through hardwood floors. Temporarily defeated, he searched for another way down. Sometimes, there were access panels so that electricians and plumbers could get under the house for repairs.

He looked in the master bedroom closet but found nothing. The foyer closet where the coats hung also had no access panel. Only Harper's room remained, so pushed through the door. The room was a pink proton rifle blast to the eyes. His eyes adjusted to the overwhelming brightness of pink as he entered. Careful not to disturb any of the piles of dirty clothes across the floor, he picked his way to her closet and pulled it open.

He could see the edge of an access panel there on the floor, under yet another mass of clothes. This mound he pushed away, and as he did, he heard a beeping noise. Something in a mound projected an image to the back wall. Even at the slanted perspective, he recognized Harper's straight black hair. Her lips moved, and he heard her voice.

"Anxiety management journal entry two-hundred twelve. I woke up this morning with a headache. Ugh, drank too much again. But in my defense, so did Torrent - I was just keeping up. That's right; I said 'Torrent.' Dr. Toussaint asked me to call him Torrent. Ow."

She winced, and a hand went up to her temple before she resumed.

"I think, maybe, we connected. We talked about everything. Well, everything except Ordell."

He noticed her countenance fall when she said his name.

"He's just been so moody. I don't know what to do about him. Canada, I mean, is a trip we can make, I think. Just the two of us, any time now. We almost have enough money! But he never seems to want to talk about it anymore. And really," she paused, "I guess I don't either. Torrent - maybe I'm getting ahead of myself. Breathe."

She took two exaggerated breaths.

"Maybe there's something there? How will I know if I leave now?"

Ordell had heard too much. He felt his face heat and eyes sting as he fished through the clothing to find the source. The device was tiny and looked like a small rectangle prism. True to what she had said, it had the words' anxiety journal' stamped across the side. He didn't want to pry further, however curious he felt. It was an invasion of privacy. He lifted a big hand across his face to clear away the emotion lingering there and focused on the work. He pulled the access panel open and found that it was barely large enough to go through.

Next, he started his timer on the communicator, then lowered himself into the hole. To the left and right, spider webs clung to the underside of the house, and no doubt, spiders lurked amidst the tangled wires that hung over his head when he was fully prone. Still, he pushed forward to where he thought the trail was, fumbling through darkness.

When he made it to a vent, he peeked through. There it

was, his freedom. A rattling noise started up near him, and he froze immediately. He had been foolish not to consider the snakes. By the sound of it, the rattler was just behind his right foot. He slowly turned his body and stared into the darkness, but only the rattle told him where it was. If he remembered, he had maybe five seconds before the snake decided Ordell hadn't heeded his warning.

Ordell turned back to the vent and pushed against it as hard as he could. The grill didn't pop out, but even if it had, it was too small. A sharp pain caught him in the right leg as the rattling stopped. He shoved his way forward with a burst of strength, and an entire tin wall on edge of the house gave, vent and all. He rolled out from under and kicked his right leg to ensure the snake was gone, though he knew it would be. The thing probably fled just after biting.

Good, he was near the trail, he could see. He checked his communicator. Three minutes and fifteen seconds. Perfect, he thought as the pain traveled up his leg. He felt his breath slipping away, and his vision began to blur. He was big, though; he knew that the bite might not kill him. He tried to get to his feet, but his right foot felt like a rubber ball when he tried to stand on it. He stumbled and fell toward the trail.

I need a rest.

The heat pounded against his skin as the fire built inside of his body. Sweat soaked through his clothing as he lay there. Dirt and sand caked his face as he struggled to get up. Finally, having forgotten what he worked for, he resigned himself to his fate.

15

Saving Ordell

Monday, July 19, 2185

Monday afternoons meant dense traffic with frustrated commuters, and this Monday was no exception. Self-driving cars crowded the roads and volantrae clogged the skyways. Harper swerved in and out of the safety zones around the auto-navigating vehicles, closer than she should. Torrent's disconnected actions and words distracted her from her task. She slammed on her breaks just in time to avoid colliding with an expensive looking Mandrave before her. A series of squeals told her multiple vehicles behind automatically adjusted to accommodate for her miscalculation.

Focus on driving.

Twenty minutes later, Harper pulled into her driveway. She noticed right away that a bush at the end seemed out of place. Her first thought was that the bounty hunters or police had come for Ordell, but she told herself to calm down. It was probably just Ordell looking around. He had to be bored sitting in the house all day and there were only so many hours someone could look over the same maps.

She stepped out of the vehicle and went up the walkway to the house. The door clicked open and she pushed it forward. There was no Ordell in the living room or the kitchen, both visible from where she stood.

"Ordell?"

There was no response. Harper's heart beat faster as she walked toward the master bedroom, calling out as she closed the distance to the opened door.

"Ordell?"

Harper was about to turn into the room when she saw that her bedroom door was also ajar. She peaked through the door of the master bedroom for a quick look, and noticed some clothes left out on the bed, laid out as though he were picking out an out fit to wear. From there, the last room to check was her own bedroom. She gulped as she entered. When she passed through the doorway, she heard the sound of her anxiety journal playing. Harper sucked in at her bottom lip as she recalled everything that she'd said about Ordell in her journal. She navigated toward her open closet where she kept the recorder, and saw a hatch opened on the floor.

Harper lowered her face through the opening and saw nothing but black. Seconds passed as her eyes adjusted to the darkness, and she made out a light piercing through from somewhere far away. As her eyes grew more accustomed to the dimness, she saw that the source was outside. She also witnessed scraggly spider webs clinging to cinder blocks and told herself that she would never be going down that hole. But she wondered why it would be open and thought that Ordell may have gone in. Harper left her room and exited out the back door to follow the porch around. There before her, as she came to where the light originated, she saw Ordell, laying face-down near the boundary of the grass and the forest.

Harper shrieked as she saw him there with his ankle swollen to the size of a basketball. She jumped from the porch and ran toward him. When she got there, she flipped him over, fearing the worst, but his chest rose telling her that he was still breathing. He muttered something she couldn't understand as she pulled him upwards with all her might. The heat emanating from his body was immense, a contrast to his cold, clammy skin, which could only mean dehydration. She pulled him up as best she could onto his right foot, but his weight nearly crushed her as he fell back to the ground.

"Get up, Ordell!"

Again he mumbled something. Sorry? She couldn't be sure, but it wasn't helping.

"Get up," she yelled at him. "Up."

He seemed to respond and pulled himself about halfway up on his left leg with the swollen ankle. With help, it seemed to support most of his weight. Still, the act of getting him onto the porch would have seemed comical under other circumstances. Harper half pushed and half rolled him onto the porch, her flats slipping against the yellow-green grass. He was able to provide some assistance as she walked him around the edge of the deck. She supported some of his weight, but the rest was supported by him slamming into the house's wall so hard she thought he might crash through it.

For the second time, Harper witnessed Ordell splayed across her living room couch on the edge of dying. This time, he didn't fall into unconsciousness when his body met it, though she would almost have preferred that complete lack of information to his endless writhing while his fever spiked and waned over and over. In her mind she considered calling for emergency medical attention, but then what? They would recognize him, and then he would go back to Emergent

Biotechnology.

Re-education was only a fancy word for torture.

"Ordell," she whimpered as she swapped out the damp cloth on his forehead with another.

"Harper," he whispered, then mumbled more incoherent syllables.

His fever spiked, and she added ice to the water and dropped the towel back into it. An emergency med kit she found in her parent's bedroom had an anti-inflammatory shot in it, so she gave him that and hoped it worked the same for models.

Of course it does, they're just humans.

It seemed effective, even to the point that the basketball reduced to a softball, but his writhing continued. Ordell's temperature came down from the 104 to 102, but never dropped past that as he tossed and turned. She poured water into his mouth only to watch him choke on it and spit most of it back out. Still, some may have gone in, so she repeated the exercise over and over until a wayward swing of his arm sent her flailing across the room. Bruised and battered, she got back up to her feet and stepped back to him. She would have to be faster with her reflexes. In his state, he could kill her and not even know he did it.

The rag went back into the ice water, then back on his forehead. This time he noticed, as his entire body shook in a terrifying heave when it made contact. A good sign, she thought, as she drenched it again and repeated the action, careful to keep his huge arms well in view.

For twelve long hours, she fought with his fever and at times with him. It wasn't until four o'clock the next morning that he finally stopped writhing and his skin regained some of it's color. The fever stayed high, but she couldn't fight it any more. She re-doused and applied the cool rag as he seemed to drift off into something that resembled sleep, reminding her to do the same. She sat in the oversized chair, afraid to leave his side, and told the house to wake her up in thirty minutes.

When she awoke thirty minutes later, he still slept. She glanced at the therm-patch on his skin to observe that it had turned yellow instead of red. The readout was only 100 degrees, the lowest since she'd gotten home. Better yet, he had begun to snore and take in deep breaths. Finally, he rested. Still, she took no chances, and kept a repeating thirty-minute check on him for the following twelve hours, more exhausted each time the alarm sounded.

The weekend wove together into an endless routine of fever spikes interrupted by vomiting while she played the barely-capable nurse. The spikes were lower though, and the normal temperature sometimes dipped into green by Sunday evening. She never felt as alone as that weekend, enshrouded in silence except for inane mutterings and unprovoked apologies that he heaped on her periodically for something she didn't even understand. He'd apparently ripped her from her life, or failed Aayushi, or something along those lines. Even flush with fever and barely coherent, he was the same obsessed man. When would he learn that it was her life, and neither he nor her mother could be responsible for her choices?

She couldn't be angry at him as much as she wanted to slap him and tell him to snap out of his hero complex. He wouldn't have realized what she was saying anyway, and reflexively might render her unconscious if she did. Harper stored it away as conversation to be had once he finally recovered. There would be a long talk, she promised herself.

Finally on Sunday night, she extended her checks to every two hours. Late in the morning, she remembered that she had a job to do. Too exhausted to handle a day of sitting in the office foyer, she contacted Railynn's communicator. Railynn didn't answer, so she left a message.

"Railynn, I need to take some time off. My…" She paused, having not thought out what to say. Then she decided to say nothing.

"…I just need a couple of personal days."

She disconnected, and stole a quick shower during her next two hour break. Refreshed but still tired, she took her post and shut her eyes for what little sleep may come.

16

Personal Days

Tuesday, July 20, 2185

"Hey Torrent, want to switch off on desk duty today and tomorrow?" Railynn asked just as he walked through the door. He'd thought she was Harper at first, so when he heard Railynn's voice, he jumped.

"Where's Harper?" he asked.

"Personal time. She needs a couple of days. I think that's fine; we don't have anything big coming up. I can do my work from here. Can you cover tomorrow?"

His pulse quickened at her response. Personal time could mean anything. He wondered if he'd said the wrong thing or the right thing the wrong way.

The situation with Harper had become weird since they started going out for drinks, and he wasn't sure what to say to her anymore. Every time he came across her at work, he longed to talk like they did in the evenings. He felt as if he had known her for his entire life, and as though they were kindred spirits. But he had to be careful. What if he was the only one who felt that way? She could be pressured to pursue a relationship with him. As her boss, he reminded himself daily that it was inappropriate to think about her any other way than as an employee. But he couldn't stop himself from feeling. Did it come through somehow that he wasn't aware?

"Of course," he replied. "Did she happen to say why she needed personal time?"

"No, just that she needed some, that's all. We can't ask things like that."

"I know, just - you both are friends, I thought she might have said something."

Railynn only smiled.

"It's kind of cute that you think I would tell you if she did."

He laughed in mock levity.

"Yeah, I guess. Okay. So you're taking today. Want me to do tomorrow?"

"That would be wonderful. The only thing that might come up is Gallatin has been threatening to visit ever since I told him that Egg Lab was done."

He acknowledged her statement with a nod.

"He always threatens to come down here. It's his way of letting us know he still believes in what we're doing. That man is way too busy making money to bother with a trip our way."

"I guess. Still, Gallatin said tomorrow might be a 'good time to take a trip.'"

"Gotcha. I guess I'll inspect Egg Lab today and make sure that it's in working order. Hate to disappoint our main funding source."

"I thought you'd feel that way."

He ducked through the door behind her and followed her hallway down toward Egg Lab. Once there, he stripped and put on protective gear in the decontamination chamber. He and Railynn had designed the man-gate to keep wayward DNA and particles as small as RNA-based viruses out. State of the art, it was the most expensive investment in laboratory function he'd made.

When he made it into the lab, two graduate students were already there inspecting equipment. He greeted them with a smile and went to work. He went through the motions, but he spent most of his time wondering why Harper had taken days off.

When he thought of her, he saw her as she was in the evenings, confiding in him about her abusive father, well beyond an employee relationship to her boss. He didn't know that much about any of the lab students. Perhaps the only other person he knew any personal background on was Railynn, and that was sparse information shared during the punch-drunk morning hours of laboratory work.

What he remembered more than the way Harper talked was the aroma of her skin. The lavender perfume she wore seemed to make sense in a way that told him, of course she would smell like lavender. The thought was ridiculous and confusing, but he felt it was accurate. Lavender was Harper, and the effect that she'd had on him at night was the effect of lavender. He relaxed; he was unprofessional and friendly, contrary to his normal tact. Work had, for the first time, become secondary to finding out everything he could about who she was and what circumstances had coincided to create her.

He forced himself to move to a pod when he realized that he was staring off into space, and the students were staring at him. He dialed up some numbers on the attached pad only to find that he still couldn't focus. There was no way he could pretend that Harper was only an employee. The way she occupied his mind was impossible. He decided then, as the pad repeatedly beeped in failure, that he had to know if she felt the same way. But he had to be discrete about it, and offer her a way out so that if he was wrong, and if she felt differently, she could say so.

As a graduate student got the beeping under control, Torrent left them to it. He should have been more concerned that a few mistypes on the pad caused the system to go haywire, but he had other goals as he made his way to the front of the lab and back through the door to the foyer.

"Railynn," he said as he passed another graduate student who also gave him a strange look. She turned to stare at him and started to laugh. That was when he realized he'd forgotten to change out of his hazmat suit, which made him smile too. He must have sounded like a robot through that thing. He pulled the helmet from his head.

"Railynn, this ethics thing I want to take seriously. Harper has to know that she can call me out on problems that she finds without retribution."

"Meaning….?"

"I'm drafting some documents to move her over to work for you."

"But I work for you too," she said. "I don't see how that helps."

"No, you don't. You're a partner as of earlier this year, remember?"

She kept acting like the partnership didn't mean anything. Torrent had made that change for a similar reason, though. He wanted independent research ideas and not sycophantic behavior. It had been mainly a formality as Railynn pretty much always spoke her mind. Still, it wasn't the token position she indicated it was.

"Okay, I guess. What if Harper doesn't want to work for me?"

"You think that will be a problem?"

"No. You're the one with the ego," Railynn smirked.

She laughed, but she was right. Torrent was the one with the ego, which she tested every few days, sometimes to the point that she made him furious. But again, that's why she was a partner.

"Okay, I'll bring the papers by later."

"In the hazmat suit?"

Thursday, July 22, 2185

By Thursday, Harper finally felt that she could leave Ordell unattended, and went to the office again. She arrived to find a nearly illegible note on her desk, scrawled in someone's handwriting. She pulled it open, unfolding the parchment twice until it was the size of a standard sheet of paper.

"Harper, I'm pretty busy this morning, but would you like to join me for lunch? I can swing by after my late morning appointment."

The signature looked like Torrent's magnetic stamp that he used to sign everything that needed signing. A squiggle followed a large 'T,' then trailed off the page's end.

"Uh, oh, what did you do?"

Harper looked up from where she sat to see Railynn hovering over her.

"Nothing that I know of. I haven't had time to do anything."

She had taken a few days off right after being "promoted," which could be considered a bad thing. And she had a lingering crush that she couldn't quite shake. Either of these warranted a conversation or more. She must have failed to keep her emotions off of her face by Railynn's response.

"Oh, I'm joking. Probably wants to go over the new position."

"Probably."

Harper's stomach knotted up as Railynn left. There was

more to it than the new position. The new job seemed so arbitrary that it couldn't be real. Nevertheless, when lunchtime came, and Torrent showed up at her desk precisely on time, she followed him to his volantrae, and the two left together. Torrent seemed unable to sit still while the volantrae lifted into traffic.

There, in guaranteed privacy, she imagined dropping the facade. She could reach out to grab Torrent's hand and explain that she didn't want to call him Dr. Toussaint in the office. She would say that he didn't need to make up a position just for them to be together. She did none of that. Instead, she stared out the window.

"Harper," he said. She turned to him and met his eyes.

"I want you to know that you report to Railynn now - not me. She's a full partner, so you don't answer to me in any way. I think this will help with your ethics duties."

"My Model Advocate duties?"

"Yes, that… and," he added, seeming uncertain, "I hope that will make this other conversation a little less intimidating."

"For who?"

She stared at him unblinking. He squirmed in his seat but didn't break her gaze.

"I deserve that. This thing between us - I mean, is there a thing between us? Don't worry, if you want there not to be, then there won't be. I'm not vindictive or anything. I think there might be…"

She put her hand up to quiet him and answered his question with a slight nod of her head.

"It wasn't you. A friend was sick, that's all."

Some of the lines in his face around his eyes relaxed away as she said that.

"Tonight then. Tonight I insist, no, beg that you go out with me. Somewhere nice this time."

In her excitement, Harper nodded her head in confirmation before she stopped herself. Ordell was still at home, and wasn't yet ready to be on his own. Partially recovered, he still needed help moving around the house.

"Thursday?"

"Thursday then."

"Okay. Somewhere nice," she replied, wondering what they would possibly talk about for the rest of lunch.

17

Night Prowler

Thursday, July 22, 2185

Ordell awoke to see Harper arranging a plate for his dinner on the coffee table. Thinking he slept longer than he'd wanted, he checked the wall clock display. No, he hadn't. The time was still just a little after five. She glanced up at him and smiled, tilting her head slightly away from him with her eyebrows arched.

"Do you think you'll be okay if I go out tonight?"

"Of course," he said. It wasn't as if he was going to do anything that might cause him difficulty. He hadn't been off the couch for days except to go to the bathroom. He was in for another evening of holovids whatever she did. The only thing different about this night and the night before was that he would not have Harper to laugh at zany situational comedy antics.

He owed her his life again. With his failure at being anything other than a drain, he couldn't begrudge her some time to herself to feel normal.

"I won't be too late."

"Torrent?"

Her ears turned red.

"That's right. An actual date this time."

"I didn't realize it was getting serious. By my count, it's two," he said, closing his eyes as he adjusted his head. "You know what the third date means."

She laughed as he knew she would.

"Thank you, Harper," he told her for what must have been the twentieth time, "for all of the things you've done for me."

"It's nothing you wouldn't have done, Ordell. I just got to it first."

"Still."

"Eat before you go back to sleep. I've got to get ready. While you have energy, please. You're recovering, and you need the food."

"I will."

He pushed himself to the upright position as soon as she went to her bedroom to get ready. She had the foresight to prepare a meal that would stand a little while without refrigeration. Spread sandwiches, and chips adorned the plate, not replicated - a good thing. It didn't look delicious, but nothing had since nausea became an integral part of his existence. He chewed the food and washed it down with some water, although he would have loved to have Vita instead.

Exhausted from the effort, he closed his eyes and drifted off. Harper woke him to say goodbye, or he thought it was Harper. The figure wore one of Aayushi's red dresses and smelled of lavender, but he was still half-asleep and may have been dreaming. He dropped back into a deep slumber.

"Odd one, wake up."

The whisper seeped into his lucid dream. At first, he ignored it. A vast landscape of open field needed to be tilled, and he was the only one to do it. Before him floated a brown and gold ball, levitating a foot and a half from the earth. A wedged iron head slid forward in the red dirt behind. As the metal ball moved, so did the wedge, furrowing the dirt into two mounds. The orb was called an 'ox,' out of nostalgic reasons, and it plowed the Martian soil, ripe for planting.

Somewhere far off, he heard the whisper again.

"Wake, odd one. You're not safe."

He glanced over his shoulder toward the house, to see Aayushi, wearing a frontier uniform of drab gray and brown, something she would never have actually worn. This jarred him, and he tilted his head, changing her clothing back into the teal sari he loved to see her in. Her smile and her eyes were directed at him as she stood in the doorway. Overhead, he knew the dome would keep out the dust storms and ice rain, when the rain did come. The terraforming wasn't yet complete. Early adopters had to take risks.

As he diverted his eyes to the far horizon, he saw the wide expanse of nothing. Red soil stretched out for an eternity, and for the first time in his short life, he felt free. In the other direction, he knew, the situation was exactly the same. No polli, no shills, these concepts were lost to him. Sounding the words in his minds evoked no reaction, because the words had no meaning here.

Even in the dream, he knew it was a lie. He rubbed his forehead with his hand before stepping forward, encouraging the ox to take a straight line. Without a satellite system, the ox had no navigation, and required guidance. Gently, slowly, he proceeded straight forward.

"Wake up!"

Ordell's eyes popped wide and he bolted up, only to have his head swim and the room go dark. This passed in a second as his eyes adjusted to the room. Darkness told him it was still night, and tiredness told him that the night had only just begun. He froze in place as the sound of clanging assaulted his ears from the kitchen.

Intruder.

He jumped from the couch and sprinted to the kitchen, ignoring the throbbing pain as the blood left his head. When he passed through the doorway, he heard the back door shut. However quickly he had moved, someone else had moved faster. He slid around the island and toward the door, to find it ajar. Pushing through, he made it to the porch just in time to see headlights fading into the distance down the pecan-tree-lined drive.

Whoever it had been, was gone. He crashed down to one knee as the excited energy began to wane. He couldn't have done anything anyway, he realized, and made his way slowly and deliberately inside. Examining the back door, he saw that the electronic lock had been triggered to release. Struggling to remember, he couldn't recall whether it had been locked or not. The front door locked automatically, but he didn't know if the back door did. Ordell pulled the door shut and latched it.

There was nothing else to do. He couldn't call the police, as he had no actual rights. Normally, Emergent Biotechnology security would handle things like this. Just to be safe, he double-checked the front door before resigning himself back to the couch. Images from his dream surfaced again.

Mars.

That was a possibility Ordell hadn't considered. The slow spin of the room came to a stop as he caught his breath from the exertion. The planet was almost a hundred years into terraforming, so people might soon be allowed to go. Out there, he doubted if it would matter if someone was a model or not - as long as one was willing to do the work, and he was.

"Holivid, Mars."

He spoke loudly enough for the holovid before him to activate and glow green as the start-up sequence tested various color ranges. A soft, soothing voice echoed out over a 3-dimensional view of the surface of Arrabia Terra.

"This is the Northern Crater, home of terraforming Station One."

The holovid zoomed into the facility, showing something that resembled a stack of sticks leaning together at the start of building a fire. Each stick was roughly the size of a small bus, but the scale of Mars made it seem like an abandoned campsite.

"Our first true Martian seedlings live in here. Station One does double-duty as a terraforming center and an experimental nursery, determining which vegetables and fruits grow better in the environment."

He recalled the freedom of the dream, and how, for just a moment, he had found what he wanted - control of his own destiny. Ordell stayed frozen to the screen as a lonely tear drifted down his cheek.

18

Free Harper

Thursday, July 22, 2185

As she pulled out of the driveway, Harper felt a sense of peace. The nurse was finally off-duty. She felt lighter as she navigated the private drive toward the main road. Twilight settled among the gnarled pecan trees dropping shadows before her, peeking through in slivers. Pavement rolled away beneath her. Harper smiled.

She had offered to meet him at the Faux Grey, a restaurant widely known to for fine dining. Her argument was that it didn't make sense for him to come out of the city just to take her back in. Harper wondered if it seemed strange that she didn't let him pick her up. She felt that if she did let him come to her home this time, it would be even stranger not allowing him inside - something she couldn't do as long as Ordell occupied the couch. Torrent hadn't said anything when they agreed on the time to meet, so the concern was likely just another of her multitude of irrational fears.

True to her nature, she arrived early. A chauffeur opened her door and glared with disdain as he realized that he would have to drive her car manually into the garage. The chauffeur's override code wouldn't allow it to self-park. She would have to remember to tip him well for his effort.

"You look wonderful."

As she stepped free of the vehicle, she heard Torrent's voice. At first she failed to register the compliment being directed toward her. Her mother's red gown and matching shoes made Harper stand out in the crowd of fashionable grays and greens. The clothes were several years out of date, and in a place like Faux Grey, Harper wasn't sure what thoughts lurked behind the sea of eyes which all seemed focused on her. She'd hoped the revolving wheel of fashion was nearing the point where the gown was fashionable again. She rationalized that trends seemed to be heading in her direction with the low-cut backs and trimmed bottoms cut just beneath the thigh. When she saw Torrent's smile, her insecurity melted away.

Torrent looked like a holovid star or a politician. He'd layered a gray coat over a zipped solid-black shirt, and his matching slacks ended an inch above high-topped dress shoes. His eyes never wavered from hers as he crossed the walkway.

"Shall we?" He extended his arm for her to take as the two of them entered the bar area to await their seats over a bottle of red wine. She couldn't help comparing between this bar, with highly-polished granite counters, and fully automated android waiters, to the seedy dive she inherited from her father. This was a bar she would love to be at, and the other was a bar one attended when one didn't have anywhere else to go.

"Alexander Toussaint?"

A man's voice penetrated the air and caused a brief look of

panic to shimmer across Torrent's face. He recovered before turning to an older looking gentleman in an expensive one-piece suit that sat behind him.

"Gallatin?"

"I didn't know you frequent the Faux Grey."

"Frequent? Oh no, I could never frequent this place."

Then the man's piercing gray eyes met Harpers' hazel ones.

"Ah, I see," he began. "So it's a date then - oh, this one is beautiful."

Torrent flashed an apologetic grin at Harper as the man stood from his bar stool and walked around Torrent to get to her, right hand extended.

"Your rude date has failed to introduce me properly. My name is Gallatin Hamilton, entrepreneur extraordinaire and funder of his little lab project."

"Little lab project?" Torrent asked. "It's the only thing moving in the direction you want to go in the industry."

The older man pulled his wrinkled face into a grin.

"Only when measured against Blackbird Bioengineering. Small in dollars, not significance. I should be more clear. And I hear great things."

"It's nice to meet you, Gallatin," Harper told him, taking his hand firmly.

"I would recognize that voice anywhere—Harper Rawls, the woman who keeps that laboratory running. The voice on the other end of the comm every time I call. What a pleasure."

Then with another grin and a side glance, he continued to address Torrent.

"I was wondering when you would wise up about this one. Mark my words - she's going to change the world someday. I'll leave you children to your romantic endeavors."

With that, he took himself back to the barstool, accompanied only by what Harper saw was about two fingers of hard liquor. He seemed content enough to sip it from time to time, and then mutter to himself or the bartender, who spent an overwhelming majority of her time entertaining him.

"Sorry about that," Torrent said. "I knew he came here sometimes, but it's such a nice restaurant. I wanted to impress you."

She was about to sit back down when a voice called out.

"Torrent Toussaint?"

"That's odd," Torrent commented. "Our table won't be ready for another half hour."

"Perhaps it's ready early?"

He raised his hand as an automated waiter navigated skillfully through the crowded bar area to them.

"Sir. If you'll follow me, someone has requested that you move to the VIP suite."

As they followed the waiter, Harper heard a chuckle behind her. She turned her head just in time to catch a wink from Gallatin, who went back to his drink and constant mumbling.

The VIP suite levitated above the city. The entire floor separated from the building below and soared into the sky. She knew that some parts of the Faux did that, but she hadn't expected to be in one. The ceiling of the suite lowered like a dome to reveal a glass enclosure. Through this, Harper witnessed the overcast sky just before breaking through the clouds, revealing the stars above.

"Wow," the pair said simultaneously, and then giggled.

"Gallatin," Torrent said. "He must like you."

"We talk sometimes," she replied, "Administrative stuff. I don't understand why he'd do this, but it's gorgeous up here."

The restaurant stopped its ascent and a door to the side of

them opened while an automated waiter brought out the first course. With the next glass of wine, Harper's guarded nature slipped away. She told him of her father's bar that she still owned, and drew some of the same comparisons she'd noticed for him to understand. He couldn't get enough details about Jarro. It seemed like a seedy, dingy joint for losers to her, but for him, it was the most amazing thing he'd ever learned about anyone. She told him about her addiction to lemon drops and her parents' deaths.

With Torrent, talking through their deaths didn't feel tragic. He seemed to feel every moment of Harper's history. She left out some parts, like Friends of Humanity visits in the hospital, or Ordell, but otherwise, she told him most of her past and he reciprocated. He told her how he interviewed Railynn to help build the lab, and why he'd made her a partner. He could be intimidating and overly intense, which scared people, so a little security helped ease opinions. He admitted being self-serving and vindictive sometimes, which was why he put barriers in place to protect him from himself. And that was part, but not all, of the reason that he'd moved her under Railynn. It wasn't all about romance.

The restaurant date ended in an intense and very passionate kiss that she carried with her all the way home. She entered the house to find Ordell sleeping soundly, having consumed all of the water she'd left out for drinking. She couldn't have asked for a better patient. Soon, she reminded herself, they would have to have that talk about why he couldn't let go of the fact that she was a friend, not an obligation.

Friday, July 23, 2185

The next morning, Harper was amazed to find Ordell up and about. He shuffled, like an older man in slippers, but still managed to move from room to room. She was even more amazed when her work day came to a close, and she straggled in to find him still awake. Then, the pair of them sat like an old married couple around the dining room table to a replicated meal of macaroni and cheese, wholly reproduced and not just dry pasta anymore.

"Someone broke in last night."

Her jaw dropped and she scanned the room for the culprit.

"Are you sure?"

"Someone was definitely here. I chased them through the kitchen, but they got away."

"Wha- who was it?"

Ordell shook his head side to side.

"I couldn't get a good look. The door was open, and I caught the car through the trees. I have to *leave* Harper."

"Ordell," she started. He moved on to take a bite of some substance he'd convinced the replicator to produce. It might have been steak. He chewed slowly and acknowledged her with his eyes. Harper's mind went back to the evening, soaring above the city with Torrent, and the feeling of his kiss.

"Are you sure you didn't imagine it? I heard hallucinations are a side-effect of rattlesnake bites."

He looked at her thoughtfully and swallowed before he responded.

"I wasn't imagining. Someone. Was. In. This. House."

She gulped down some juice and broke eye contact. A lump formed in her throat.

"Maybe it just seemed like someone was there."

"This is about Torrent?"

She instinctively shook her head no, but her eyes betrayed her as they fogged up. Ordell sighed and his massive shoulders slumped forward.

"You don't have to do anything. I'm making my own

arrangements."

"What arrangements?"

"Freedom Underground. I've contacted them, and they're going to help me get to Canada. It won't be too much longer."

She drew in her breath sharply.

"When were you going to tell me? What is a 'Freedom Underground'?"

Ordell had contacted some random organization that probably claimed to be able to help him. As he explained it, they were nothing but an urban legend. How could a man so old be so naive sometimes?

"There's no such thing as an organization that helps models escape. It doesn't exist."

"They called me back, Harper. And I've chatted with them. The people I spoke to - they look like models to me."

"Really?"

"Yes. One looked like me, and the other looked like a friend I went to Didactics with."

"Staged, Ordell. Or, wouldn't other models just do what they're told? Let me look into them before you do anything, okay?."

"I'm not an idiot. Live your life. You don't have to be concerned about me."

Her eyes filled with tears as she considered the cruelty of his words. They streamed in rivers down her face as she screamed at him.

"There's no way that I will ever stop caring about you. It's not a burden to care about somebody. It's what we do for each other."

"That's not what I meant."

"It's what you *said*, Ordell. I'm here - we can do this together."

Even as the words came out, she felt a knot forming in the back of her mind. Maybe a week ago, the two of them could have left and made their way northward, to try for Canada and freedom. Jarro - the house - the job - none of these things felt permanent since her parents died. But now there was Torrent - things change. She wiped her face dry.

"I don't have time for this right now."

Before he could respond, she stood up and left him at the table. She hadn't even gotten to the part about why he had been under the house, but the more she talked to him, the more aggravated she felt.

Breathe.

She had another date to get ready for - a fun one. It wouldn't be as extravagant as Faux Grey - that would have been hard to top. Tonight they were going to Chewy's Toffee House, a dining establishment that specializes in making toffee. It was in old town in League City's, with its quaint historic duplexes embedded in the Poplar trees. She didn't know what to wear but settled on a bright green dress with a yellow scarf. She donned her makeup and perfume, and left, passing Ordell without a word.

They were seated immediately, close enough to smell the batch cooker working to reduce the necessary ingredients into toffee. The aroma of caramel soaked into everything around them. By the time she arrived, the fight with Ordell had seeped into her and Torrent seemed to pick up on it.

"Are you okay?"

"Yeah. I just had an argument."

"Is this the same friend who you took care of earlier this week?"

"Exactly the one," she sighed.

"Seems like she should be a little more appreciative."

"He could at least try."

Torrent looked at her and smiled, and she realized then that she had let him keep his assumption that her friend was female.

"More like a friend of my parents," she followed up, "friend of the family, you know?"

Then she bit her lower lip as she recognized her second mistake. Torrent, being an orphan for his entire life, wouldn't have had friends of the family.

"I know what you mean," Torrent said, rubbing her bare shoulder with his hand. "You're here now, and the most you have to worry about is whether to eat toffee before or after dinner."

"You're right." She resolved not to let the fight interfere with her date. That would be complicated since dating Torrent was one of things that spurred the argument in the first place. Harper forced the thought from her mind. She insisted on having fun, a task that was much easier than she thought. They decided to have toffee before and after dinner. The pre-dinner toffee was English, buttery, and creamy with a thin chocolate layer. The meal was bland pasta, but the desert toffee more than made up for it - Cashew White Chocolate toffee, rich and smokey, and almost too sweet to eat. It was so good that she ordered a bag to take with them.

The evening ended too soon. The only thing she had waiting for her at home was Ordell and the unfinished fight. She sighed into her after-dinner coffee, distracted from whatever Torrent was telling her about his experiences at the academy. The idea of walking back into that frustrating situation sucked the fun out of her evening. A few seconds passed before she realized Torrent had stopped speaking.

"I'm fine. Just thinking," she said.

"About anything you want to share?"

She shook her head no as she lifted the corners of her mouth.

"It's nothing. Sorry - you were saying about the dormitory at Fouriedon University?"

"Not important. I was talking, that's all. Filling space. You've been distant this evening. Are you sure you're okay?"

Even without explicitly thinking about it, Ordell loomed in her thoughts. Pauses in the conversation had brought her mind back to him, and had been since she sat down.

"I'm sorry."

"You don't have to be sorry. It's that guy, isn't it?"

"Yeah, I just don't understand him sometimes."

"Talk to me about it. I'm interested in everything about you, not just the good stuff."

She longed to tell him then, and share everything. But at the same time, to do so would have ruined what was left evening and possibly their lives together. Instead, she reached over and took his hand.

"Can we get out of here?"

"Absolutely! Where do you want to go?"

"I was thinking about your place."

He swiped his hand over the table and pulled out a data coin, plopping it down on top of the automated itemization of their bill. Thirty seconds later, they rode in his volantrae, ascending into the skyway.

What am I doing?

There would be no going back after this. Harper tightened her grip on his hand, and he pulled her closer. She let him do it and turned from staring out at traffic to staring into his eyes - blue, like two lapis lazuli stones embedded in his eye sockets. Her mind replaced his eyes with rocks, and she stifled a laugh. Just then, she realized how close he was when his lips closed over hers. She let go of all her thoughts then and inhaled him. She pulled her hands around his head and kept him there, kissing him again and again.

19

Doubts Already

Friday, July 23, 2185

The snake bite disrupted Ordell's sleep cycles causing him to sleep whenever he could, independently of day or night. He used what waking time he could to plan his departure. Ordell examined the map lines carefully on the tabletop screen before him. He rose to his feet and stretched his arms and lower back in a tight back-flex, then shuffled toward the kitchen table to take advantage the better usability. Technically the house itself was a computer, as was the holovid-coffee-table-combo and the salinization unit, though the interface for both was quite a bit more challenging. The kitchen table had the best interface, and the option to pivot from two-dimensional to three-dimensional display. Better than that, it had a chair that wasn't the couch he'd been laying for 5 days.

The chair scraped across the floor as he dragged it back from the table, and creaked when he lowered his massive frame into it. Ordell tensed his legs at first sit, just in case the chair gave this time. It didn't, so he let the rest of his weight fall to to it. He slid his hand lightly over the table's surface, and the white was immediately replaced by a black background and something that resembled a sound wave rippling in the middle.

"How far is it to Winnipeg?"

The vocal prompt shimmered and then the table responded.

"One-thousand, four-hundred and twelve miles."

"What about driving?"

"There's no direct route from League City, TX to Winnipeg, Canada."

Ordell knew this was wrong. He thought back to where the old I-29 highway had crumbled - somewhere around Souix Falls.

"How far to Souix Falls?"

"One-thousand, one-hundred, and five miles."

"What about Watertown, North Dakota to Winnipeg?"

"Four-hundred and thirty miles."

That wasn't much better. Best case scenario, that was two charge-ups for Harper's car, or worst case, four. At approximately twelve-hundred dollars per charge, that was forty-eight hundred dollars he needed. Add to that five-hundred dollars per meal and that's an additional fifteen-hundred dollars. That was only if all went well. A trustworthy car would cost a couple of million dollars. Ordell hunched over the table and rested his chin on his palm.

"So that's all?" He asked the question out loud, as though the appliances could tap.

"Yes, that's all."

The response made him laugh and jump slightly in his seat.

Buying a car was out of the question. Harper didn't have

that kind of money, unless she finally decided to sell Jarro, which would take more time. She could have probably earned it in half a year. Well, he didn't *need* two million dollars for a car. Two-hundred thousand dollars might be enough for a one-way clunker. So far, two-hundred and fifty-three thousand dollars was his total. Harper made that much in a month.

But he didn't have a month, and he had no money. Experience in the jungle told him that trying a desert on-foot wasn't something he would be able to accomplish. He needed to be patient - while whoever was stalking them continued to do so.

He milled about the house, cleaning and taking the occasional peek outside to see if their visitor returned. Bored with his fruitless search for escape routes, even chores no longer interested him. He'd given up on the day and sunken into the couch for a nap when Harper walked through the door. Ordell began his slow rise to greet her, but she motioned for him to stay where he was, came to him and sat by his feet.

"I'm sorry about the other day. I know you're scared. I'm scared too."

"It's not just for me, Harper. If I get caught here, it's bad for you."

She nodded as her lips met in a single line, curved up at the ends in a weak smile.

"I went by the bank today," she said. "Look."

Harper held out a small rectangular box and tilted it over her palm. Seven cash-coins fell into her hands, which resembled like data-coins but with the faces of dead presidents etched into their surfaces.

"This is the Canada fund," she said as she dropped the first six back into the box.

"How much?" He asked, curious of how closely it got to his

estimate.

"Right now, altogether we have one thousand forty-three dollars. It'll build fast though. You're right that we need to get moving on this."

The next question was evident, and she answered it before he asked.

"Forty thousand, I think. That's how much we'll need to get to Canada."

"I count two-hundred fifty-three."

"Why so much?"

Ordell explained his thinking that a car would be the most expensive part of the journey.

"We can just use my car."

He looked at her askance.

"Are you planning on going?"

Harper stared at him for a second, wheels spinning as she looked down and to the left, weighing her options. Instead of answering, she changed the subject.

"We can use my car. That brings it down to around fifty-three thousand by your count, and forty-thousand by mine."

"How long until you think we can get that together?"

He asked the question, but the question he really asked was how long it would take her to make that money and give it to him for his escape. He grimaced inwardly while she considered the question.

"A month should do it," she told him. "It might not even be a month if we can stop eating."

She shrugged nonchalantly, and then grinned at him. Ordell's heart lifted as she held open her arms for a hug. He leaned forward on the couch, and wrapped his arms around her, surprised at how little she seemed then. Harper pulled back away from him after about thirty seconds.

"I want you to know that I'm going over to Torrent's tonight. I'll be back in the morning to check on you."

He smiled.

"He seems like a nice enough guy."

"*You* haven't met him."

"When are you bringing him over?"

"Okay, Ordell - you're not my mom."

Harper laughed as she said it, and Ordell laughed too. Then she left him to another evening of bad holovid movies.

20

One Possible Future

Monday, July 25, 2185

Harper felt a gentle push against her calf. She consented and pulled her leg back over Torrent's hip, where she had left it wrapped around him during the night. Still half asleep, Harper became aware of him pulling the loose blanket up around her so that she wouldn't get too cold. She squeezed her eyes tight against the knowledge that if she opened them, then morning would begin and bring with it the end of the weekend. Another day of deception and misdirection among co-workers approached with the daylight.

A pale pink glow flowered against her closed eyelids as a sliver of sun breached a gap in the blackout curtains. The wayward beam lay like a warm, thin rope across her thigh. She refused the invitation to rise. No memories of death lingered in this tiny apartment. Nor was there responsibility to Ordell with Canada looming between them. At Torrent's home, she was just a woman in a relationship and could be as selfish as she wanted. And now, she wanted to postpone the morning.

Harper turned toward him, opened one hazel eye, and flashed half a smile.

"What are you staring at?" She asked.

"Your endless beauty."

He exuded charm sometimes. Usually, such a mood involved a glass or two of wine in the evening, as they recounted how fortunate they were to have found each other. In the morning and wine-free, Harper had learned the response more likely meant that he only partially invested himself in their conversation, and probably worked on one of his theories in his head. Another reason for her to hate mornings.

She shut her eyes. Torrent didn't have a gear-shift. He was either on or off. Harper passed through at least twenty gears from the moment she awoke to when she was ready to do anything useful.

"I'm just thinking through what to do once these models are done baking," he said absently. She opened her eyes again when she heard the phrase. Torrent made cloning sound like a cooking show.

"The Firsts are in already?" she asked, with thoughts flashing through her mind about the risk that national attention would bring to Ordell.

"Not yet. Today's the day we transfer to Egg Lab."

"How many?"

"Sixty in total. Half are back-up."

She pulled her arms across her body.

"What do you plan to do with thirty children?"

He pulled her hand free and took her fingers between his own.

"My Model Advocate in action."

"And?"

"Staying on plan. Rai has been working on placing them. We have homes for most already. We're matching them with families - it'll be okay. That's not what concerns me. I was thinking..."

She didn't hear the next part. An unwelcome thought surfaced that the children were Railynn and Torrent's babies. She pulled her hand back and turned around to hide as her eyes teared up. It wasn't fair for her to feel the way she did, as though he'd cheated. She knew he would never do that. Sixty models created in a lab with a mix of DNA from Torrent and Railynn wasn't the same as a torrid affair.

Cold rationality kicked in. Harper's sensible side told her that she was involved in a summer romance. Eventually, Ordell would leave for Canada. Would she go with him? If she did, then there was no future with Torrent. But if she stayed instead, would she someday have to explain thirty half-siblings? And how could Ordell make a journey like that without at least one non-model helping to rent rooms and buy food?

The thoughts irritated her. Two weeks into a clandestine relationship with her boss, and somehow it was the appropriate time to even think of a future together. She controlled her breathing, and her heartbeat followed, slowing with each breath. Fingertips drummed along her waist as she noticed that silence replaced Torrent's monologue.

"What's bothering you?" He asked her.

"It's fine," she said over her shoulder without turning back. "Sometimes I forget. Jesus, I can't wait for this experiment to be over."

"Soon, Harper," he told her. "Only six months once we get these eggs going in Egg Lab."

"I know." She let out a deep breath. "You'll be late if you wait much longer."

He pulled his hand away and walked toward the shower.

"Forty-percent opacity," she said as soon as the door closed behind him. The blackout curtains lightened to let in more sun, which warmed her chilly, exposed leg.

Harper didn't want him to go into the office angry, and especially didn't want him to see Railynn when they had just had a soft-fight about her. When he came out of the shower, she stood and pulled the sheet off, standing unclothed before him. She slowly walked toward him, swaying her hips and carefully placing each step in front of the other. Then she grabbed the back of his head just above the neck and pulled him forward into her for a kiss.

Afterward, he dressed quickly, tripping over his clothes as he ran out of the door. Harper watched him, longing to go in with him instead of waiting the prescribed time to keep up appearances. Until the experiment concluded, they had committed to keeping their relationship a secret. She couldn't remember whether they both had decided this or just him, though she had her suspicions. Alone in an empty apartment, she wondered about the wisdom of the choice. Would it matter if anyone in the lab knew about them? How much simpler would it have been to share a ride into the office in his volantrae?

She forced herself up and into the shower, then slung herself back over the bed to grab her black canvas bag of necessities from the floor. Then, swinging her legs up and over the blanket, she freed herself from the tangled mess of bed linens, bag in tow. It would have been much more straightforward for her to keep her stuff at Torrent's house instead of lug her cosmetics from location to location. That was another conversation she'd yet to even have with Torrent. And what if someone else happened to show up and see her stuff?

Harper's communicator chimed. She retrieved it from the nightstand beside her. The projected number was Ordell's "burner com" as he liked to call it. The communicator was something Harper had bought at a convenience store for about two hundred and fifty dollars and no registration.When she called the number back, the connection went to a generic prompt, indicating a full mailbox. Harper took a deep breath and exhaled slowly. She did it one more time, pushing out air through pursed lips. She would try again later. Probably he'd called her by accident and they would have a good laugh over it.

She sprayed on her Lavender Path Parfum Spray, an expensive spray that reminded her of her mother. Then she pulled on fitted beige slacks which were only saved from mediocrity by a bright blue camisole that she'd chosen the day before because it went so well with Torrent's eyes. And then she set out for work, resigned to the fact that she probably wouldn't see him at all that day since the Firsts were moving into the Egg Lab. She would be alone, in a desk, counting people as they entered.

21

Moving the Firsts

Monday, July 25, 2185

As Torrent arrived at work to move the Firsts, Railynn greeted him at the door.

"Ready?" she asked, exhilaration apparent in her wide blue eyes.

"Let's do it."

When they peeked through the window of the Egg Lab, Torrent saw the egg-shaped chambers into which they would transfer thirty of the cell clusters which had matured into zygotes. Though more resilient now, they could still easily be damaged during the move from the compact sample cases to the ceramic containers. Something as simple as improper decontamination could ruin the previous several months of lab work.

"Torrent, are you coming?"

Railynn held open the door to the sanitizing station. He nodded and stepped inside. Once the door latched behind him, he stripped to his boxers and socks, and she stripped as well, and then the chamber sprayed a fine mist for thirty seconds. Afterwards, both donned the white containment suits that hung from the wall.

Railynn shuffled across the floor to the wall vault that housed the 60 viable samples left from the first stages. She pushed three buttons, and a tray that resembled a Petri dish popped out partway. The grips on the gloves made it complicated for her to grab the plate, but she succeeded, and walked toward another machine to slide the sample into a slot for analysis. Torrent watched her pull up the sample on a screen that he couldn't make out as he passed through the decontamination gate. The way her shoulders slumped told the story. Even in the bulky suit, he could see that she was disappointed. She turned to look in his direction.

"This one didn't make it."

That wasn't a good sign. Torrent shuffled to the massive storage vault to collect a different sample. He pulled out A2 and followed the same journey that Railynn had, as she passed him to go back for A3. Their eyes made brief contact, and he could see tears preparing to fall. He felt the same. Still, he slid the dish into the slot and held his breath. The monitor popped on, and at first, he thought A2 had died as well. Then he noticed a little wiggle from the cell group and couldn't stop a grin. Then the numbers slowly ticked across the screen – viability at 99.8%.

"Rai, this one's alive," he nodded to the screen. She stopped mid-stride and pivoted to come back to where he stood. She squeezed in beside him to see the screen, and he could hear her breathing quickening through his speaker.

"Yeep!" she exclaimed and then cut out.

"Yeep?"

"Yes. Yeep!"

He nodded.

"Yeep, then," he told her and pulled the sample out of the machine. 'Yeep' may have been the correct reaction. He grinned as he carried the tray through a white door and into the next room where they kept the eggs. Three feet tall, and just short of a foot around, they were lined up like a garden, in six rows five across. A mass of wires connected each pod to a neighbor. At the endcaps, the cords wrapped around to the next row.

"Dorothy, open pod one," he said, addressing the lab's only robot assistant.

"Sure thing, boss," Dorothy replied, and moved to the egg directly in front of him, and grabbed the lid with her metallic arms, twisted the top off, then rolled it aside. He approached slowly, to ensure that he didn't drop the sample. It would be a lot of work wasted if he did.

Six inches away, he slowed his approach. He poured the contents from his sample dish into the open pod. The pus-colored liquid in the cell solution blended into the translucent green and blue fluid in the pod's base.

"Close pod one," he called to Dorothy, who immediately rolled past him and twisted the metal lid back on until it clicked. Torrent lamented silently how clunky the transfer method was. It seemed inelegant that they dumped the cell mixture into the eggs. Had he trusted the lab robot more, even having her do it would be better. He'd never taken the time to program her, so the only thing he trusted her to do was open and close containers, a task for which her inhuman strength guaranteed an air-tight seal.

"One down, Rai," he said. "Twenty-nine to go."

"This one's good too," she replied. "So we only need twenty-eight others. It's a good thing we kept sixty. So, are you going to tell me?"

"Tell you what?"

"It's just the two of us. Who's the mystery woman?"

Torrent didn't have to look to know that Railynn smiled mischievously behind her visor. The conversation caught him so off-guard that he nearly dropped the new sample he transported over to the monitoring machine.

"Just get your work done," he responded amiably. He closed his eyes, took a breath, and re-focused himself. If he failed to stay attentive, they could compromise the experiment.

Before the two of them finished, eleven o'clock at night had come and gone. Even by Torrent's workaholic standards, it had been a long day. The two of them had opted not to break for meals to avoid the time cost it took to change into and out of the suits, but the work would not be rushed. The remainder of the samples transferred without incident, justifying the slow and deliberate approach. All of the remaining 28 colonies proved viable, which would mean a 98.3% success rate in the later stages, unheard of in modeling - if carried through to the hatch. They planned to keep the remaining 30 samples as backups in stasis. Given the hurdles they'd overcome, success seemed guaranteed, a thought Torrent barely dared to entertain.

Hungry and exhausted, Torrent was too excited to think about going home yet.

"Thai food?" he asked Railynn as he removed the hazmat pants to pull back on his regular jeans.

"This late? I think all the ones near here closed half an hour ago."

"Yeah, maybe you're right. Jo and Beth's should still be open. Scrapple?"

"Ugh. I'll go, but no scrapple for me."

As they left for dinner, he picked up his communicator and noticed three missed calls, all from Harper. The last call had been from an hour and a half earlier. Whatever it was she had been calling about; Torrent was sure that she would let him know about it later. She hadn't bothered to leave a message so it couldn't have been critical. Calling this late would only wake her up prematurely.

He dropped the communicator into a compartment in the car before they approached the doors of an ancient-looking diner. A dense billow of smoky air accosted them with the smells of burning scrapple on a flat grill. The cook grinned as they approached to seat themselves on bar stools. The restaurant was a multinational conglomerate but still kept the homey atmosphere.

"I thought you two found a new place to eat," he admonished them. "What'll you have?"

Late nights and sparse options had made Jo and Beth's the go-to place for Torrent on many long nights and weekends, of which there had been quite a few. Though Railynn had joined the lab late, she had more than made up for the missed time by keeping pace with Torrent's excessive hours. As a result, the two of them had come to know the cook pretty well, and he knew about their experiments, in broad strokes though he didn't have the scientific background to understand the details. He seemed to follow the 'big picture' okay, or at least he nodded and smiled a lot.

"I'll have the usual," Torrent told him. "Liver and onions."

Railynn made a face to this but didn't say anything. Torrent had convinced her to try liver and onions once before, and he wasn't sure that she'd forgiven him for the experience several months after.

"I'll take the Scrambled Hot Mess if you don't mind," she told the cook.

"Coming up."

Torrent turned to her.

"Really? You'd rather eat that than liver and onions?"

"I'd rather eat the barstool than liver and onions," she responded. Then, changing the topic, she whispered, "We did it."

He could tell from the whisper that she felt as apprehensive as he did about the downhill research slope on which they now found themselves. The lab could practically run itself from this point. Still, the corollary meant that if anything went wrong, they couldn't recover.

"Yeah," he acknowledged solemnly.

"What's next?"

He turned his attention to her just as a fresh cloud of smoke wafted across his face.

"I'm glad you asked."

"Consciousness research, right?"

He nodded.

"Yes. But we're going to change it up I think."

"How?"

"Using models - I'm not really sure about the ethics on that. Harper and I have been talking about an alternative."

Railynn's face fell and she squinted her eyes as she looked at him.

"Oh, all of that Model Advocate stuff. So what's our new plan?"

"Nanite filaments."

"What?"

"We can grow the module. Start with a pill. We'd just have to work out how to cross the blood-brain barrier and lodge. Then we can treat it like any other drug."

"I see what you're thinking. That could be painless and easy to administer," she told him. "It could be a pill. Take a pill, and join the experiment."

He nodded and swallowed a sip of water.

"That's what I'm thinking. In pill form, we could do it without causing physical pain at all. We would grow a network in the brain instead of drilling through the skull."

"Do you realize what that could mean?"

"Yes. Less pain for models."

"No. Well, yes, but we could use volunteers. Without having to cut people open, you could get thousands or possibly millions of volunteers to participate. It would be just like testing a placebo drug, except we'd be mapping consciousness. It would have a wider reach and be more conclusive once the data comes in, even with the wider variability."

The reason he'd wanted to use models was to take advantage of the overwhelming similarity he could create in artificial conditions. He'd estimated perhaps a hundred models would be necessary to get the answers he was looking for. To achieve similar results using brains which had nearly nothing in common, he thought perhaps two orders of magnitude might be enough, or ten-thousand or so volunteers. If they offered a bonus, like maybe, added memory that neurons could link into, the trade-off for taking a pill might be enough to entice millions of poor college students.

"Memory," he said to her. "We can integrate memory. Make it a test to see if the memory-enhancing 'drug' works, versus some placebo. Put together enough paperwork to cover us and use nanites to do the wiring. This could be huge."

The cook plopped down a massive pile of liver and onions directly in front of him and a large pile of something he didn't recognize for Railynn.

"Are you seriously going to eat that?" he asked, motioning with a gristle-laden fork.

"Yep, probably all of it. We haven't eaten all day, and I'm starving. Are you going to eat that?"

She pointed back at his mound of brown slimy livers draped generously with caramelized onions.

"Yep, all of it," he said. Un-replicated food was expensive, but worth it. He smiled as he cut another chunk of the liver. It was decent, and just chewy enough to get a workout, but not so challenging that he couldn't eat it. The iron content alone made it worth eating, especially after such a long day. How she justified her pile of gravy-covered eggs, hash browns, peppers, hot sauce, and whatever else was hiding in it, he had no idea. That conversation was one that they'd had many times in the past, so he didn't feel a need to press it further.

Torrent only managed to eat about three slices of the six pieces of liver placed before him. Those, plus the smokey haze, brought home to him the fact that he was a lot more tired than he thought. The excitement of the Firsts waned, and the thought of curling up in bed next to Harper grew more and more enticing. One glance toward Railynn told him that she felt the effects of a rapidly filling stomach as acutely as he did.

"How long do you think it will take us to understand consciousness enough to model it?" She asked him the he caught her eyes.

"Ten years, at least. Getting approval for the massive study will take some paperwork and cooperation with a few different schools. The modeling stuff should create enough buzz to help there, I think. But then we still need the implants to stay in for a while to get enough data. Not to mention we'll have to pay for the electron probability computation bandwidth to process all of those data."

"I'll be nearly forty then," she muttered, but he couldn't tell if she was talking to herself or him. He nodded regardless.

"Me too."

"Do you ever think about a family? I mean, eventually?"

Torrent had thought about it a lot lately, but he hadn't decided if he could see a future with Harper yet. Something in the way she behaved seemed like she was holding back. His perception was that she would come to the edge of revealing some secret, only to shut off and back away. Of course, he had no reason to believe that. Nothing he could single out and say 'this is what I mean.' He told Railynn most of what he was thinking, without revealing Harper's name. She continued on as if she hadn't heard him.

"I mean, I'm an acquired taste. I know it. You know it. I'm super animated at times, and really, kind of like a weird science-seeking robot."

Torrent considered whether that was true or if she was hard on herself. He decided that perhaps a little of both was accurate. Railynn continued.

"Sometimes, I think that my chance won't come. I think about how good it would be to have someone. When I look forward, it seems that I can either chase this idea of consciousness to the end with you, or I can give it up, and follow a more 'traditional' path."

"You're not 'traditional.' You would be miserable."

"I know, I know," she replied. "Never mind."

"You're amazing, Rai. Without you, this project would have failed ages ago. You inspire folks around you to be better – I've seen it. When the right guy comes along, he'll see it too."

"You....do know that I'm a lesbian, right?"

The subject had never come up. Torrent felt himself flush a little as he cut into the fourth piece of liver. Never had the thought occurred to him to wonder about her sexual orientation. To him, Railynn was just Railynn, and a bag of assumptions he'd brought with him. Or not really. He knew he was right that she'd had at least one heterosexual partner.

"I guess not," he muttered. "Sorry. But, what about Dave?"

"A mistake," she said, haphazardly glossing past it. "I'm not just talking about relationship stuff. I mean, it's children too. Don't you think about it? Eventually, I'll be too old, and yeah, you will too. I guess you're doing something about that, though."

Torrent swallowed the hunk of meat he'd chewed on for

less than the requisite amount of time. The morsel slid down his throat and slowed at his windpipe before forcing its way past. He felt it stretching his esophagus as it traveled down and considered if he could find a simple way out of the conversation.

"Well, we've got thirty children to put somewhere," he joked but choked back his laugh as he caught her eyes, which wrenched up into a glare. He thought she directed the look at him, but then she lifted her left hand to her temple and rubbed in a circular motion.

"Headache?" He asked the obvious question if only to absolve himself of his inadequate attempt at humor. Railynn nodded and she squinted her eyes tightly as if she had just walked into direct sunlight from a dark room. A moment later, she slid off of her hard wooden stool. Torrent grabbed her left arm, allowing her to swing slowly down. She immediately popped back up to her feet, and, blushing, took her seat as though nothing strange had happened.

"Tired, I guess," she muttered, and dove back into her Scrambled Hot Mess breakfast-dinner without making eye contact.

22

Missing: One Model

Monday, July 25, 2185

Harper parked the car in the driveway, gathered her bag, and quickly covered the ground to the door.

"House, open the..."

A thin sheen of light told her that the door was already ajar. She slowed, and as she stepped toward the opening she felt her pulse in her throat. Harper cautiously pushed with her fingertips, and was temporarily blinded as the door swung open and light flooded through the opening.

"Ordell?" she called, as she waited for her eyes to recover. She thought she heard the thick deep undertone of his voice before realizing that it was only the cooling system spinning up. The house swallowed all of the other sounds. She called out again, but still received no response. Was he angry, and not replying on purpose? He had the right to be. Harper hadn't been home for more than a day's stretch in weeks, but his nature didn't usually bend toward the passive-aggressive.

Her heart pounded against her rib cage. The couch lay overturned on the floor, moved nearly a foot from where it should have been. Something red stretched out from beneath it. A fresh bloodstain? She dropped her bag and drew her hands to her lips. Images of her parents' deaths assaulted her mind and took her breath away. Harper collapsed to her knees before the destruction.

"Ordell..." she tried to call out but discovered that she'd stopped breathing. In vain, Harper struggled to pull fresh air into her deprived lungs. Patches of light materialized from nothingness and disappeared as quickly, sure signs that she would pass out soon. Some lingered and flew around in tiny circles before her eyes. More and more cluttered together until somehow they became a single point, which then began to fade as though she entered a dark tunnel swallowing up the sunlight. She tried to think of anything to wrench her mind free of the parade of deaths, first her parents', then Ordell's.

Only he wasn't dead. If it was blood, the new spot was too small for blood loss to kill him. It was only the size of a coffee cup ring, she told herself. He couldn't be dead from that. She tried to breathe, but her throat still wouldn't let the air pass through. She gasped desperately. The tiniest tendril of oxygen made its way between her panting lips. As anemic as it was, that cold air was enough to keep the darkness closing in around her at bay.

She staggered slowly to the overturned couch and pulled one edge, breath coming easier to her now. The furniture rocked back easily because of the off-balance way it had landed. Nobody lay beneath.

Breath by painful breath, she recomposed herself. The blackness faded back into the dull light that her parents' house always seemed to be in, since neither she nor Ordell ever bothered with the window tinting For all the effort and weariness, Harper had only so far inspected a single room. It wasn't fair to Ordell for her to fall apart yet when the house was over two-thousand square feet and several rooms remained unchecked. She remembered with a shudder finding him snake-bitten and incapacitated in the yard.

Slowly, she pulled herself up. In her heart, she knew what she would find. There would be no Ordell. The idea of even beginning such a futile search crushed her will, but compelled along by a naively hopeful voice somewhere deep inside, she did it anyway. A few minutes of going from room to room confirmed what she expected. Ordell was nowhere to be found.

Back in the living room, Harper sank into the chair, holding herself and rocking as an earthquake of sobs shook her body. She chastised herself for her relationship with Torrent. The happiness it had brought her wasn't a worthwhile trade for Ordell's freedom. The man had waded with her through an emotional darkness and saw her to the other side. She should have insisted that they flee a month and a half ago – as soon as she got her first paycheck. They would be at the border by now, and coyotes would have taken them across for a few thousand dollars. She had been selfish, and Ordell had let her.

No time for rumination.

When Harper had Ordell back, she could self-deprecate at leisure while they made their way safely toward Canada. Now, she had to act.

Her mind fixated on the possibility that he'd been captured by bounty hunters. To confirm, she immediately turned on the holovision to discover whether anyone had claimed the reward.

"News on Ordell Bentley," she stated.

Ordell's face slid across the matrix of her holovision, and blocky three-dimensional text displayed the new high bounty of six-hundred thousand dollars. She had time. Whoever had taken him had not turned him in yet. Would they? If the culprits were the Human Pride Movement or Friends of Humanity, what would *they* do? She'd heard horror stories of models hanging from trees in the western states.

Her mind once again betrayed her. She saw Ordell's body swaying gently in the hot sun as a summer breeze lazily swooned in from the ocean. She couldn't think. But she needed to think. Her enemy mind refused to stop jumping from guilt to guilt and fear to paralyzing fear.

Harper picked up her tote bag from near the door where she'd dropped it. She fished through to retrieve her communicator and called the only other person she trusted. Now that Ordell was gone, there was no point in keeping him a secret any longer. Torrent would have to help.

But he wasn't there.

She paced rapidly through the rooms again, this time without hope and driven by desperation. She thought she looked for clues, but blurred eyes made her barely able to see, as overwhelming rage and fear concealed any rational thoughts. Again, she found nothing, and two thousand square feet were beginning to feel like two.

Her legs throbbed from pacing and her mind ached from thinking in circles. She tried to call Torrent again but received no answer. When she hung up, she called one more time, and this time it went straight to voice-mail. She screamed into the receiver. "Where the fuck are you?" She threw her communicator at the couch, and it bounced down to the floor. That's when she saw that a piece of paper lay just under the edge, as though it were trying to escape notice. At first, Harper had taken it as one of those do-not-remove-this-tag tags. She missed her mother with nearly crippling intensity when she saw the 'tag.' The woman had been obsessed with not removing them, no matter how much Harper tried to convince her that the tags were for the manufacturers only. In a perfect world Harper could have turned to her mother. But the real-world truth was her mother wouldn't have been any help. Her defeatist advice would likely have been to wait and see if he came home, advice Harper couldn't take.

She retrieved the note and examined it closely. Handwriting scribbled across the front of the tiny piece of thick white paper showed the first three numbers as her address. On the alternate side, she saw the neatly printed name Doppler Reclamation Services.

Reclamation Services. All of the bounty hunters called themselves 'reclamation services,' as though humans were like cars or rent-to-own holovisions instead of people. Defeated and alone, her heart raced beneath her chest as she struggled through the options. It took her a minute to go through her list. She could pursue the bounty hunters, but what would she do if she caught them? She was the outlaw, and they probably had licenses. Alone, how could she help the situation? She would track them down for the sole purpose of watching them laugh at her.

There was someone else she could call. She had Railynn's comm number, but she didn't think she could ever return to Toussaint labs if she made that call. She felt her teeth clench as she recognized the pull toward normalcy that even then found her weighing the return of someone she cared about against her life's comfort. Railynn at least liked her enough to invite her to lunch from time to time.

"Hey, who's there? Just kidding. I'm busy. Call me back."

"Where the fuck is everybody?!" she yelled. She sank, crying into the couch, as another unfounded suspicion that the two of them were together somewhere washed over her. But they *were* together. She checked the time by glancing at the clock above the mantle. They were probably still working on the Firsts. Anger coursed through her as she plotted her next move, then frustration rose as no clear path carved itself out of the red mist in her mind.

A sharp whisper pierced her thoughts. She turned toward the sound, expecting that, of course, now, the police would show up. Whoever had captured Ordell had also turned her in for harboring. The noise morphed into a voice that mimicked the sound of her name.

"Harper?"

There was a tenor of sadness beneath it, like the stain in Harper's heart she carried with her every day. She stared into the dim light, straining her eyes to prove to herself that the impossible was still impossible.

"Harper, I'm so sorry."

Harper blinked as an outline formed.

"My baby, I couldn't protect you."

It looked like her mother, standing near where the couch had come to rest when Harper released the teetering thing and conservation of energy re-positioned it. Her mother's gentle face smiled at her, complete and whole as before the incident that stole her away. Her deep-set eyes centered on Harper, who gazed back in awe. Those eyes seemed slightly more hollow than usual, tired almost. The sari she wore revealed the sharp lines of her knees beneath the folds of a silvery-blue material.

The woman floated across and wrapped her thin arms around Harper. A chill spread through at the touch with the quickness of a lightning strike. Harper lurched away sharply.

"Are you real?"

Her mother didn't answer the question. A profound sadness projected from the downcast features as her mother slowly backed away. There wasn't a person in the world who Harper felt she needed as much as her mother, but the fact was, her mother was dead, wasn't she?

"Harper, your father wanted me to tell you. Be careful, don't be too rash."

It seemed like her mother, deferring to her father, supplicant to his domineering. It made her sick to think that even in death, the woman had not managed to shake free of her shackles.

The room grew colder, and icy fingers scraped down her back. She recognized the feeling of dread as that gnawing insecurity that followed her every day of her life, only intensified a thousand times. She remembered her father's presence. The apparition of her mother vanished and, along with it, the chill that had pierced Harper's body. In death, Harper's mother was still protecting her from him, too, she felt. Harper let out her breath slowly into the cold room. She then shook her head violently to clear the fog lingering there and made a decision.

She almost collided with the front door on her way past, holding no plan in mind except that she would get Ordell back before the worst could happen. She jumped into her car and sped away between towering pecan trees lining her driveway.

The car skidded at the bottom of the drive, where it joined the main road. She narrowly missed sliding into a shallow ditch, recovering on the next turn. The last left before merging onto the interstate caught her off guard. Harper felt herself lose control, and then the car began to skid. She sensed the lack of responsiveness as the car shook on the turn. Moving in slow motion, Harper stepped on the brake, and milliseconds stretched into hours as the vehicle drifted against her will. She slammed down the parking brake in response, but the act did nothing to reduce her forward momentum. For a brief second, the car went airborne, like swinging over the peak in a wooden roller coaster, before it collided in a dull thud with the water's surface just off of the shoulder of the road. There, she and the car stopped.

Something warm and sticky trickled down her eyelids. The rear-view mirror had twisted to an odd angle on impact. A spent airbag drooped over the steering wheel. A red streak followed along the edge of the sun visor, still trembling from the accident. She checked over her body and didn't feel as though she had injured herself too severely. However, her eyes refused to focus on anything before her. The sound of dripping caught her attention with its relentless metronome-like consistency. The engine sputtered just once, and then hissed, and steam filled the cab.

She tried to pull off her seat-belt, even though she couldn't see it, still dazed from the collision. The clasp refused to release on her first try. On her second try, her hand slipped from the grip. Rising water now hid that hand from her, so she pulled at the canvas belt in an attempt to free herself, but nothing happened. She frantically yanked at the tough fabric as hard as she could. She only succeeded in tightening the belt across her lap, and her legs began to lose feeling. When she glanced into the mirror, she noticed blood streaming down from a cut on her forehead. The flow increased and decreased with her heartbeat. She felt herself growing tired and light-headed and almost laughed at the irony of the possibility that she would die trying to save Ordell.

The car slowly sank further into the reeds. She no longer even knew to look for the clasp and had stopped feeling her legs altogether. Harper found herself strangely calm and curious about how far down the car would go into the dark earthy water. The last fuzzy, barely comprehensible thought she had before she lost consciousness was how nice it was that the water had retained at least a little of the day's heat. She would be warm when she drowned.

23

Unravelling

Tuesday, July 26, 2185

The bright-pink glow of the morning sun diffused through her closed eyelids and interrupted Railynn's sleep. She opened her eyes slightly and a bright white crescent penetrated her eyelashes. Rapid blinking adjusted her eyes to the incoming light. Thirty seconds later, she sat upright, scaring her tabby Levi. He jumped off of her husband-pillow to land silently on a hardwood floor. Blankets and sheets clung precariously to the side of her orb-shaped bed. A smile slid across her lips.

We did it.

They had tucked the Firsts away in their ceramic eggs, with fine-grained temperature control, one of her many contributions, keeping them safe. They'd done the hard part, and now daily monitoring and logging would pass her time until the batch hatched in May.

Railynn rolled toward the windows and slid her feet into

rainbow-colored Alpaca slippers. Just as she attempted to stand, her breath rushed out, and the room began to spin. She sat instead and counted to thirty, while she waited for the fit to pass. The attacks were happening more frequently. The night before, she had almost lost complete control of her body, falling from a stool in the process. A few days before that, she had vomited in a bathroom in the office. That one was hard to explain away. Her usual self-rationalization of being overworked didn't account for purging the contents of her stomach.

If she had been in the grip of a heterosexual sex life, she might have concluded pregnancy from the symptoms. She planned to see a doctor if it came to it, but also stubbornly held the belief that work stress caused the problem. The Firsts sucked up more of her energy than she'd expected – that was all. Railynn shook off the dizziness and made her way to the kitchen to start some victory pancakes in the replicator.

These, she smothered with maple syrup and whipped cream. As she lifted the first delicious-looking bite to her lips, she noticed a flashing light on her communicator. "Call back," she called out, and the cylinder beeped and connected.

"Hi! Harper here. Not available, but you can leave a message," came the audio from the other end.

Railynn's eyebrows furrowed as she stuffed the wedge of pancake between her teeth. Harper never called her. She'd forgotten that Harper even had her number. The girl exuded anxiety and never opened up.

"Harper, if you want to talk to me, give me a call back," she called out with a mouth full of food.

She'd done her duty and returned the call, so she turned her full attention back to her victory pancakes, which were starting to get cold. She shoved another bite into her mouth in defiance of that fact, dismayed to discover that the pancake had already reverted to room temperature. She briefly debated using a microwave, but the idea of spongy pancakes was even more disheartening than that of cold ones.

She heard a distilled monotonal version of Lonely Planet by Jenny Kensey floating through the air. It took her a moment to comprehend that the melody originated from her communicator. The song was maudlin, and about youthful friendship, as was a lot of classical-style music. Friends and relatives alike had chided her from her obsession with the "really, really oldies." Antique music defined her childhood. Most people didn't know who Jenny Kensey was, but the 2140's as musical years went had forever changed the landscape of Counterpoint Mega. Her communicator chimed again, and she picked it up to connect the call.

"Railynn, I need your help."

"Oookay... with what, Torrent?"

"I'm at Harper's house now, Rai. The door is open, and it looks like a tornado blew through. Someone knocked over a couch, and there's what looks like blood on the floor," he continued.

"Did you call the police?"

"I – I'm not sure I should. I've been looking through the house. I found - something. I can tell you when you get here."

Annoyed at the interruption, and feeling guilty about it, she carried the rest of her pancakes to her car. At least she would be able to eat her pancakes in peace.

Fifteen minutes later, she finished up the last of her victory food as the automobile rounded a short curve. Before her, the video screen panned over the ground in front, showing uninterrupted wetlands and reeds with half-destroyed cat tails poking up out of the water. Something shiny flashed quickly across the screen, an unnatural intrusion in the otherwise scenic landscape.

"Car, pan back," she said, and the video screen moved backward and confused her body into believing the automobile moved in reverse. But she saw the distortion again. What she was looking at was an unnaturally thin metallic reed, or...a car antennae?

"Car, stop, back up seventy yards and pull over," she said. The car pulled over to the edge of the road, a safe distance into the shoulder, and then the doors unlocked. On her side, gravel and pavement fought for control of what little non-road space existed. She walked across the pavement and to get a better view of the antennae. The roof of a car, concealed mostly by weeds, cleared the water. Her arms trembled as she approached the vehicle, which was a deep cobalt blue, the same color as Harpers' and about as old. Never before had she wanted so badly to be wrong. Railynn waded into shallow water in her flats and through the marshy weeds toward the vehicle to see more. Deeper and deeper, the cold water lapped around her ankles, then calves, and finally the backs of her knees. Goosebumps prickled on her upper back in response.

She took a deep breath when she made it to the driver's side door. Her eyes tried to close and shut out the image, but she forced them open as she peered through the window. A seat belt was all that kept Harper's face from submerging into the water. Tiny ripples of her breath on the surface were the only indication that she was still alive.

Railynn discovered a hidden cliff by probing with her foot and realized then that the front wheels seemed suspended over nothing. The angle that Harper's car had gone in was perfect for sinking the front end into either soft mud or over the edge of a steep drop-off. A few more inches forward and the car, and Harper, would have disappeared completely. There would have been nothing left to see.

"Wake up, Harper!" she yelled, but nothing happened. Minnows had gathered around a pink pool beneath her face, and a trickle of blood seemed to trace her nose into the water, still dripping slowly. Her normal brown skin seemed washed out and pale.

Railynn's first thought was to call the police, but then she remembered what Torrent told her. She backed away from the vehicle slowly, to prevent knocking the car over the ledge by accident. Back at her automobile, she contacted Torrent.

"I found her. But I need your help."

"What do you mean you found her?!"

"Come back toward the highway and you'll see me," Railynn told him, as calmly as she could, given the circumstances. "It's bad, Torrent."

There was silence on the other end until she heard a deep breath. "I'm coming."

Railynn examined the situation more carefully but kept three feet between her and the car to avoid accidentally knocking it over the precipice. From her vantage, she could see that a shoulder belt held Harper in place. Nothing else seemed to contribute, by the unnatural angle of her body. Undoing the restraint might make Harper fall forward into the water and drown before Railynn could pull her up. Or worse, she could shift her weight in just the right way to take the car over. They had to get her out soon, but Railynn couldn't do it alone.

All she could do was wait. In her line of sight, Harper moved her head, and her eyelids fluttered, but they didn't open. Her breathing stopped suddenly, and Railynn paused her own, listening for Harper's to reconvene its steady rhythm. After thirty seconds, the slow rasp of Harper's breath recommenced, weaker than before. If Harper's breath stopped again, Railynn decided she would have to try to get Harper out by herself.

Ten minutes of steady, weak breathing later, she saw Torrent's volantrae descend and pull next to her car on the shoulder. He jumped out, leaving his vehicle blocking the highway on-ramp, and ran to the side of Harper's car.

"I can't get her out; she's too heavy," Railynn told him.

"Oh no...." he trailed off, and for a moment, Railynn thought he wouldn't do anything. By then, she'd figured out who the mystery woman in Torrent's life had been. She had a thousand questions she wanted to ask.

"I'll release the buckle, and you keep her from falling under," Rai told him, which shook him from his stupor and caused him to move quickly to the passenger's side door.

"Be careful - there's a drop-off," she told him, and he slowed his movement from a sprint to a walk.

He pulled the door open. Once he was in place, leaning in carefully through the opening, Railynn reached in to find the seat belt. The cold water completely soaked her shirt through to her skin. When the wet t-shirt slapped against her chest, she gasped and nearly let go of Harper completely. Torrent kept one knee on the passenger's seat, with both his arms wrapped around Harper's body.

"Got her," she heard him grunt.

"Unbuckling now."

She shifted her weight to move her leg under Harper's inert form as much as she could before she freed her left hand to fish around for the seat belt latch. When she found it and pressed and winced as her hand slipped down forcefully, the latch digging into her knuckles. The second time, the belt clicked open, and she wrapped her free arm around Harper's body to help keep her face clear of the water.

The 120-pound dead-weight of Harper's body challenged them, yet they managed. While standing in the marsh up to her knees, painfully aware of the risk of water moccasins or alligators, Railynn helped Torrent to drag Harper from the car and to the dry grass by the highway. Only then, once Harper was on dry land, did Railynn call an ambulance.

While they waited, Railynn watched. Torrent knelt next to

Harper and placed her head in his lap, with her damp straight hair falling around his bare knees. She could tell by the way that he held her, with his arms wrapped protectively around her body, trying vainly to warm her up, how much he loved her. Love was fickle, she decided, and could happen to anyone, so she let him keep his private thoughts. But she had to know about the police.

"Why no police?" she asked.

Torrent looked up at her, with red and tear-threatened eyes. The way his face looked at that moment reminded her of her latest ex-girlfriend when they'd broken up for the third time, and the woman had finally figured out that it was likely to stick.

"This," he told her and stretched out his free hand. Railynn took a data-coin from him and recognized the logo stamped across the front.

"Friends of Humanity?"

"I found it in her bedroom. Why would she have that?"

Then she understood. Torrent must have thought that Harper collaborated with one of the anti-modeling organizations. He must have thought that finally, someone had succeeded in infiltrating his lab. The idea was plausible. But wouldn't that be an argument *for* calling the police instead of against it? The idea of sweet, nervous little Harper participating in one of those organizations in any real capacity was ludicrous. Maybe he'd thought it was a plant, although researchers were as varied as citizens in their feelings about cloning.

They all walked a fine line as modeling researchers. By advancing the technology and making cloning easier and cheaper, research increased the profit margins for the industry. So implicitly, she supposed, modeling scientists all would seem very pro-modeling from the outside. Nobody ever asked researchers how they felt about the modeling industry. If they had, and if the scientists had answered honestly, Railynn suspected a good many of them would be critical. The correct answer to any question about modeling was always "science isn't good or bad." She remembered getting that lecture repeatedly in graduate school.

Harper stirred. She snuggled her head into Torrent's lap in a move so practiced that Railynn wondered how long the underground relationship had gone on. Then she then muttered the words "Doppler" and "Ordell," and drifted off again. Her breathing seemed better, and some of the color had returned to her cheeks, though the massive gash in her forehead still hadn't closed and would likely require stitches. Or so Railynn, the modeling scientist and notably not-a-doctor supposed.

Something white protruded from Harper's tightly-closed left hand. When Railynn pulled it free, she saw that it was a thick, crumpled piece of paper. She could make out the words "Doppler Reclamation Services."

"Torrent," she told him, "did you see that?"

He nodded as she flashed the paper toward him.

"They are a clone retrieval service. I've passed their office before. Seedy downtown by the fifth avenue."

"Does any of this make sense to you? Friends of Humanity and a reclamation service? What's an Ordell?"

Railynn shook her head slowly, then paused as something sparked.

"Ordell Bentley."

"Who?"

"You don't watch the news? The model that's been missing for almost six months. There's a six-hundred thousand dollar reward."

The hand that stroked Harper's black hair halted against her forehead, then continued tremulously a few seconds later.

"It makes sense, Torrent. HPM must have been threatening

her as they threatened you."

Railynn had other ideas. Harper wasn't the first in a research lab to step over the line of cautious impartiality. The more Railynn thought about it, the more she realized that perhaps harboring a fugitive model was precisely the sort of thing Harper might do. The idea seemed to fit within her quiet and unassuming personality. Never the person to go out of her way to cause trouble intentionally, their Model Advocate nevertheless didn't keep her opinions to herself. She must have been miserable in her perpetual anxiety of being found out. Harper had been in trouble for the entire time she'd known the girl and it never came out. Railynn glanced at Torrent. The secrets seemed unending.

Railynn looked away to the broad, gnarly oak trees that lined the road. Moss hung down in giant curtains from the trees, saturated by the nascent marsh, barren except for their moss cloaks shimmering with dew in the morning sun. The chill in the water would be gone as soon as the sun broke the tree line.

An ambulance arrived with lights flashing. It pulled to a stop beside Torrent's volantrae, and from within sprang two EMS workers. It took only ten minutes to load Harper into the back of the bus.

Torrent tossed Railynn his keys as he climbed in beside Harper.

"What are these for?"

"I'm blocking traffic the other way. Can you move my volantrae?"

"Sure, I can do that. Just send it home?"

"Yeah, thanks Rai, for helping," he continued. "This isn't how I wanted to tell you about us."

Railynn nodded but didn't feel a need to reply. She'd never felt as empty as she did at that moment, watching the ambulance drive off, alone on the highway and responsible for three different vehicles.

What was Harper trying to do? Railynn turned on Torrent's volantrae, dropped the keys inside, and told it to go home. It lifted up carefully, spun, and then straightened itself on the on-ramp before speeding up into the skyway. She thought about whether to send her car as well, and then get a tow-truck for Harper's, or leave Harper's little blue car half-immersed in the bog.

Railynn padded softly toward the water's edge, thinking about how the car could have gotten into the ditch. From the highway, the car would have been nearly impossible to land in the gutter like that. The ramp was bi-directional up until a point, but she would have had to turn completely around to get the car into the bog facing the direction it was. If she'd left her house, though, and traveled the other direction? She might have been trying to head downtown, possibly to Doplar. Railynn looked for tire-treads and didn't see any evidence that Harper had ever considered slowing. Convinced of the correctness of her assessment, Railynn now had a hypothesis. The only thing left to do was to prove it.

And really, it was time for Harper to get another car. She considered pushing it over the ledge, but the wind changed and took the choice away. Railynn became the solitary witness to the vehicle sliding silently into its grave.

24

Soldiers of Misfortune

Tuesday, July 26, 2185

Ordell bolted upright from his slouched position and pulled against his bonds, which didn't give. He surveyed his surroundings. Morning announced itself by a white glow penetrating a crack beneath a far door. The room separating him from freedom consisted of silhouettes as what little light there was failed to illuminate the entire space. The air smelled of take-out Mexican food and caused his stomach to grumble.

The spacious room had the general atmosphere of an inner-city pawn shop. Ordell's eyes adjusted slowly, materializing images from the haze. Directly in front of him, sitting at a little round table, two man-shaped shadows took shape, one tall and thin, and the other shorter and thick like a rugby player. The tall one wore a black coat with a band collar topping gray slacks and glistening black shoes. He looked less like a bounty-hunter and more like a priest or a band director. The other person, denser and squatter, looked like a more traditional bounty hunter, with a coat made of synthetic black fibers that shimmered, and an opened cut-away collar. Ordell couldn't see anything below his torso from his positioning at the table. When he shifted his body to try for a better look, tight ropes reminded him that his hands and his feet were both tied to his chair.

He tried to squeeze one hand out and then the other, but it was no use. Then he tested the ropes around his legs and came to the same conclusion. He only succeeded in tightening the bonds around his wrists and his hands began to numb.

If the men were going to kill him, they would have done it already. The worst of what he could imagine at this point was that he would be sent back to Emergent Biotechnology for 'reprogramming.' He'd heard of reprogramming at his Convocation Ceremony. A model from another squad had tried to run away halfway through training.

"They caught him quick," Lancaster had told them, growling out the words.

"How?" Ordell asked.

"They found him hiding in an attic of polli."

"How did they find out?"

"Funny. The polli heard snoring coming from where he hid."

That seemed kind of funny, at the time, he remembered thinking, but the memory offered little encouragement to his situation. All of the stories of escapees inevitably led to their capture and return.

"What happened to him?" Ordell asked.

"When he came back? Reprogramming," Lancaster had said. But when Ordell asked him to explain what that meant, it was Rochester who answered. Rochester was a skinny man with thin fingers. His model occupation code (MOC) was that of an engineer, so his physical characteristics were under-emphasized to make room for more intellectual pursuits. Though they shared Convocation training, Didactics for the man would be completely different than what Ordell would experience. Being big wasn't mutually exclusive with being smart, but Ordell had never met a large model who was exceptionally bright. He long suspected they dumbed down the big ones on purpose.

"Two weeks of intense behavior modification training," Rochester told him. Ordell exhaled quickly. During Convocation, they'd had only three days of moderate behavior training, which involved electric shock with long poles through cages. He didn't want to think about what two weeks of intense training was.

"Hey shill, we're orderin'. What do you want?"

The tall skinny man's voice penetrated his fog of remembrance and pulled him back into the present. He debated feigning unconsciousness, but it was too late for that. Besides, he was hungry.

"Where are you ordering from?" he asked.

"Taco Madness. Burrito?"

He met the man's expectant eyes and nodded slowly.

"With a Vita?" he asked.

The man scowled.

"What would you want that crap for?"

Vita was an impression of a fruit drink that only models consumed. That was probably because it was all they had to drink in Convocation – Vita and a strange soy-based protein that didn't have flavor. It was something like tofu, but chewy like a hangar steak. The high nutritional content meant that Ordell craved the drink sometimes, and he figured right now, he should get what he could. He was more in a beer mood, but he doubted that their generosity would extend that far.

He declined to answer the man's question, though. It would have been impossible to explain his history, nor did he think the man cared. Instead, he chose to comply and change his order since he was a prisoner.

"Fine. Cola then."

A mysterious voice from the next room bounced toward him.

"Ordered. I'll pick it up and be back in twenty."

Ordell could hear a door open. In the brief second before it closed, he registered the sounds of traffic and birds. He locked away the knowledge that there was another way out that he couldn't see, other than the way they'd come in. That might be useful. They would have to untie at least his hands to eat unless one of these men wanted to feed him, which he doubted from the looks of them. He couldn't imagine the priest or the bounty hunter holding a burrito to his mouth.

The priest sat next to him and positioned himself close to where the knots were in the rope. He started loosening them.

"They're not going to kill you," the man told him quietly. To this, Ordell only nodded, so the priest continued.

"We're returning you to Emergent Biotechnology. I don't know what *they'll* do – probably reprogramming, I guess. But you seem smart. A couple of weeks in the hole should be a breeze."

Ordell felt slack in his wrist constraints and pulled his arms forward. They swung around in front of his face, but he didn't have enough slack to do more than that. It struck him as strange that the man bothered to encourage him.

"Why do you care?" he asked.

"We may seem a little rough, but we're not that bad. Just doing a job. Doug's got a real confusing sense of humor, but we're not trying to make it bad for you."

"Doesn't feel like a job to me."

The priest grimaced slightly, which made Ordell wonder

just how long he'd been doing reclamation work. Anyone who could see capturing another human being as 'just a job' was difficult for him to understand. He supposed it had to be "just a job" or nobody would do it. A stone-faced sour expression returned to the man's face. Then the priest pushed back away from the table without another word.

Back in the cramped office and out of his head, he turned to see something interrupt the glow under the door. The something moved forward and backward on the other side as though pacing. He scanned the room, and neither the priest nor the bounty hunter seemed to have noticed. Just then, the door sprang open, and Ordell went temporarily blind. Silhouettes reformed, slowly materializing into images against his retina.

A short woman with sandy-blonde hair stood in the revealed opening. She wore a confused expression, which made it seem as though she hadn't expected the door to open at all. Judging by the speed at which the massive wooden door had slid out of her way, Ordell guessed that the door opened automatically on approach. She folded her arms self-consciously but didn't back away.

"Who are you?" bellowed the bounty hunter, clearly to intimidate.

"Railynn Marche. Who are you?"

"Doug." He motioned to himself first, then the other. "Tyler. And this here's our bounty."

"Ordell?" the woman asked, looking past the pair and focusing her light-brown eyes on him. He nodded, and the men pulled themselves to their feet.

"You know him?" the priest asked.

"Not really. But we have a mutual friend."

She turned her attention to the priest, or Tyler, as the squat man had pointed out.

"Shills with friends. Why are you here, girl?" Doug growled at her, but if the woman was intimidated, she failed to show it. Instead, she pointed a slender finger in Ordell's direction.

"Here to take him back home," she said, which brought a laugh from both men simultaneously.

"Sure, you can have 'im," Doug said, "when I get my six-hundred thousand."

"That's a lot more than I have," Railynn replied to him. "I may be able to get forty."

"Forty thousand?" Tyler interrupted. "That's not even worth having this conversation."

"Go away," retorted Doug in agreement.

The woman stood there and didn't move.

"Look lady," the priest told her, "the only way we're giving this guy to you is if you can top the reward, and we shouldn't even do that. Capturing escaped models is all perfectly legal. Handing him back over to you isn't."

She flashed Ordell a quick smile.

"Don't worry, I'll be back," she told him. "I'm a friend of Harper's."

With that, she turned and walked back into the blinding light. Ordell peered after her for as long as he could. The brightness grew to be too much and forced his eyes away.

"She won't be," Doug said sourly. "They always say that. They never come back."

"Yeah," Tyler spoke to Ordell now. "I wouldn't get too excited about that. You're a model, after all – there's only so much work that woman's going to put into you. If she's starting with only forty thousand, there's no way she'll get to six hundred. Seen that a lot too."

Ordell wasn't listening to either of them. He was instead trying to place the name Railynn Marche since something about the name seemed familiar. Harper's friend. He hadn't known that Harper had any friends aside from Torrent, but the woman had to have been someone with whom Harper worked. Then he remembered. Harper had once confided in Ordell her feelings of jealousy towards the woman. It was interesting that she showed up here looking for him.

"Hey, shill," came a voice from the same direction as the front door. Ordell looked up toward the brightness one more time to see a burrito flying toward him in an aluminum foil wrap. He caught the projectile with the loosened restraints; then he glanced up to see if the soda had followed suit. Sure enough, a can of soda sailed through the air at him, which he barely caught with his right hand.

"Craig! With food!" Tyler exclaimed.

The third man had returned.

"Who was the girl?" Craig asked.

"Some woman wants this one back," Tyler said, and motioned with his thumb. "She only has forty thousand."

"Harper Rawls?"

"Nah, someone named Railynn Marche," Doug said. "Sad story, no money."

"Hmmm, seems like things could get messy. Any word from Emergent?"

"Not yet, left a message," Tyler replied.

"Call them back. I don't want to get wrapped up in any ownership dispute. Let's get rid of this guy and get our reward."

"Yep, no problem," Tyler answered, and put a communicator to his head.

Ordell couldn't hear the conversation clearly, but the result was unmistakable.

"Eat fast," Tyler told the group. "They're sending someone in the next thirty minutes. We've got to pack up and go meet them halfway."

As he wolfed down his food, Ordell considered the

likelihood of rescue within the next half-hour. The idea seemed pretty unlikely, so he settled himself as comfortably as he could into the chair beneath him.

Aayushi had warned him. She'd told him that bad things were coming. With that knowledge, he had failed to prevent anything. How would Aayushi judge him? Her daughter had found happiness, and that had to count for something. Yet here he was, despite his intentions, the catalyst for more despair.

Ordell considered spending even more energy working on his bonds. His first thought was that perhaps, now that they were looser, he might get somewhere. The fact remained that the men here were all seasoned bounty-hunters, whatever they looked like, and even the priest would be a formidable opponent. Three of them together, and he doubted very much that he could overcome, even if he managed to rend himself free of his constraints.

He would have to be patient. Eventually, his opportunity would come. He had, after all, survived trudging through swampland. This captivity was only another obstacle, and though Aayushi had spoken of bad things, she hadn't mentioned how bad. The bounty hunters might be the worst of it, he thought. Any moment, the key to his freedom would appear. He needed to be patient, and he could do that.

25

Sabotage

Tuesday, July 26, 2185

Railynn returned to her car, and and watched the door for movement. Two different sketchy-looking men had approached her and tapped on the window. To her, they looked like beggars. If she'd come across them in everyday life, when she wasn't staking-out a bounty-hunters' lair, she might have given them some. But she thought it was in her best interest to keep her windows rolled up and her eye contact to a minimum.

Somebody had beaten the man in the chair badly. His left eye was bloodshot, and the fact that his right eye didn't match meant that something hefty had collided with that side of his face. He was so large that it must have taken all three of them to bring him down. As encouraging as she'd tried to be, Railynn felt none of the optimism she offered. She didn't have six-hundred thousand dollars, and even if she did, what would she buy with it? When the reward kept going up, surpassed a million, perhaps, would Harper find herself in a similar situation all over again? Railynn didn't even know Ordell Bentley. Maybe he was a genuinely nice guy, but he was also a fugitive. That brought by itself a level of desperation that she imagined might trump any number of moral convictions. A voice inside screamed 'not my problem.' Railynn pushed that voice down until it became only a whimper. He was Harper's problem, and Torrent's problem, so he was her problem too.

Her communicator buzzed loudly.

"Remember how I told you about my parents?" Harper's quiet, hoarse voice sounded in the as Railynn connected.

"Harper?" Railynn felt her heart jump. "You're okay!"

Harper continued as though she hadn't heard.

"There's money," she whispered. "Lot's of it, upstairs. Go to get him back."

"Six-hundred thousand dollars?"

"No. Only a little over ten thousand saved. But we can get more. I can sell the house and our family restaurant."

Railynn watched as a short man with a mustache exited with the empty bag and placed it into a nearby dumpster. She considered what they could do with that kind of money. Anyone expecting the six-hundred thousand wouldn't blink at ten. But something the man had told her stuck out. He'd said what they were doing was 'legal,' as though that were the appropriate measure of the price of a person's freedom. She wondered at that. Was it as legal as they claimed?

"Hire a lawyer," she said. "Fifty thousand would be a good down-payment on a lawsuit."

"Fifty?"

"Yeah, yours plus mine."

Her forty-thousand represented her life's savings after supporting herself between jobs. It wasn't much, but she might be able to convince herself that parting with it was the right thing to do.

"Maybe," Torrent replied in the background. Sometime during the conversation, they must have switched to projection. A certain listlessness in his mumbling response told her that the man who overcame all odds to become a nationally known scientist drifted away. If Harper died, Rai guessed that there would be no more Toussaint Labs, and their experiment would never see the light of day. It was selfish to think, and guilt-inducing to consider, but she affirmed that she wouldn't let that happen. She disconnected the call.

The Firsts suffered no immediate danger, though, and Harper's friend swam in it. Unless Harper or Torrent happened to have a college friend on track to partnership at a distinguished law firm, Railynn was the only one who even had a way to act. Sighing to herself, Railynn picked up her communicator and entered a number she had memorized from repeated over-usage. In slightly more than a second, someone picked up.

"Brigid?"

"Hi Rai," Brigid Kostic answered, "it's been a long time."

"It has been. How are you?"

Silence.

"Busy. Is there a reason you're calling me?"

A friend might have been a little bit of a stretch as a description of Brigid Kostic. They had shared a study group once in a senior class, and both she and Brigid competed to steer the group. The chaos that followed had very nearly cost her the 4.0 that she'd managed to maintain for her entire college career. Brigid, since then, had assisted in a Supreme Court case and was widely considered one of the best lawyers in League City, if not Texas. Railynn wasn't a lightweight professional either, though, with several papers already published in peer-reviewed journals. They were both winning at life, but from the sounds of it, Brigid may have harbored some hostility still.

"Can you help me? A friend is in trouble." Railynn described the events as she understood them. "Do you think we have a case?"

"No."

Railynn's heart fell below her stomach as she digested the straightforward response. Then, Brigid spoke up again, somewhat hesitantly.

"Well, not with the Madison Rule in place. But something is happening in modeling sentiment right now nationally. The time might be right to challenge the rule, or it might be absolutely wrong. Not sure yet."

"We have about fifty grand. We can pay."

There was a moment of silence on the other end. Was fifty-thousand-dollars insulting? She heard Brigid talking with someone away from her communicator, but couldn't make it out. Then she came back on.

"Craig Moody is here with me."

"Hi, Ms. Marche, how are you?" A man's voice spoke up.

"Fine. Have you decided?"

"We have. We do a certain number of pro bono hours every year that we use on passion cases, changes we'd like to see. This case is fascinating to us, and we're willing to take it. Save your money. Your friend, the one with whom Mr. Bentley stayed, is she prepared to be a claimant?"

"I'll ask her."

"When you do, have her call us back. Do you have anything to write with?"

She grabbed a pen and jotted down two communicator numbers Craig dictated.

"That first one is my direct, and the second one is to Jim Moody. Of course, you have Brigid's number, but if you can't get her, then you can always try one of us. Very interesting.

Winning this case would put Walsh and Moody in the history books."

That was the extent of the conversation. It was over so quickly that Railynn stared at her communicator for a minute after disconnecting, half expecting Brigid to say something else. Eventually, she gave up on the idea and shifted her gaze to more store-watching.

Another volantrae pulled down from the skyway and nearly hit her roof as it pulled into a spot across from her. She saw two more burly, angry-looking men exit and go into the building. The volantrae was as tall as it was long, a feature reasonably common in the flying vehicles. Black and unmarked, it may have belonged to a company.

The door opened again, and one of the men passed through the opening. Behind him walked Ordell, who seemed to have trouble, possibly because of the ropes she had noticed around his feet. He had a kind look and the sort of face prone to smiling, sometimes probably even at inopportune moments. His jaw was straight and chiseled, except for a scar that covered most of the left side. He could have been handsome except for that.

It bothered her how perfect he looked. Stocky, but not overweight. Cut too, and by the way he examined the parking lot, alert but not jumpy. He was beautiful in the fluidity of his movements, even as he struggled against the ropes that bound him. Watching him between the two brutes seemed surreal. The one behind him forced the Ordell's head down, pushed him through an open door into the volantrae, and then climbed in behind.

Railynn watched the flying box drift upwards. When it got so high that it looked no bigger than a loaf of bread, it zipped higher and joined in a stream of similar dots in the skyway. She watched in frustration as the volantrae disappeared. Torrent's could catch them, but by the time she got back to it, they would be well into their journey. Railynn had an idea where they were going anyway - likely to Emergent Biotechnology. Instead of following, she turned onto the road toward St. John's to check in with Torrent and Harper at the hospital. Before she'd even left the parking lot, she changed her mind. Harper and Torrent were out of commission, and they had a lab soon to be full of researchers that someone needed to let into the building. She told her car to take her to the office instead.

The parking lot was empty, as she'd known it would be, save a police car parked in a far corner. She swung the front door open, and the first thing she noticed was the heat. The building had warmed more than usual, a sure sign that there was no power. The automatic lights were dark as well. Panic set in. No lights meant no power, which meant no temperature controls in the Egg Lab. She sprinted through the foyer and turned down the hall.

The Egg Lab maintained residual coolness from the evening before. If the eggs weren't receiving power, they would slowly adjust to room temperature. That meant that all of the Firsts might die without intervention, but it was possibly not too late. Railynn dashed into the room, pausing in the decontamination chamber long enough to put on her gear. She approached the first pod. The readout screen shone brightly, which meant that the battery backup was working. The temperature on the screen read comfortable ninety-nine degrees. It was a shade cooler than she would have liked, but not fatal.

"Dorothy, how long has the power been out?" she asked the lab robot.

"Four hours and twenty-three minutes," Dorothy replied, and rolled toward her.

"What's the status?"

"Battery backups are on. We're within operational parameters. Two more hours of battery remaining, and the temperature is rising at a degree every half-hour."

"Why didn't you call me?" she asked. The question was unfair, as Dorothy wasn't sentient and wouldn't have thought of calling without being programmed to do so. Dorothy responded anyway. "The situation is not yet critical."

Railynn's first call was to the power company. Was a bill not paid? She could have sworn that the traffic lights were working on the way, but she sometimes didn't pay attention to the monitor when she rode in her self-driving car. She might have been wrong.

"League City Power," came a voice on the line.

"Yes, when will power be restored to 6917 Poplar Avenue?"

"Let me check, ma'am."

She heard the noisy beeps of a touch interface in the background. She thought about navigating to the power outage maps on her communicator instead. Just as she was about to start, the androgynous voice re-emerged.

"Uh... ma'am, there's no power outage on Poplar."

"Well, I've got no..." she started to say, but then it occurred to her to check the transformer behind the building. Was it possible they had overloaded something?

"Got to go," she told the voice and disconnected.

She jumped up and raced back out through the decontamination chamber, and followed the semi-circular hallway to the back exit. As she was about to push through, she thought about it again. What would she be able to do about that? The door gave easily as she shoved through and stepped back out into the hot sun, then turned to the left to examine the panel beside the door. She wasn't an electrician, but nothing seemed out of place. The numbers which tracked the wattage use still slowly turned over. She puzzled over it for a minute; then it occurred to her to check the fuse box near the courtyard entrance.

She could feel the time slipping away. Every running step she took seemed to take an eternity to place, and then lift again. It was as though she ran through molasses, just when every second counted. The eggs were getting colder since it was clear that the battery backup wasn't enough power. There would be no more eggs in a couple of hours and no more reason to come to work.

She reached the fuse box and yanked it open. Someone had flipped off the main breaker. When she flipped it back on, the lights came on. The storage units would be back on as well, but the outage had destroyed all remaining samples except the Firsts. There was no battery back-up on those - a prioritization decision. As she expected, when she checked the storage units for signs of life, there were none. The remaining samples, in temperature-induced stasis, were no longer remotely viable. There would be no do-overs if the Firsts didn't work. The Firsts were it, so she hoped that they would succeed. As a precaution, she circled back to the Firsts again and verified that they were online, and the pods were functional.

The question of who had turned off the main breaker shattered her momentary relief. Only she, Harper, and Torrent had keys to get in after hours. The building wasn't a fortress, though. Anyone who had access to the building could have flipped the breaker. The janitorial staff perhaps?

Then she had another thought. She raced back to the foyer and peered through the glass. She thought she had seen a police car parked in the lot before entering, but it was gone now. If the cop had been there all morning, he might have some idea of who had disabled the breaker. She backed away from the foyer and settled into Harper's chair behind the desk.

Torrent would have to hire security guards. Railynn wasn't

sure how much money he still had from his sponsor, but security had just moved to the top of the list. She contacted a security company and they offered to send someone right away. Hiring someone without Torrent's approval would test her partner status, but he said it wasn't a token position. They'd invested too much in the lab work already to risk success by being cheap.

26

Legal Challenges

Friday, July 26, 2185

The lies were over. As Harper lay reclined on the hospital bed, Torrent sat right there with her, holding her hands. An occasional shiver passed through her body as it fought to regain temperature control. She wanted to sleep, but the cold and the beeping of machines prevented it. Instead she lay there and pondered the fact that all it took for her relationship to progress was a near-death experience. There was something sad in that.

"You're awake?" Torrent's voice pulled her attention to him. She shifted her eyes so that she could see his, steeped in tears that never fell across his freckled cheeks. The poof of his hair actually could become messy, she realized, as one side stuck flat to his face where he'd spent the night laying on it.

"I have been," she admitted.

"I thought you were trying to sleep. I didn't want to wake you."

"Thank you."

Harper offered a feeble smile for him, but couldn't keep it.

"The doctor should be back soon. He's running some tests."

"I heard."

As if on cue, the doctor re-entered the room. She tilted her head to get a better look at him. He was a tall man in his early eighties, with the spryness of a seventy year old. Age therapy had smoothed the wrinkles in his face, but the tell-tale lack of plasticity in his knuckles was a give-away. The thought made Harper lift her own hand before her face, and examine the folds of her skin. Her knuckles were still smooth, though they seemed clay-like, probably due to the blood loss.

"How are you feeling, Ms. Rawls?"

"I'm fine."

She lowered her eyes back to Torrent, and tried smiling again. This time she kept it on her face for about a second.

"Good," the doctor responded. He then turned to Torrent.

"We need to get into Harper's medical situation. Can you please wait in the other room for a moment?"

"Y-yeah, I can."

Torrent jumped to his feet but Harper didn't let go of his hand.

"Doctor, he can stay. I give permission."

"Fine. Good."

The doctor took his place standing beside Torrent's chair.

"It's a good thing your friends found you when they did. You lost a lot of blood, and as a consequence, your internal temperature regulation suffered. The combination of blood loss and cold water - well, you were hypothermic when they brought you in. Coupled with shock."

"Thank you, doctor."

"There's more. We ran some tests - lots of tests, actually - because of your age. Maybe it's better if your friend waits outside?"

Something in the way that the doctor paused made Harper relinquish Torrent's hand. The doctor was clearly uncomfortable disclosing more information about her in front of him.

"Torrent, I'll fill you in. Can you get me some coffee? If that's okay doctor?"

He nodded briskly.

"Coffee is fine, yes."

Torrent stood and squeezed her hand lightly before he left her alone with the doctor, who gave him a few additional seconds just to be sure before he continued, in a low voice.

"You're pregnant. I'm not sure if you wanted him to know that. Is he the father?"

Pregnant?

Her jaw went slack and she felt her eyes widen as she mentally reviewed every sexual encounter that she'd had. Torrent was the only man in her life, and as she thought back, she recognized one or two occasions where they might not have been as careful. Torrent was a driven man, and Harper could only imagine the scandal now. Dating is one thing but getting a subordinate pregnant? Even in modern times, that was a career destroyer. She nodded dumbly at the doctor.

"Do you want him to know?"

"N-no, it was a one-time thing," she lied, and could tell that the doctor knew she was lying, but played along anyway.

"Okay, I won't write prescriptions then. But you need to get pre-natal care. Vitamins, you know. And start making some appointments. The health of the child is extremely important, especially at this stage."

"What stage?"

"Right. So he's about a month along now, so there's not much happening yet. You may not have even noticed. Bioscan indicates that the child isn't experiencing any trauma from what you've gone through. In fact, he may be contributing a bit to your condition as he's your body's number one priority right now."

She squeezed her lips together until they hurt as the doctor explained more about proper child care. Tears pervaded her eyes, and she blinked repeatedly to keep them from plummeting down her cheeks. Harper shook her head no, it couldn't be possible.

"Are you okay, Ms. Rawls?"

"Can I have a minute, please?" She asked the question in steady words, enunciating each syllable quietly so she would only have to ask once.

"Of course, I can come back later. There's one more thing."

Harper steeled her mind for the next blow as the doctor took an unnaturally long time deciding how to phrase whatever it was he had to say.

"While technically you could check out today, we would like to keep you here for observation. You know, for the baby's sake."

"I thought you said he was fine."

"Just preliminary, that's all - being careful."

With that, he stood and clacked his way out of the room in his white shoes, leaving Harper alone to weep shamelessly, a temptation she nearly entertained until she remembered that Torrent would be back any minute with her coffee. Then she would have to explain the source of her newfound tears. She gulped down the pain and quickly dried her eyes using the edge of the sheet that covered her. Sandpaper, always, the sheet irritated the corners of her eyes and she was sure made them red. As soon as she finished, Torrent entered the room again.

"What'd the doctor say?"

"It was silly. He just wanted to make sure you aren't an abusive boyfriend."

This made him smile. Harper followed suit with a smile she didn't feel and Torrent didn't seem to notice.

"Me? I hope you corrected that idea."

"I told him you beat me nightly."

She spit the words out without understanding the impact. Images sprang to her mind of her own childhood, and her mother cowering beneath raised fists. Somehow, she kept her demeanor as Torrent chuckled, oblivious to her torment.

"Nightly, huh? I'm sure. I'm glad you're feeling better."

"Yeah, me too."

"Oh, here's your coffee."

As he pushed the coffee toward her, Harper's communicator erupted. At first, she didn't know where it was, but then found it on the table beside her. She kept him at bay by holding up a single finger while she answered.

"Harper, you're there. Good."

"Railynn?"

"Yes. Listen, I called Walsh and Moody - a girlfriend works there. Well, ex-girlfriend technically, I guess. Anyway, they're interested in your case."

"My ... case?"

"Ordell, Harper. They can help you save Ordell."

She grinned and looked up at Torrent, who couldn't have known what the conversation was about because she'd answered on private mode. Harper flipped the mode to broadcast and set the communicator on the table. The device then projected an image of Railynn across the room onto the far wall.

"You're live, and Torrent's here. How can a lawsuit help Ordell?"

"They said something about the Madison Rule."

For two seconds, neither Railynn nor Torrent said anything. Harper's smile faded as she understood why. The Madison Rule was a huge part of the reason research on models was possible to the extent that it was. Future modeling research may not be allowed if the law was challenged or chipped away at. Railynn's image seemed ponderous before a wide smile came back onto her face.

"That would be amazing," she suggested. "Could you imagine how historic it would be if that law was overturned?"

"Historic and fatal," Torrent interrupted. "For us, anyway."

"How can you still think of your consciousness research when a man's life hangs in the balance? They could be killing Ordell right now," Harper told him.

Torrent flushed and he put her coffee down on the bedside table.

"I didn't say you shouldn't do it," he remarked defensively. "I only said that it would be bad for our research. That's all."

"Oh Torrent, don't act like that," Railynn reprimanded him. "You know we've worked out a solution for that."

"It's a *possible* solution, Rai."

"It will work. And anyway, how could you ask for more from a Model Advocate than overturning the Madison Rule. It's kind of your fault."

This brought a smile to his lips and he moved closer to Harper. He picked up her coffee from the table and handed it to her.

"Thanks, Railynn. You're a true friend," Harper told her image, and then flashed a scowl at Torrent. They may be able to joke about it, but Ordell was her friend. She wasn't smiling.

"What do I do?"

"Call them. Ask for Brigid Kostic. She'll fill you in. Oh, and guys. You should know there was a break-in at the lab. Nothing was damaged, but I hired a security guard and he's there watching the place now."

"That's only going to get worse," complained Torrent.

"When this get's out, we'll be targets everywhere."

"Did either of you happen to lose your lab keys?"

Harper's eyes shot open as she thought back. She couldn't remember the last time she had her lab keys. She always showed up after the morning rush, so she didn't need them.

"Torrent, can you hand me my purse?"

Dutifully, Torrent grabbed her purse from beside one of the buzzing machines. She pulled it open and rifled through it, but found no keys.

"Not here. How long have we been here in the hospital?"

"Ever since this morning. We came straight here from the accident."

"Torrent, think. Has anyone been around here who seemed out of place?"

"In a hospital? Lots of doctors, nurses. A couple of policemen."

"Wait. Police? Was one of them dark-complected, with deep brown eyes and close-cropped hair. Kind of like yours, but shorter?"

"Yeah, Officer Agemba. Nice guy - we chatted for a while. I completely forgot that - he said to tell you hi, and that he hopes you get well soon."

Iciness rushed down her spine.

"That was him," she told them, "I'm certain. He's Friends of Humanity."

Harper filled them in on her previous hospital stay after the deaths of her parents. These were confidants - people she felt that she could trust. She hadn't ever had that before, and realized now that she'd treated them both poorly by keeping her secrets to herself. Torrent confirmed when he spoke.

"I can't believe you were dealing with all of this."

"Harper, you need to call Walsh and Moody. I'm hanging up."

Railynn's image disappeared.

"That was abrupt," commented Torrent.

Harper ignored Torrent's comment and retrieved her communicator, then switched it back to private mode. She held it up to her mouth.

"Call Walsh and Moody."

A few buzzes later, and the line connected.

"Walsh and Moody. How can I direct your call?"

Harper couldn't tell from the tonality whether the voice was a real person or a bot. She decided to be polite just in case.

"Brigid Kostic, please."

"One moment."

A few clicks and beeps sounded before she heard a woman's voice.

"Brigid Kostic here."

"Hi Brigid. My name is Harper Rawls. I understand you know Railynn Marche?"

"I do. Do you have a moment to talk?"

Harper looked around the hospital room, in which she had been invited to an extended stay.

"Yes, plenty of time."

Torrent shrugged and took his seat as the two of them spoke.

"What are our options?"

"We've discussed that at length in the last hour or so. We think there's a good chance, given the temperament of the country, that challenging the Madison Rule could make it all the way to the Supreme Court. But that's not the only option. We could also settle out of court. I'm sure Emergent Biotechnology doesn't want this plastered all over the news."

"What do we do *now*, Brigid?"

"Now?"

"Yes. Railynn saw them taking Ordell, probably back to Emergent Biotechnology. You know they torture them, or kill them. How do we stop that?"

"We start the lawsuit. If he's key evidence, then it might offer him some protection. But I have to be honest here. There's not a lot we can do. We'll file and include our concerns about his mistreatment, but it's up to the courts to decide."

Harper shook her head no. She let out her breath and slumped her shoulders forward from her seated position on the bed. Torrent looked at her, and she stole a glance long enough to see her concerns reflected in his eyes. She felt the hairs on her arms prickle up and her chest constrict as she wished beyond hope that she'd already left with Ordell. In her alternate past, she and Ordell drove her little car across the desert to freedom. By Canadian law, he was granted full citizenship and a place to stay, and money to use for his first year. He could be a free man.

"Are you still there, Harper?"

"Yes, I'm here."

"Do you want us to contact Emergent Biotechnology on your behalf?"

"I don't have much money."

"Railynn didn't tell you? We didn't ask for any. This is our pro-bono for the year."

"Yes, then. Please get to them as quickly as you can."

"We will. Don't worry, you have Walsh and Moody on your side."

They said their goodbyes and disconnected the call. Torrent had taken an interest in the machines beside him now, so Harper had a moment to collect herself. She imagined what Ordell must be thinking. He could be free, if she hadn't wasted her time pursuing a relationship. He would never actually tell her anything like that, of course, but who can tell what someone is actually thinking? Right now, he had every right to hate her. She even hated herself a little.

"You should go to the office," she told Torrent, anxious to be alone with her feelings. With him there, every tear or sigh would be questioned, especially the build-up she'd been working towards all morning.

"Are you sure?"

"Yeah. If there's trouble at the lab, you should be there."

"I know. I just don't want you to be here all by yourself. What if Agemba returns?"

"I'm safe enough. I'm pretty sure they think I'm one of them."

Torrent looked at her askance, awaiting an explanation that she had no intention of giving. She only shook her head from side to side.

"Okay, I'm off then."

He gathered his things and left her alone. She waited until she heard his voice far away greeting a nurse in the halls before she threw her body backwards onto her pillow and let out the grief and confusion in quiet, throbbing sobs.

27

Secret Admirer

Tuesday, July 26, 2185

At least one other person was in the back of the van with Ordell. By the clinking of the chains, he guessed other prisoner.

"Can you hear me?" he whispered in the direction of the sound. The other person only grunted in response. Ordell then felt the wind knocked out of him as a something hard struck him in the side.

"Shut up, shill."

The pain from the blow intensified sharply when he tried to recover his breath. Ordell accepted the lesson that he should only speak when spoken to, and felt around blindly for a seat. His hands, chained together behind his back, found purchase with a wide, flat surface and he twisted quickly to plant himself on it.

Twice before it lifted off, the van hit bumps and launched Ordell into the low ceiling and then out into the middle of the floor. He righted himself each time, and nobody offered assistance. If he hadn't managed to negotiate his way back to the bench, he would probably have received another kidney punch, and his side still hurt from the last one.

Otherwise, the journey passed in silence, which gave him more time to think of another way to escape. Being tired and hungry, his mind seemed to have a different agenda. It drew his thoughts to Harper and how much she would miss him, and then how much he would miss her. He wanted to believe that without him, she was no longer tethered to the house where her parents died. In his imagination, she would transplant herself somewhere new and somehow be happy, maybe move in with Torrent.

Inevitably, his mind turned back to Aayushi. What now seemed like ages ago, he remembered the two of them naked and unashamed in that tiny bed in his small apartment, as if destiny commanded it, while the rest of the world moved along beyond his dirty curtains. Her face became so vivid in his mind that he could make out her lips moving in the darkness of the bag, her smiling lips forming words he couldn't quite understand. But originating in memories, he already knew what they said.

They talked of Royal Roses, he recalled. Neither of them understood how it was possible to keep roses from dying for three years, nor whether a thousand dollars was worth the sentiment they produced. It was a pointless conversation, since neither of them had the money to purchase such a frivolous thing. It was a conversation of lovers each talking only to hear the voice of the other in return.

He nearly toppled over as the van began its descent. Then, its momentum ceased suddenly, and the extended elbow of the person beside him saved him from falling to the floor by digging painfully into his ribs. The darkness lightened to a more opaque brown, as a blast of light made it through the translucent bag.

"That one," a voice cried out, commanding and unused to being questioned.

Someone grabbed him by the shoulder and pulled him up to his numbing feet. He struggled to catch his balance on the uneven, carpeted interior, standing quickly to do so. Instantly he regretted it, as he banged his head into the ceiling. He had to remember he was still in a van. He ducked back down and followed where he was led, afraid to lift his head again, even when fairly certain he had stepped down to pavement as a blast of heat told him he'd left the air-conditioned confinement of the volantrae. The bag was lifted from his head, and the light rushed in like water from a failing dam.

"Ordell Bentley?"

He addressed his response to the darkened outline of a man enveloped in the unforgiving sun.

"Yeah."

"Your lucky day."

He felt someone behind him manipulating his shackles and then they fell to the ground. A scraping sound accompanied them being picked up again.

"Don't *feel* lucky," he observed, now able to make out many more of the man's features as his eyes adjusted.

The man in front of him wore sun glasses, aviator style. The suit he wore was flawless, and so was his manner. Outside in the Texas heat of at least eighty degrees, he didn't see a single drop of sweat along the man's salt-and-pepper hairline.

"You could be going where *he's* going."

The man nodded his head in the direction of the van, as it closed up. The other prisoner hadn't moved, bag firmly in place.

"Instead, you get a room a the Akson Regency here in League City. I'd say that's pretty lucky."

"Who are you?"

"Sorry, yes. Jackson Grayson. I represent Emergent Biotechnology."

"Represent?"

Jackson nodded in confirmation as he responded.

"While we figure out what to do next, you, my friend, get a luxury, all expenses paid, *guarded* stay at the Akson Regency hotel."

With that, three men, who Ordell assumed were armed because of their extremely uncomfortable-looking and oddly lumpy suits, escorted him into the lobby. They checked him in, and then accompanied him up to what he guessed would be his room.

The "room" was really a suite, and easily nicer than his apartment. Possibly it even gave Harper's house a pretty good run for luxury trimmings. When he walked through the entryway, he encountered a door to a bathroom on the right, which contained a large Jacuzzi tub within. He saw from his line of sight that if he traversed the living room to the back where the bedroom sat, a king-sized bed waited. The top surface of the dresser was the largest holovision he had ever seen before. As he stared wide-eyed around the apartment one of the guards addressed him.

"What are you carrying?"

"Why?"

The guard was only slightly smaller than Ordell, and seemed intimidated by his size. The man approached him slowly and cautiously, before reaching into Ordell's pockets to retrieve everything he had stored in them. His communicator came out first, followed by the set of house keys Harper had given him, which used to belong to Aayushi, with her butterfly charm still attached. Opalescent wings reflected greens and blues around the room.

"Cutsie boy, huh?"

Ordell had the sense to keep his mouth shut. These men seemed like the type who liked whatever power they could get, and right at that moment, they had all the power in the room. When the guard started to slide the keys into his own pocket, Ordell had to protest.

"Hey! Those aren't mine."

"Now you're catching on. They are the property of Emergent Biotechnology. You're lucky we're letting you keep your clothes, shill."

Ordell drew himself up to his full height, and the man took an involuntary step back. One of the other guards raised his plasma rifle.

"Stand down!"

"That's not mine. And it's not yours either."

"Relax, shill, we're returning them to the girl."

The girl. Shill and the girl. The terminology shook Ordell. He slouched back down and let the guard continue to search him. All that was left to find was a pen and a blank piece of paper, which the guard threw on the floor.

The trio exited into the hallway, leaving Ordell to sit in silence, and wonder what might happen next. But nothing did. For five minutes, then ten minutes. Finally after thirty minutes, he turned on the holovid.

"Holo, play news."

After a few seconds of commercials, his face floated in the matrix with the word

"APPREHENDED" stamped in red across it. Then a breaking news prompt flashed beneath it.

"Holo off."

"Communicator, call 281-755-9802-9982"

"Outbound communications are not allowed from this room. Please contact your company for more details."

Ordell then understood that he was now in prison, regardless of the extravagant niceties. Just then he heard three knocks on the door, rapidly. He heard the door swing open, and the wheels of a cart entering. On the way back to the living room, a plate awaited him, covered with a stainless steel dome, perfect except for the single hole in the top, for spiriting the lid away. The rising odor wasn't filet mignon, which he would have reveled in, but it was his second favorite, a New York Strip.

"Ordell Bentley?"

"That's me."

The man handed him a note folded neatly in a white paper envelope, then turned and left the room. Ordell pulled the note free, and opened it to expose two handwritten words.

A friend.

That was good – he could use all the friends he could get. His immediate thought was Freedom Underground, but the idea that they would have been able to find him so quickly when they'd been so slow to do anything else seemed unlikely. It was safe to say, he considered, that Emergent Biotechnology probably *did not* send him a steak. He didn't know what their plans were, but so far, but he didn't expect treats or casual visitors. He wanted to ask someone besides the guards what had happened to the other man in the van, but there was no opportunity. Was that man dead now, and if so, what was the difference between him and Ordell?

Ordell surveyed the room. If the man had only just left, he would have to go down the same way Ordell had come up. That would take about thirty seconds. A window hid behind some curtains by the couch in the main area. As soon as Ordell drew the curtains back, he saw the man step into a volantrae and rise up into the skyway. The vehicle seemed expensive, and didn't make the usual jet whirring noise, meaning that it used an ion distribution engine. Very few types did that, and only high end - which made him even more curious about his new found admirer.

The ground didn't seem that far down. He looked at the latch on the window, and noticed that it wasn't fastened. As prisons go, his didn't seem secure. At least, until he lifted the window and poked his head through. The ground swelled up farther away, and near the hotel, he was definitely higher than a livable jumping height. With little else to do, Ordell slumped back to the couch and sank into the cushions. His heart raced and apprehension ate away at the back of his mind.

Wednesday, July 27, 2185

The next morning, Ordell found himself on the couch, face in a damp spot on the pillow where he had drooled. The previous day hadn't been a dream. His stomach growled and his mind raced as he considered his possible choices. There were none. The men outside took away any possibility he might have of escaping. In the kitchenette, a small table-top replicator sat waiting to be used. Ordell made his way to it across the plush carpet, driven by the gnawing in his stomach. He punched in some numbers, and nothing happened.

"Replicator, make some eggs."

The box sat there mocking him, doing nothing. Ordell wrapped his arms around his stomach as it growled loudly, and contemplated the guards outside. He considered how he'd been treated before. Nothing would give them more satisfaction than for him to ask them for anything so they could have the opportunity to deny. He rummaged through the cabinets, searching for anything that might have been overlooked, and found nothing but dried tea bags from some previous occupant and some glasses. Tea would have to do. Ordell filled the glass with hot tap water and dropped the tea bag into it. The tea would take forever to brew at the warmish temperature from the faucet, but he had time to burn. He slid into a chair at the kitchen table and tried his hand at waiting.

He was lousy at it. Ordell squirmed in his seat, and every few seconds checked the cup to see if the water had darkened. His unsettled stomach growled at him ferociously, and in response he patted it down until the grumbling stopped. How many days would he have to spend sitting, staring and wondering? At least he had the news to stay informed, but there had to be a better way.

Waiting, seated in the chair, watching tea brew, reminded Ordell of a meditation session he'd attempted with Aayushi. She sat with her legs crossed, propped up on a folded pillow with her knees touching the floor. She wore gray-blue yoga pants with a broad pink waistband, while her straight black hair fell across her shoulder down the front of her light-pink form-fitted shirt. She smiled, flashing those straight white teeth at him, before closing her mouth and breathing in through her nose.

"Like that," she had told him, after a moment of rhythmic breathing.

"Okay."

He crossed his legs, apparently the wrong way, ankles crossed in the middle. Her correction was soft but unmistakable.

"You can sit any way you like, Ordell, but if you sit like that your legs will fall asleep in less than three minutes."

She pulled another pillow off of his bed and tucked it under his bottom.

"Use that, shift your weight and keep that blood going."

He remembered the smell of her hair, and the feel of her breath as she leaned over him, adjusting his position bit by bit until he had it properly. He remembered at the end, trying to reconcile the elegance of this woman, who was so much more than he had ever known, with the wife of man filled with so much hate and rage that it had overflowed and corrupted everyone around him.

Focusing on the memory, he tried to settle into a lotus pose. His mind circled around Aayushi, no matter how he pushed her away. His stomach settled, though, and his hunger left as he breathed deeply into his belly.

"You're doing it, odd one."

He snapped his eyes open at the whisper of her voice, but she wasn't there. It was only him, and the curtains, and the tea that had finally decided to leech out into lukewarm water.

Friday, July 29, 2185

Ordell didn't see anyone from Emergent Biotechnology the next day either. He improved his meditation practice, splitting his time between watching the news, and then meditating so that he could soothe his frayed nerves. The news cycle focused on his capture and the pending court case.

On Friday, room service arrived with a stale sandwich from the hotel gift shop. The man who dropped off the sandwich had wrinkled his nose up while entering the room, prompting Ordell to obligatorily sniff his under-arms after the man left the room. He concluded that he had begun to stink. He stripped his clothes off and washed them in the bathroom, then hung them over the balcony, mildly amused at the spectacle he must have been - a massive naked man carefully hanging clothing from the rail to dry in the sun. Then he meditated some more, clearing his mind and thoughts, all the while listening for Aayushi's voice, but no longer hearing her.

After meditation, his clothes still weren't dry, so he decided to occupy the time by doing squats in front of the news. His normal lifetime routine had never involved squats. Even as large as he was, he'd always had the job to keep him fit. Faced with his denuded body in the bathroom mirror, and without any other time commitment, Ordell realized that one big fat roll wrapped around his midsection.

He'd just showered and dressed before his door buzzed and opened. In came a cart with a steak on it, and a note.

"Who keeps sending these?" He asked the man with the cart, who only shrugged.

"Whoever it is, thank them for me. This is the only food I've had today."

The man, saying nothing, nodded and backed slowly from the room. Without the supplemental protein supplied by 'a friend,' Ordell doubted he would have had the energy to do any physical exercise at all. The paltry portions provided by Emergent Biotechnology weren't enough for someone half his size.

Ordell settled into the couch to eat his steak and catch up with the news. He was shocked to find a picture of Harper spinning in the holovid void.

"We have additional information that names the claimant Harper Pavina Rawls."

Steak slid into his windpipe and he coughed it back out.

"Turn it up," he told the holovid.

"...lawsuit against Emergent Biotechnology for, get this, discriminatory conduct and inhumane treatment of a human being in their employ. That's right... the lawsuit claims that Ordell Bentley, the model who we've discovered had broken up Harper's parents, is a human and entitled to all of the benefits of being human. This is *revolutionary*."

"Revolutionary that a person could be a person?" Ordell asked the question to no one. The only thing revolutionary about the lawsuit was that a polli cared enough about a model to intervene into the legal system on his behalf. Any model would have made the same mental connection. If Ordell was found to be too human to be discriminated against and treated unjustly, then that meant that Madison Rule could no longer be applied, down to the mauled bar code on his wrist.

The newscast answered a few questions for him, as he now understood the difference between him and the other model from the back of the van. The other model was by now dead or being rehabilitated – though he guessed probably dead, and that he'd barely escaped a similar fate. Certain things were made more complicated by Harper's involvement, such as he now had to put aside his nascent plans to escape. Ordell could only imagine the damage fleeing would do to her lawsuit.

A wave of relief washed over him. With impossible speed, Harper had negotiated a stay of execution for him. Whatever her plan was, so far her strategy kept him alive, so he would do his part and be a well-behaved captive while events moved forward. That would give him plenty of time to ponder the identity of his secret admirer.

And so his days progressed, one into the next, with the exception that meals did suddenly start arriving regularly after that news segment ended. His routine was to wake up, watch the news, then eat what passed for lunch. Mediate while his clothes dried, work out, shower. Eventually he worked naps in. Eat what passed for dinner. Occasionally he would eat some actual food in the form of a flank steak.

It was an ascetic existence. Hours passed, days passed, and his routine never faltered. He had enough to eat and drink, though none of it had flavor except for the occasional steak, which inevitably brought with it notes of encouragement. The last one had a card attached which said, "hang in there." The idea reminded him of a poster of a kitten he'd seen ages ago, perhaps it was at Convocation. The steak was always brought by a different person, and the person never stayed long enough to talk. He was surprised that the men outside allowed the steak in, but then as guards, they may not have known that he wasn't to have it. And for all he really knew, it was a trick of Emergent Biotechnology to lure him into a sense of security.

Every morning he thought of Harper, and every evening he thought of Aayushi. The time in between, he spent making sure he didn't forget any more of his history. Maybe some day the ability to tell his story, which he felt rapidly coming to a close, might be important to someone.

28

The Settlement

Saturday, July 30, 2185

The offer had come in the form of a sealed envelope slid beneath the door of Torrent's apartment. Harper had been sleeping the morning away, recovering from her recent accident and fights with the insurance company, who finally did replace her car with "one of similar value". They matched value almost exactly, as her new car wasn't a volantrae, and although technically capable of self-navigation, the feature didn't actually work. They called it an upgrade, and she was too fractured to complain.

Her emotions battled for ownership of her mental state. She would have to tell Torrent about his child some day. The thought made her quake with fear as she knew already what the reaction of the ever-professional accomplished scientist would be. He wouldn't be able to handle it. He would, of course, help - and as importantly, let her make the decision of whether to keep it.

She'd already made the decision. And she had a name for the child. Bodhi Pavina Rawls, after her mother and her grandfather who had immigrated from eastern India. She felt a growing urge to gather clothing for the child, and prepare a room for him - but she could only do that in her home, as her newfound obsession would make Torrent ask questions in his small apartment. Returning would mean facing the empty house where her mother had died and her best friend had been stolen from her. Her only comfort came was to sleep, which she spent entire weekends doing.

Three quick knocks caught her attention, and then a brown envelope slid beneath the door frame. She stood to go investigate, and popped the envelope open.

Dear Ms. Rawls,

We regret that our actions have caused you such distress. Please know that we do understand your loss and the friendship that you've established with Mr. Bentley. Although it is currently illegal for us to free him to his own recognizance, as that would be in violation with section 12 of the Madison Rule, we would love to present him as a gift to prosper under your guidance.

We hope that together, we can put all of this behind us and move on to a brighter future. Please reach out to us and we can get the appropriate paperwork together to remove this stain from our relationship.

Many regards,

Jackson Grayson

Below that was an ansible number for her to call. She sat down on the couch, lightheaded after her rush to the door. Then she read the letter over one more time, pondering why it had come to her and not to Walsh and Moody. As she thought about it, her communicator rang out.

"Hello?" She didn't know whether to expect sleazy Jackson Grayson or Brigid Kostic, but she was glad to hear the voice of the latter.

"Emergent wants to settle."

"I know."

"Do you want to?"

Yes, oh god, yes.

The words sprang to her mind but died on her tongue. It wasn't her fight, and having come this far together, she had to talk to Ordell. Would Ordell really want to be tethered to her for the rest of his life, without agency for his own destiny? Of course, she could steal him away to Canada and set him free there, to make a future in an unfamiliar land. That was, after all, their original plan - and settling would make that a much simpler task.

"That depends. How much of a chance do you think we realistically have at overturning Madison Rule?"

"Things are looking really good. The bench has been liberal for some time. The only thing preventing this rule from being thrown out is a lack of cases."

"I can't make this decision without Ordell," she heard herself say, hating the words as they escaped.

"We'll get him a communicator, and I'll have him call you. Harper, this is great news. It means our case is strong enough to distress them."

"Good." Harper repeated the sentiment, but wondered

how good it really was to frighten a multi-national corporation. She disconnected the call, and placed her communicator beside her on the cushion, waiting anxiously for Ordell's call, knowing that it would take longer than a few minutes to get a communicator to him. Five minutes later, her communicator buzzed itself into the cushion crack. She feverishly pulled it out and clicked the button, to be treated with a view of Ordell's unclothed torso hanging in the air before her, wet hair dripping down into his face.

"Harper, is that you?"

"Ordell?" She squealed his name.

"They told me to call you. The communicator in this room was blocking calls, but seems to be letting them out now. How are you doing?"

"I'm okay." She paused, and didn't follow it up with any additional information.

"Still okay here, I guess. Mostly ignoring me. You may not believe that your mother once again is helping me. I'm meditating every day now, Harper, just like she taught me."

The mention of her mother brought tears to her eyes and a smile to her lips. Even in the grainy projection of the communicator, she could see the love he'd had for the woman. Suddenly all of the petty arguing they'd done seemed like wasted time. She wiped away a tear.

"That's great, Ordell," she said. "There's something I have to ask."

With that she explained the note, and the reason for the call. And at the end of the entire explanation, he asked her the question she'd hoped he would answer.

"What would you do?"

"That's what I'm asking *you*, Ordell."

"I'm all right here, Harper. The food isn't great, and now that I've learned to deal with the loneliness, I can wait if that's what it takes."

"To go after the Madison Rule?"

Harper wanted to scream, but she resisted the urge. She bit her lip and furrowed her eyebrows into a gentle arch.

"Are you sure?" She continued.

"I've been thinking the last few days... I realize now that it's not about me anymore."

Really?

"I understand, Ordell. I'll tell Brigid that we're still going to pursue. Be careful."

She disconnected from the call, took a deep breath, and laid back into the soft couch cushion. She closed her eyes, and willed sleep to take her.

"Harper, this is great news!" Torrent woke her up with his proclamation. She shook her arms and looked around the room. She was still on the couch, in Torrent's apartment, staring at the ceiling. She turned her head to see him grinning and holding her letter in his hands.

"We're not doing it," she said, in a matter-of-fact tone.

"Why not?"

"Ordell didn't want to. He wants to take on the rule."

Torrent's face melted into disgust before he could recover to an angry scowl. For a second, she saw her father's hostility before it faded. She backed into the cushion, pushing herself deep in and away from his reaction.

"I'm sorry," he followed up, "but isn't it *your* case? Settle. That way, he's free, and you're free."

"It's not my decision to make, Torrent."

"Of course it is. *He's* a model. *You're* the only one entitled to a choice."

She gasped as his calloused remarks, and turned back into the sofa.

"I didn't mean ..."

"Go away," she told him. "Leave me alone. I - I just need some time."

"Harper…"

"Don't you have some eggs to check on?"

She listened as he wandered around the apartment, and then eventually left. Harper closed her eyes again, shut out the world, and slowly drifted back off to sleep.

29

Frustration

Tuesday, August 10, 2185

"Harps, please get up," Torrent pleaded with her uselessly. Every day since their fight, she interacted less and less. He wanted to support her but wrestled with his his irritation at her for giving up. Torrent struggled to contain his aggravations while trying to coax Harper back into the world.

He understood Ordell's importance to her, but the man had not been important enough to mention before placing Torrent's entire laboratory at risk. Or perhaps it was the reverse. Maybe Torrent was not important enough to be informed. Torrent found it difficult to determine his current status in her eyes. It was precisely the wrong way to think about the love of his life, currently pinned to their bed with depressive symptoms.

"Not today," she told him and rolled back over into her pillow. His ever-present frustration mounted as he bit back on what he might have said. Instead of chastising her, he tried to implore her to a minimal level of self-preservation.

"Okay, but at least eat something?"

"I will, I promise. Just....not right now."

Work alone kept his mind from the various levels of gray that every day with Harper had become. As he passed through the door into the foyer, Railynn greeted him with a smile, a cup of coffee, and a warm hug.

"Hi Rai," he said flatly, not feeling much like smiling, but he forced a weak grin anyway as he rescued the coffee from her grip.

"I talked to Brigid yesterday."

"Really?" he questioned, unsure of how successfully he'd hidden his disdain for the woman who had replaced him in Harper's life. He was keenly aware that this also wasn't a fair way for him to think of Brigid, who only did Harper's bidding. She was a trial lawyer, and he was a boyfriend or something. He mattered more, even if the only thing that enticed Harper from her trance-like depression was a call from Brigid.

Why Railynn continued to be involved in the trial process remained a mystery to him. With Brigid, it made three. They reminded him of the fates from Greek literature, weaving and cutting while lives unraveled around them with every pull of the thread.

"She said it'll take time to get started. But she, uh, they, feel like there's still a good shot of overturning Madison's Rule. Even with Ramsey's constant dribble, the tide is starting to shift."

Torrent nearly spit his coffee into her face but choked back the simmering beverage at the last moment.

Railynn grinned from ear to ear like there was something to celebrate. All Torrent could think of were the years and years of deliberation ahead, court appearances, negative press about Toussaint Labs. He tried to imagine what his investors' reactions would be. They likely would be "very disappointed," just before cutting funding. How would Harper make it through years of court appearances and national scrutiny? She barely functioned as it was. How would he? How would they?

"Why go that far? Why can't they fix this problem and get Ordell out?"

"There is no way to 'fix' the problem, Torrent. They've got to change the law."

That wasn't true. Torrent wasn't sure why Railynn kept making that argument every single time they'd talked about the case. The law could stay in place, and the millions of models impacted by the law could remain impacted. There was no reason to let the case continue to be a political and public firestorm. Emergent Biotechnology didn't want that any more than he did. The most frustrating part was the simplicity of the solution.

All Harper had to do was sign a piece of paper, and Ordell would be free, and Harper would be out of bed. She wouldn't, though, because Ordell wouldn't actually be free. Instead, Ordell would be officially and legally her property since no legal mechanism gave Ordell agency. She could still have Ordell back, along with a healthy amount of money. Her stress and anxiety would end, he was sure, as soon as Ordell gained freedom. That was yet another argument that he'd failed to win convincingly.

"Harper's already a wreck, Rai. It'll take them months to even decide whether to hear the case. Can you imagine what more of this will do to her?"

Railynn flashed a frown.

"Her, or you?" it seemed to say. Torrent sighed and looked away.

He acquiesced and feigned indifference as he gave his best

'yeah, you're right' smile. He supposed Railynn admired Harper for going through with the court case. The consequences weren't real for Harper in the same way they were for him, but Railynn should have known better.

"Also, more good news," she told him.

"That was good news?" he scoffed, but she didn't seem to hear or didn't care.

"I found a home for the last two of the Firsts."

"Oh, that is good," he said, breathing a sigh of relief. Another thing that a pending national trial impacted was the desire of otherwise happy couples to adopt experimental babies from controversial labs. It had become challenging to place the last of the Firsts. Most families didn't want to take the chance of being caught in the national spotlight, despite the non-disclosures and other contractual precautions.

"Who's taking them? The Orphan Program?"

The Orphan Program had been his upbringing. He had no parents and no siblings except the other children who ended up in foster care as he had. He didn't even know his real name. Alexander Toussaint had been a great-grandfather of one of the nurses who had found him deposited on their doorstep, wrapped up in a tiny Moses basket. If he believed the story, he had never cried once when the woman discovered him lying there and brought him in. Even when he was hungry, the most he ever did was reach out with grasping hands.

"Nope," she grinned and paused for a moment with a look that may have been a smirk. Finally, she spoke up.

"Me."

"You?"

"Yes, me," she said again, and frowned at his skeptical tone. "Why do you say it like that?"

"No reason, I guess. It just didn't cross my mind... can't you have children?" he asked her cautiously. Just at that moment, an embarrassed looking graduate student coughed, pivoted, and left the room.

Railynn lowered her voice to a whisper. "Of course I can have children if I want. But I want these children. Think about it. We made them, mixed up DNA, created them ourselves. They are my children already."

"They're not my children. They're my experiment."

Then he slowly pondered over a conversation that he and Harper had had ages before. What were the rules for these children? Perhaps he should have paid more attention.

"You don't have anything to do with it—my children. And I've already got names picked out. Are you ready?"

"Sure, I can't wait," he quipped, half-joking.

"Larken and Oliver."

"Is Larken a real name?"

"What kind of name is Torrent?"

"Fair question. Did I ever tell you how I got it?"

"No, not yet."

It didn't feel appropriate for Torrent to bring up hosting a pornography hub in college while speaking of her new adoptive children.

"Maybe another time," he suggested. "Shall we check on Larken and Oliver then?" The two of them walked together, slowly following the outside curve of the facility. They pulled up the internal view of the pods C1 and C14, otherwise known as Larken and Oliver, when they made it into the Egg Lab.

Something caught his attention as he studied the growing fetus on the monitor. He wished he'd spent more money on was monitoring equipment. If he'd had a holo monitor instead of the flat one, he could have been more confident. Only having two dimensions was limiting, but he was still pretty sure of what he saw.

"Rai, we might have a problem," he told her no longer

joking. "Those are three-month-old fetuses, and they've only been in there a month and a half."

"Oh no," she replied. "Hold on; let me check."

"Temperature is good. Cell division rate is accelerated, though. How did we miss this?"

"I haven't been in here for a while; it's only been the grad students and the lab robot since this mess with Ordell started."

"Everything else looks normal. I don't know what it could be."

"Should we crack one open and have a look?"

"I think we have to. What if something terrible is happening here? What if developmental processes are being skipped or short-circuited?"

"Okay, which one?"

"One of the ones going to the Orphan Program. They won't miss one less orphan."

Rai flashed Torrent a look that was a combination of apology and embarrassment at how quickly she pivoted from thinking of the Firsts as children and back to experiment subjects. He had made the same mental transition she had and only nodded knowingly. The look they exchanged would not change what they had to do.

"A4," Torrent told her. "We have excellent metrics on that one."

His eyelids felt heavy as he prepared for dissection in the decontamination chamber. The experiment was his one positive thing in a sea of apprehension. It took most of his strength to stretch the thin rubber gloves over the fingers of his right hand. He cursed as he realized he should have donned his booties first. One glove snapped as he tried to pull it off to adjust his shoes, so he had to pull another out of the dispenser as soon as he was done, and start that part of the process over again.

By the time he made it through decontamination, Railynn was already looking over the stream of digital numbers on the side of the A4 egg. He joined her and Dorothy, who seemed aware that something was amiss, and hovered nearby. A full fifty minutes later, and they thought they had their answer.

"It looks like…," Rai began. "Wait a minute. I think it's because of the mixing agent I added to prevent fixing to the side of the pod."

"Do you think it'll continue once they hatch?"

"I don't think so. Really, they shouldn't. They won't be exposed to the agent anymore. I would expect it to slow. They look fine, right?"

"I don't see deformities," he told her. "Everything looks ok in A4. The sample just aged more than we expected."

"You know what this means?"

"Yes. Double our observation rate to make sure nothing else goes wrong."

"No," Railynn said. "Well, yes. But also, these will hatch in another month instead of six. And we haven't lost a single one yet, except this one."

As she motioned to the still corpse on the table, Torrent's eyes widened as he went over her words in his mind. The development changes meant that, if things continue, they will have hatched nearly 100% of their late-stage models in half the time that it usually took. Something else occurred to him.

"These will hatch before the trial starts," he told her. "That's the absolute best news ever!"

She glared at him, but only for a moment. The fact that they had just discovered yet another scientific breakthrough was intoxicatingly good. Torrent thought that she couldn't get too mad at him after such good news.

If he hadn't thought it would be crude, he would have done a full-body happy dance right there in Egg Lab. Instead, he did a little swivel-and-spin as his mini, personal happy dance, and Railynn laughed at him when he finished his revolution.

Torrent wanted Ordell to gain his freedom, but the future of all who worked in the lab depended strongly on timing. If they mired themselves in controversy before the experiment succeeded, the entire thing might become a footnote to history. Graduate and undergraduate assistants depended on him, on his word, and his research reputation to further their careers. Whether his name would still mean anything after the Firsts hatched would rely a lot on timing. A breakthrough just before trial would be precisely the thing to offset the bad publicity a trial would inevitably bring.

In that light, the hastening maturity of the Firsts was good news, and in the sea of bad news that his life had become, he welcomed the deviation. After they'd cleaned up and made it through decontamination, Torrent pulled out his communicator to call Harper. He hesitated. He couldn't tell her the 'good news' about the hatching while Ordell was in detention. There was no actual good news for her except Ordell's pending release, which as yet wasn't secured.

"Hi, Torrent," her voice muttered into the communicator. "I've eaten, I swear."

He scrambled for what he was going to say and decided that perhaps it was time to let her know about the Madison Rule after all. He sighed inwardly.

"I know," he told her, grasping at what to say. "I have news."

"Good news? I could use some."

"I suppose, yes," he continued, "and no."

He pulled off his gloves while his communicator perched on a shelf nearby. He picked it up and walked toward the exit into the hallway.

"I'll clean up, Torrent," Railynn said. "You guys talk."

In the hallway, he and Harper continued the conversation.

"Walsh and Moody called Railynn. They are expanding scope again. The Supreme Court is looking at the case."

"Did they say when the trial is going to start yet?"

"They may not hear it. They're reviewing it to decide whether or not to hear it. Look, Harps; this will mean more international attention, spotlight, death threats – more of the same. It's going to be long and painful, and everything about you, Ordell, us, it will all be out in national news."

"More than it already is? I don't care, Torrent. Why are you still trying to talk me out of this?"

The bite in her voice made him cringe.

"I'm not," he protested, even though he was. "I just want you to understand it will get ... messy."

"We have to get Ordell back. What would you do if it was someone you care about?" she snapped at him.

Sign the settlement was his immediate thought, followed closely by the second. Probably turn him in. Part of him wanted to remind Harper that Ordell wasn't her blood relative and that she barely knew the man in reality. He was some guy who showed up at her house with a sad story. But Torrent knew better than to let any of that come out of his mouth. For the moment, he kept his tongue.

"Torrent, I love you. I'm sorry."

"I love you, Harps. It's just this whole thing you..." he stumbled through, and didn't know what he could say that he hadn't already tried.

"I know I've been a lot. I'll get better, I promise," she told him. Torrent nodded as he listened. When he replied, he hoped that his head's bobbing motion translated into his voice as confidence. He wondered if she could tell that he didn't believe her.

"I know, I'm sorry too," he said.

With a little effort, he could convince himself that there

was hope and that eventually, something like normal would come back. He needed to believe that they could stabilize, or at least, he needed to believe that she cared enough about their relationship to know what she did to them. Even as the tiny flame of hope re-emerged in his chest, somewhere within him was the unwavering knowledge that the resurgence would be short-lived. He felt the flame already beginning to flicker.

30

Hatching Day

Wednesday, August 31, 2185

The days marched forward, pulling Harper along in their wake like driftwood. As weeks formed, the idea of a trial morphed into adolescence and screamed for her attention, selfishly unresponsive to her own needs. More calls with Brigid begat more communicator calls with Brigid, during which Brigid accosted Harper with questions that grew more intrusive. Harper wondered whether she was the defendant instead of Emergent Biotechnology. Brigid wanted to know everything about her, from childhood indiscretions to the college boyfriends who didn't return her affections. The worst were the mock-interviews, which always left Harper exhausted and just short of crying. Today's was no exception.

"How long have you been sleeping with your boss?"

Harper sucked her breath in and looked away from the accusing eyes. Her heart raced, and her palms grew slick with sweat. How was that anyone's business?

"Harper? Answer the question."

"Why are you doing this? What does any of this have to do with Ordell?"

"We have to be prepared. I'm doing nothing less than I expect Emergent Biotechnology to do. They will attempt to eviscerate you on the stand, and we have to make sure you're bulletproof."

"But I'm not bulletproof."

"You don't have to be. You only have to *seem* bulletproof."

No matter how many times she prepared, memorized her responses, and fought with Brigid, the woman always found a way to her core. The mock-interviews were like having her heart slowly flayed into thin strips with dull knives.

After the session ended, Harper stared forward at the holovid matrix where Brigid's face had been moments before, her body shaking uncontrollably from anger. Even knowing how the attacks came did nothing to temper the edge on Brigid's words.

The doorbell shook her from her stupor. Harper stood slowly, rickety, and raw on her cramped legs, to cover the short distance to the door of Torrent's apartment. As she nudged the door forward, she saw a lock of blonde hair barely hiding a bright brown eye.

She pulled the door open farther to reveal Railynn in a t-shirt and shorts. Her thin, light t-shirt presented a worn image of a vase of flowers across the front. Five tiny white flowers spotted a background of green and blurry red.

"Brigid called me. She said you had a rough time. Uh - are you going to let me in?"

"It's a mess in here," Harper told her instinctively, moving her body to block Railynn's view into the apartment.

"I knew Torrent before you did, Harper. I know how he lives, and I definitely won't blame you. Besides, I brought this." Railynn pulled an arm around in front of her. Clutched between her fingers was a bottle of red wine.

"It's a Chianti. From well, Chianti, Italy. There's a backup in the car if we need it."

With that, she shoved her way past, or Harper moved first, the reality was unclear. However, it happened, Railynn very quickly made herself comfortable and produced two wine glasses from her other hand.

"Want to tell me about it?"

"Tell you about it?"

"Sometimes it helps to talk, let it out, and be heard. Remember what that's like? Friends?"

She did remember. A lifetime ago, when problems arose, she had always had her mother to talk to, however imperfect. Afterward, it had been Ordell filling the void of friend and confidant in the limited way that he could. Torrent possessed far too much energy to be a good listener, though. Harper plastered on a permanent ingratiating smile around him. When he 'tried to help,' he was more interested in hearing himself talk.

"I...guess," she muttered, accepting a glass of wine and pulling it to her nose. The fruity oak scent relaxed her shoulders.

"I'm listening. Go ahead," Railynn told her, and poured herself a matching glass, then sat silently beside her.

The words were a salve for Harper's still-bleeding heart. She poured her worries out onto the table, where Railynn, who never seemed to notice that Harper limited herself to a single glass, dissected them until the bottle was empty.

Railynn came over more often after that. With Railynn's support, Harper gradually found the strength to return to work in time to witness the births of the Firsts.

Friday, September 30, 2185

Torrent disconnected A3 from the power. A wayward surge might end months of hard work. The lab robot removed the top part of the pod over ten minutes, gently unscrewing a thin ceramic lid from the rest of the container. Looking into the egg, Harper found it hard not to think of it as a uterus. The upside-down baby poked tiny toes up in the opaque greenish-brown mucus-like fluid. A transparent plastic sack enveloped the child. The lab robot cut A3 out of the faux-placenta and lifted the infant deftly up by the ankle with one rubberized claw. In the same motion, it half-handed and half-threw the screaming baby at Harper.

Harper grabbed it out of the air and clutched it close to her chest. The baby was tiny, helpless, and warm, like a guinea pig or a kitten. She immediately wrapped her arms around it and carried it to a nearby baby unit. From the sounds of the screams, the child had no trouble breathing. The tiny girl clutched at Harper with ten perfect fingers. No bar-code tattoo committed the child to a lifetime of servitude.

The sight of her unmarred wrist prompted Harper to think of Ordell's tattoo. The difference between freedom and slavery was a tattoo.

She handed the child over to Railynn, turning away before Railynn had a chance to question her. As she moved on toward the next child, Railynn's voice caught up to her anyway.

"Is there anything I can do?" her friend asked, her voice dripping with concern. She'd seen the emotion in Harper's face.

"No," Harper said, just as her eyes fell on the C1 and C14 pods, upon which were taped the names "Larken" and "Oliver," respectively.

"Larken?" she muttered barely loudly enough for her to hear the way the name sounded.

"And Oliver," indicated Railynn, nodding her head toward

the other container.

"And Oliver," Harper repeated with a whisper.

"These two are the two I told you about," Railynn beamed. "A little boy and a little girl."

Harper wanted to be the blindly supportive friend that Railynn expected. She flashed a smile convincing enough to conceal the fact that she persistently repeated in her mind that these children were no threat to her. The children were real now, and no longer a vague aspiration. In less than an hour, both of them would be on their way to Railynn's condo, their new home. Now, exactly two of her boyfriend's illegitimate children would be in her life for as long as Railynn was.

Harper's body involuntarily shook. When she refocused her eyes on Railynn, she saw that Rai had continued along to the next pod. She hadn't noticed Harper's latest fumbling.

Another baby screamed from across the lab and pierced through her concentration. She yanked her head toward the noise and made eye contact with Torrent, cradling one of the children to his chest with one arm, and wrapping up little legs with the other. He looked like a father. Harper looked away.

Saturday, October 8, 2185

As with all great discoveries, there had to be a celebration. For Harper, there was little to celebrate. The lab had become a chore. She only maintained the responsibility out of her obligation to Torrent, a commitment she wasn't sure she wanted to keep. Without him, she would be alone, and without the lab, she wasn't entirely sure she would still have him. So she planned to celebrate with them.

Railynn's visits grew rarer, with her her new responsibilities. Harper knew the children, *his* children, required more and more of her time. If the situation had been anything like normal, Railynn should have taken a maternity leave and disappeared altogether. Railynn reduced her work schedule as Egg Lab emptied to only a few days a week as the children took over her life.

Torrent insisted on the celebration. Despite Harper's frequent and consistent complaints, Torrent arranged a press event publicly recognizing the revolutionary modeling process the lab had discovered. The way he'd justified this to Harper was by "paraphrasing an ancient proverb of scientific funding" - the tree that falls in the forest with nobody around to witness does not get the budget. It wasn't a real saying, but an effective way to communicate the point. Harper understood that, even if she didn't like it.

On the night of the celebration, she tried to make the occasion special. Torrent, for all of his previous accolades, acted like the success of the Firsts was the most important thing to happen in science for a century. Nearly a hundred percent success in the later phases was a capability of which was previously unheard. If nothing else, the rate of modeling would increase exponentially if other scientists could duplicate their process. Harper was confident that a duplication effort was already underway.

As they prepared for the event in his tiny apartment, she tried on a veneer of fatuousness.

"Your apartment is too small," she laughed while attempting to sidestep and pull her slip on at the same time.

"I know," he returned her smile. "It's the only way I can afford to stay downtown. It's paid for with grant money, and they hate things like actual rooms in an apartment."

"What about publicity events?"

"Oh, people who fund research love publicity events to show off how amazing they are. You can bet that our donors will be there, toasting their success and hobnobbing together with other givers."

"Fah fah, fa fa fa fah," she muttered with an aristocratic air, her wrist up holding an invisible martini.

"You nailed it." His grin widened. "Exactly that. Also, speech, speech, speech, speech…."

"Can you help me zip up?" She spun around to let him pull up the zipper on a sparkly silver evening gown.

"Nice dress," he said, and leaned in to kiss her on the neck.

"Thanks, some rich guy bought it for me. I mean really rich, but also stingy."

"Not fair," he told her. "It's not my money; it's just my bank account. And that *was* expensive."

"The things you tell a girl."

Then Torrent must have seen her countenance fall as she found herself dragged back to thoughts of Ordell and what might be happening to him while they played at trial.

"Ordell?"

She nodded as she stoically tried to force the grin back. Torrent responded by rubbing her bare shoulders gently with his palms.

"We'll get him out, Harps, one way or another," he told her, as sincerely as if he cared nearly as much as she did. She let herself believe for a moment that his feeling was genuine, and let the gesture wash over her, although she knew better. At least he'd made an effort to sound authentic.

She eventually succeeded in bringing her smile back. However, she found herself wondering what "other way" Torrent thought they might try. She didn't say anything about it.

"Tonight is for celebration," he continued.

"Tonight is for celebration!" she echoed, wondering if it came across her lips sounding as fake as it felt to say.

Later, at the event, Railynn arrived in a sleek orange dress with brown heels and a orange coat. It was too much orange, Harper thought. Still, Railynn pulled off looks that Harper couldn't even dream of, even though Railynn had often complained about how much prettier Harper was than she. Objectively, that was true, but Railynn had distinctive features which completed some outfits. The orange dress and coat were the right combination for her.

The first speaker was Gallatin Hamilton, the leading donor for establishing Toussaint Labs. He spoke of vision, hard work, and the usual novelties that self-important men talk about to seem even more critical. The entire time, Torrent, Harper, and Railynn whispered like school children, occasionally giggling about some witticism or another. They progressively got louder as the champagne flowed until finally, the announcer called out from the microphone.

"And without further ado, the man of the evening, Alexander Toussaint, and his partner, Railynn Marche, who found every speech tonight extremely amusing."

They stood, and Railynn blushed a bit and gave Harper a look somewhere between anxiety and excitement. Then, she made her way to the stage and stood beside Torrent as he took the microphone.

"Almost a year ago today, we began this project. We had an idea of a way to revolutionize modeling. With what can only be called genius insights of Railynn Marche, we have our first ever batch of models with a one-hundred percent success rate."

An audible murmur traveled through the crowd.

"But that's not all. We also developed the Firsts for a third of the cost. And we finished the models in half the time of anything industry has right now. The lowest error rate in history means freedom. It means now we can produce experiments in the academic community without requiring corporate partnerships and ambitions."

Silence.

"Not that we don't love you guys."

He stopped to wink at the corporate sponsors, who fidgeted in their chairs.

"The new process will help you, too. You can stretch that dollar and fund more studies for much less money. So you might ask what's next?"

Harper was amazed at how he handled the crowd. As soon as he said the words, the entire audience of over three hundred people went almost entirely silent.

"Have you ever heard of the hard problem of consciousness?"

He paused again. The audience held a collective gasp.

"Yes, that one. We're doing to cognitive science what you just saw us do to modeling. That's a promise."

The room filled with applause and Harper felt her hand shake as she lowered her crystal flute to the table. She couldn't help feeling betrayed that he hadn't told her that he planned to start so soon, especially with the trial just around the corner.

"And now, I'll take questions."

Hands shot up in the back of the room.

The first reporter asked if they planned to solve the hard problem of consciousness or do another interim paper.

"We will solve it within a year. You can bet on it."

The next reporter asked about cloning and licensing the technology.

"We'll license to whoever can use the technology responsibly."

A third reporter's hand raised.

"Is it true that Toussaint Labs is backing an ACLU lawsuit intended to overturn Madison's law?"

Without skipping a beat, Torrent responded."No."

"But the plaintiff is there at your table. Do you expect us to believe that Toussaint Labs, who work in cloning, don't have a position in this lawsuit?"

"I'm sorry. Do you have a question about our research?"

Harper stood up, flustered, and left the room, but not before she saw Railynn scowl at the reporter from the stage. Her heart may have been in the right place, but the reporter was only part of the problem.

"No more questions. After all, we are celebrating!" Harper heard from behind her.

Harper found herself alone on a balcony somewhere in the hotel, away from the noise and the lights. She was only there for a moment before she heard the clicking of Railynn's high-heels on the shiny marble floors. Harper felt a jacket laid gently over her shoulders in the frigid night air.

"I'm sorry," she said into the night air. "I shouldn't have done that. Now it'll be on the news tomorrow for sure."

"That's fine," Railynn comforted her. "He had no right."

"Exactly. Should I ask the reporter to leave?" Torrent asked. She hadn't heard him follow Railynn out, but Torrent must not have been far behind.

"No," said Harper. "That'll make it worse. I ...want to leave, though."

"No," Torrent said to her, which caught her off guard before he back-pedaled. "I mean, please don't. We can still have fun. It's been so long since we've relaxed. That's the only time anybody is asking questions, I promise. After this, they'll get just as trashed as the rest of us. Come on; I'll introduce you around. I'm sure Gallatin would love to get to know you better!"

"I'd rather not," she told him. "I mean, not see him."

Torrent made an fair point though. She had to admit that they hadn't had much fun in a while, and the fault, was mainly hers. The trio turned to head back in through the doors when a thin buzzing sound caught their attention.

Harper reached into her handbag.

"Harper," she heard as soon as she picked up her communicator.

"Ordell!" she practically yelled. "How are you? Are you okay?"

"Yes, I'm fine," he told her. "I've been watching your award ceremony. Congratulations!"

She hadn't seen the cameras in the lobby, but she guessed that it made sense. The intersection of a modeling breakthrough and a high-profile court case would of course lead to extensive coverage.

"Thank you!"

"I miss you, Harper."

"Me too, Ordell. I can't wait for this whole thing to be over."

"Yeah, I know. You look beautiful tonight," Ordell told her. "Your mother would be proud."

"Thank you! It was a gorgeous dress that Torrent got for me. I think it was perfect."

She flashed a smile toward Torrent and felt it in her chest. It was a real smile.

"It is," Ordell told her, as his voice cracked though he was trying not to cry.

"Are you okay, Ordell?"

"They're treating me well enough," he told her, "Nothing fancy, but they mostly leave me alone. I'm just missing you, that's all."

"I miss you too. Can we visit?"

"No. I would be escorted, probably shackled. I'd prefer not. Good night, Harper. It's so good to see you enjoying yourself that I couldn't resist calling. I'm sure I'll hear from Brigid tomorrow."

"Ordell, wait..."

Harper found herself talking to an empty line. She put the

communicator back into her purse, surprised to find that the smile hadn't left her lips yet. Harper rode on the feeling through an evening that turned out much better than she could ever have expected. She and Torrent laughed and joked while dancing until the press corps was gone, and well after the VIPs trickled away. Finally, the time had come for Railynn to retire to her children. Children! Of all the people, it was still strange for Harper to think of Railynn with children.

"I can't believe you have children!" Harper blurted out excitedly.

"I know! Isn't it wild?" Railynn responded. "They're so... wonderful, but sleep-depriving. I'll see you in...late tomorrow, probably."

Railynn grinned as her car pulled away, and the window rolled up between them.

Harper's mind went to Railynn and her two babies, glowing little fat babies with eyes full of love. At least, that was her imagination of the children whom she secretly hoped to never meet.

"You're smiling a lot tonight," Torrent mentioned.

"I am?"

"It's a nice change. Are you really having that good a time?"

She thought about the question. For a whole hour, since her conversation with Ordell, she hadn't thought once about how horrible a friend she was to do things Ordell couldn't, or how he wouldn't be imprisoned now except for her. Harper looked past Torrent and up at the tiny beads of light swinging from the ceiling just on the other side of the glass entryway.

"I guess I am," she said, watching their slow-motion swaying. Harper pivoted her gaze to Torrent, wearing a slight smile. "What do you think?"

"I think it's great that you're able to relax."

"No, not that. About children. Do you want to have any?

Not now, but eventually."

He circled his arm around her waist and stared into her eyes.

"Yes, someday," he replied. They stood like that, eyes locked together, as Torrent's volantrae arrived to shepherd them home.

Sunday, October 9, 2185

The next morning, Harper awoke to find her elegant clothing strewn across the tiny apartment, her lace underwear spread out on the table. She grinned as she pulled herself from her bed and let Torrent sleep. Then she popped on the news to have something to listen to while she got ready for her meeting.

"...and we'll have more on this breaking story."

She heard the voice from the background in that typical accent-less, and over-enunciated newscaster vernacular. Turning, she caught a glimpse of her and Torrent, climbing into his car with arms around each other. She stared fixedly at the screen, appalled at the insinuation that she knew they were trying to make. Behind her, she thought she heard Torrent stirring, so she turned to look at him.

"We're in the news," she said.

"So what?" he asked, though he immediately jumped fully exposed from bed and ran to her side. As he got there, she motioned to the holovision. Across the bottom, in the news banner, was a message.

"Lead scientist announces breakthrough, in relationship with employee..."

"We knew this would happen, Harper," he reminded her. "This isn't going to be the worst of it."

"That doesn't make me feel better, Torrent."

At that particular moment, she didn't know that there was

anything that would ever make her feel better. After a few minutes of awkward silence, she spoke again.

"Just leave me alone right now."

"Fine."

And he left. The few moments of understanding and support from Torrent the evening before were transient, and the real Torrent was back, in all of his obtuseness. Harper turned away from the television in time to watch him leave. She didn't try to stop him or explain that she'd never seen herself in the news before. For her, this was the feared opening round of a long battle to control public opinion. The first thing anyone was going to think about her was that sleeping with her boss was the way she managed her career. That impression would be impossible to shake for some many.

How would that influence the trial? She didn't know, but she was sure it wouldn't be in a good way.

All she needed was a little reassurance that their relationship was real. She wanted it to be. She felt the way he looked at her sometimes still, but she wanted more. When he didn't deliver, or couldn't deliver, she wondered how it had ever been that she'd chosen him over supporting Ordell, consciously or not.

Harper stood up from the table, determined now to push away her doubts. There was a lot of work to do – she had an interview with the lawyer that morning at ten. She wondered if he forgot about that, and then her communicator buzzed. She picked it up without looking at the number.

"Hello."

"Harper, I'm sorry," Torrent said, and it sounded like he meant it.

"I'm sorry too. With everything going on, it's hard sometimes."

"Yeah, I know," he replied. "We'll get through. Good luck

with your meeting this morning with Brigid."

She smiled as she disconnected and felt stronger than she had in a long time. Half an hour later, she clutched her sensible tan purse and walked out the door, leaving the still cluttered apartment behind her.

31

The Ordell Bentley

Sunday, October 9, 2185

Ordell wasn't a soldier. For most of his time among polli, he hadn't considered himself much of anything besides a construction worker. He might have been a boxer or a football player in another reality, but construction workers were in demand, so that's what he was awakened from his second birth to do. The nation was in the midst of a construction boom as it built and then rebuilt, trying to keep ahead of global warming. Without global warming, Ordell surmised that he might never have emerged from the second birth pod. These were some of the thoughts that kept him company in his isolated room.

Lately, his first birth had captured his focus more than his second. Ordell had ample opportunity to reflect on the earliest years of his life. Those years had been full of machines and measurements as Emergent Biotechnology prepared him for a life that would ultimately be delayed. He remembered being carried through white halls by strong, metallic arms, devoid of human presence. Ordell saw a crumpled body at the end of a bright-crimson streak across the floor as the machine took him past. He didn't have the words to describe death then, as he'd only just entered the world, but he knew now that the body was a clone who hadn't survived the first birth. Other details were fuzzy and malleable, but one thing he was confident about was that his world was glacially cold. Even wrapped in blankets and mostly dry, the air chilled him through. He understood now that the compound that had brought him into the world had been hospital-cold and sanitized to keep the possibility of bacterial growth at a minimum.

Past that, memories of the earliest years of his first birth were sparse. The lights were always flickery and dim, and he was perpetually cold. Over the following years, he attended endlessly dull classes taught through pre-recorded lectures. Robots led his cohort to and from classrooms. Replicators delivered bland food and Vita.

Those memories delivered little emotional nourishment.

Ordell chose instead to focus on his time with Aayushi. Even the most banal of these filled his heart, and one in particular frequented his mind. He and Aayushi had decided to learn Italian for a trip out of the country. Like so many other fantasies, the journey could never happen, but she imagined it for them. In repose on his second-hand couch, she struggled to follow along with a holographic instructor. The man mouthed words, and then the holovid emitted three-dimensional pictures of what each meant. She failed to pronounce 'biccicleta' in a way that didn't sound like the bastardization of 'bicycle.'

The word rolled from Ordell's mouth almost instantly, which earned him a glare.

"Mi dispiace, ma non parlo bene l'italiano," he told her, and then translated, "I'm sorry, I don't speak Italian well."

She groaned and then laughed. The joke wasn't funny, but she laughed anyway. Her laughter alone made it worth the two days Ordell had spent practicing.

"You know Italian? Why did you let me buy all this stuff?" she had asked him.

"I don't. It was in the books. That's all I know."

She had laughed at that too. Trapped again in the tiny hotel room, the warmth of the moment washed over Ordell and brought a smile to his lips. He witnessed his smile through half-closed eyes, reflected in a glossy picture frame.

He surmised that he would still be a happily ignorant model without her. Ordell could easily see himself spending long days working and hard nights drinking, with no real ambition for change. What could he change, though? Aayushi had never fully understood how he absorbed daily abuse without complaint. She had always been free. Laws didn't keep her trapped in slavery.

"Do you ever want more?" he remembered her saying.

"More?"

"More. Like, to make choices for yourself. Travel if you want."

"Where would I go?" he asked her, all conviviality stripped away.

"Wherever you want to."

"No, I mean, I don't know anywhere to want to go."

As a model, his universe was his work, and the idea that he was part of the rest of the world's population was a foreign way of thinking. Everything except Aayushi pigeoned him into his little slot. Aayushi dared ask 'what if' with such frequency and determination that eventually he'd internalized the notion without even realizing it. What if he could have a lover? And now, after all of this time, what if he could be free?

He recalled Gregory Ramsey's voice.

"They're less than animals."

The argument was self-reinforcing. Humans treated models like animals taught to jump to orders at the fear of bodily harm. Anyone looking in from the outside would come to the same conclusion. There wasn't truth in that thinking, though. Ordell knew it from his love with Aayushi. Lancaster, as dumb as he had been, had known it before Ordell could even imagine. Perhaps Ordell had been the slow learner of the two.

The communicator buzzed and projected an image "UNIDENTIFIED" across a far wall. Had it not been for complete boredom, he would have let it buzz without consequence.

"Hello?"

"Ordell Bentley?" came a heavily distorted voice.

"Who is this?"

"Do you know what happens to shills who get out of line?"

The projection sprang to life, painting "HPM" on the wall. Ordell's heart raced. Someone had discovered him - someone who he had to assume intended to do him serious bodily harm. This time he had no escape strategy or go-bag.

He shuffled to his feet and sought out something useful with which he could defend himself. He'd been through the cabinets multiple times before, but desperation bred denial. He pulled several different varieties of tea from the cupboards onto the counters. There was nothing there that he hadn't seen before. In the other cabinets, the ones over the stove-top, he knew he would find glasses and generic-looking coffee cups. Glasses might be promising in a pinch, but neither seemed useful against a proton rifle.

* * *

A knock outside of his room roused him from his routine. Ordell carefully placed a little saucer, also useless as a defensive weapon, down on the counter and stepped quietly toward the door. When the lawyer had come by, he recalled - that one time since he had arrived in the room – she had used a card key. The security guards just let themselves in the same way. Nobody ever knocked.

But he heard the knock again, distinct and sharp. Peering through the peek hole and saw a thin, younger man on the other side. The man didn't appear threatening, so he pushed the door open a crack. A woman around the same age stepped into view beside him. The man wore a League City Legends baseball cap emblazoned with an astronaut patch across the front, with short, blond hair tucked neatly up inside. Both wore bellhop uniforms, and the man carried a large wooden tray, with two plates covered with silver domes.

"Morning, Ordell," the man greeted him, then nodded to the woman on his left.

"I'm Dan, and this is my trainee, Mara," he said. "Where would you like me to put your food?"

Breakfast was usually cold pastries and juice, on the days that anyone remembered to bring it to him. The salty, metallic smell of steak and tomato salsa escaped through the hole in the top of one of the plate covers. Ordell motioned to them to bring in the cart. The woman quickly slipped through the door and cleared an area as the man moved the tray from the cart to the coffee table.

"You are Ordell Bentley?" Mara asked, with a faint undertone of admiration.

"Yeah, that's me," Ordell replied while helping himself to some of the pancakes.

"*The* Ordell Bentley?"

"I guess," he said, puzzled at the question.

She seemed to fade a little under his less-than-enthusiastic response. Ordell saw Dan encourage her with a soft nudge in the back. She made a sign across her chest in half-triangle that spurred something in Ordell's memory, but it was faint, and he couldn't quite recall. The gesture, which the woman had used to give her courage presumably, seemed familiar.

"Maybe you should fill him in," the man told her.

She nodded and made the sign one more time before she began to speak.

"You're famous," she explained, lowering her voice more if that were possible. "We're all hoping for you to win. All of us, thousands, hundreds of thousands..."

"Hundreds...of...thousands?"

"All of us," she repeated, making the sign again, and kneeling slightly at the end. Then Ordell finally recognized it. He was first exposed to it at Convocation, as one of the other Bentleys tried to recruit him. The motions were a sign of religious commitment used by members of the Siblings of the Natural Order. They believed that models would only ever find equality through violent uprising. This made them unique from most models, who never sought equality and accepted their position as non-citizens. Others also believed in equality with polli and thought that peaceful organizing would work. However, it hadn't been effective so far, and everyone who tried to organize ended up recycled or reprogrammed.

"Mara used to be a sex worker," Dan interrupted his thoughts.

Mara pulled down the collar of her shirt, exposing the beginnings of a massive scar between her concealed breasts, starting at her sternum and continuing toward her bellybutton.

"When you're not a citizen, there are no rules," Mara told him. "I'm not doing it anymore. I can't do it anymore."

She didn't go into details about it, though Ordell understood not to ask any questions. He only nodded somberly, giving a grimace that he hoped communicated that she didn't need to explain further.

"Your case," she told him. "We're all, and I mean every model in the United States- not just us, waiting for it to start. Rawls v. Emergent Biotechnology. Your case can change everything for us."

"Nobody else has done that before," Dan continued. "Never."

"Why?"

"Because it doesn't work," Dan replied. "You know models don't have the right to sue. If you don't have a citizen who's willing to sue for you, then you may as well not bring it up. And you know how big the industry is? If you didn't have to, would you invite a fight with them?"

In all, Ordell did know that the industry was currently worth about one-hundred-twenty billion dollars on the low end. That seemed like an infinite amount of money to Ordell.

"This case is going to be hard," Mara told him. "We came to offer our support. Whichever way it goes, we're here and watching."

He supposed that they meant to give him comfort, but the Natural Order a national terrorist organization. The label was well earned by multiple violent uprisings, ultimately as unsuccessful as the non-violent protest attempts, killing models outright instead of recycling them after show trials by kangaroo courts.

Ordell longed for the simplicity of his earlier life. Work. Bar. Home.

"Another delivery, Mara," Dan motioned toward the door. Ordell hadn't noticed him take a communicator out, but he now stared at it with longing. Dan stuck out his hand to Ordell, who took it, and the two shook, just like citizens entering a deal.

"Thanks, Ordell, from all of us," Mara told him, as she threw her arms around Ordell's neck and gave him a wet kiss on the side of the face. Ordell felt his cheeks grow hot with embarrassment as she pulled away, but she had already turned. The two exited through the door, chatting excitedly between them. The security guards seemed not to notice or care about their departure. At first, he wondered why, until one of the guards turned toward him briefly and flashed a grin and a mock salute. This wasn't one of the men who had deposited him rudely in his room the first day. Ordell noticed a bar code stamped across the man's wrist, and the pieces clicked into place. The guards were models too, and probably members of the Natural Order as well. It was much cheaper for Emergent Biotechnology to place models than to retain expensive polli as guards.

Ordell's hotel-furnished communicator buzzed. He let the door swing closed behind him as he turned to answer.

"Ordell speaking," he answered.

"Ordell? Is that you?" He heard Harper's voice on the other end, and his heart jumped as she continued. "Are you okay?"

His heart jumped. He'd lost count of how many days he had been without her. Now he realized what an emptiness her absence had created in him. A lump formed at the back of his throat, and he bit it back and gave himself a second before responding. There was no reason to upset Harper more than she must have been already. Ordell could only imagine, given his stress level, what her anxiety was doing to her.

"Well enough," he told her. "They're not beating me or anything. The food is kind of bland."

Except potentially for whatever was under the plate covers, rapidly cooling to room temperature. Ordell's stomach grumbled as he eyed the silver domes.

Harper's laughing response brought him back to the conversation. He thought he could make out a tinge of pain beneath the surface. She carried pain in her voice the same way Aayushi had in her eyes.

"I'm sorry I haven't called before. Brigid says that we shouldn't talk as long as you're in Emergent's custody. Is there anyone there with you?" she asked.

"No, I'm alone."

"Good, then what she doesn't know won't hurt her. I don't know if anyone told you yet – we're meeting tomorrow."

"Tomorrow?"

"Yes, around lunchtime. Emergent made another offer, Ordell. This one is better. We'll talk about it in person."

He wondered what that offer could be. He put his hand against his face, where the scar across his cheek reminded him that it wasn't so long ago that Mark Ruby targeted him for death. That thought further reminded him of the threatening call a few minutes earlier. Such things were useful to remember when he started thinking his situation might improve. The winds might shift at any moment.

Monday, October 10, 2185

The next day, a new security detail escorted Ordell to Meitner's Bistro, the type of establishment that brought out lunch in four separate courses. He found himself seated at the head of a table in a private dining room. They left him entirely alone for fifteen minutes, sipping on cucumber-flavored water from a glass cupped between chained hands.

He was in-between sips when Harper's unmistakable hazel eyes searched through the glass walls to meet his own. As he smiled back, she broke out into a run to the door and swung it open quickly. She wrapped her arms around his neck as soon as she was close enough, in a way that reminded him vaguely of Mara, absent the lingering smell of violets.

Harper squeezed his hand, then sat beside him. A man walked behind her. He seemed to be eyeing the security guards suspiciously. Another woman, plain next to Harper, walked last in the line. He recognized this woman as the same brave person who had shown up at the reclamation warehouse.

"Ordell, you're okay! I was so worried."

"I think I'm fine, but so bored. I have a holovision, a stationary bike, and a bed, and that's pretty much all they allow me."

He lied about the stationary bike and wasn't entirely sure why. The hotel had a fitness room, but it was two floors below, and even the model guards wouldn't take him down to it. He supposed he wanted her to feel like he was okay.

"I believe it," she told him, just as the intense-looking man who he now recognized from the television coverage of Toussaint Labs.

"Torrent Toussaint? And....Railynn Marche?"

"Yes, and yes," Railynn replied with a broad smile.

"Correct. It's a pleasure to meet you in person," Torrent started with a handshake.

"The same," Ordell replied, flashing his chains to show that he wasn't rude by not shaking.

Ordell watched Torrent survey the room. He stared at the first course before them, then at the pillars leading up to the cathedral ceiling. It occurred to him that Torrent, like he, wasn't used to an establishment like the Bistro. The only person who seemed at home was Railynn, who didn't even seem to notice the expensive-looking tableware.

"So, a deal?" Ordell chimed in, intent on understanding the details and privately figure out a course of action before the opposing lawyer arrived. Harper seemed a little set back by Ordell's directness, and at first, deigned to respond. Or perhaps, he considered, thinking of the distraught girl he had stumbled upon months before, the context had switched too quickly for her to follow.

"Yes, Ordell," she told him. "Your freedom, and you will never have to work again unless you want to. You can leave with us today if we take the deal."

"What's the catch?"

"None that I can see," Torrent interrupted. "It's pretty straightforward. Our lawyer went through it yesterday, and she says it's reasonable."

"What about the case?" Ordell asked. "What would happen to that?"

"Nothing," Harper told him. "We just walk away. All of us walk away from this room together. I become your legal guardian, and you get a bank account balance which any citizen would be envious of."

"No case?"

She shook her head.

Ordell thought of Mara. He thought of the hundreds of thousands who watched his case, and then the millions of models in the United States who had no idea any of this was happening. What became of them if the legal case didn't go forward? What became of him if it did?

He wondered if the Natural Order had known of the settlement before they reached out to him. Perhaps they had staged the previous day as a preemptive strike of sorts.

Just before he could respond, the door opened, and a tall red-headed woman in a lime-green pantsuit walked in.

"Sorry I'm late," Brigid said, and flashed a grin at Ordell. "Hi, Ordell."

He smiled back at her. Since they had first met, there had been something about her that he genuinely liked. She leaned in and shook his hand before seating herself to his side opposite of Harper.

"Should we accept the deal, Brigid?" he asked, without giving her time to settle. He had meant to catch her a little off her guard. He wanted to see what she thought, and he never would if she had time to compose herself. Brigid's face revealed what he'd hoped it would. She wanted the case, and she seemed to think they had a chance at winning.

"I would accept this deal," she told him without wavering. Her facial expressions had settled to her lawyer's face, but he felt that he knew where her sympathies lay.

Less than a second afterward, the door opened again, and a tall man in a dark black suit, with a blood-red tie, walked through. This man had silver, wolf-like eyes and a measured pace that seemed to render his body into a posture that seemed as though he would pounce at any moment. Ordell recognized him as the man who had escorted him from the van into the hotel lobby. The man had seemed sleazy then and still oozed foulness.

"Hey everyone, are we ready to sign some papers?"

He seemed in a festive mood and made absolutely no effort to introduce himself to Ordell. It was clear what he thought of models by the way he scrunched his nose when his eyes fell on Ordell's wrist tattoo. Ordell instinctively turned his wrist, so the tattoo was against the table, and immediately became angry with himself for doing so.

He looked at the man and then at Brigid, and then turned to Harper. He'd made up his mind about what he wanted to do, but he didn't know how she would react or if she was willing to commit to his choice when such an easy out sat on a piece of paper right in front of her. One signature and her life became simpler. Ordell thought perhaps his resolve wasn't as firm as he would have liked. His stomach began to rumble and toss, and he thought he might be sick, but he swallowed and addressed her anyway. He already regretted what he was going to say.

"Harper, I can't tell you what to do. But this isn't about me anymore. There are millions of us, and so many suffering every day. The status of non-human makes us expendable and renders us invisible."

Ordell selected the words the best he could. Aayushi had been so much better than he was at such things. Harper seemed to understand, even while the blood sucked out of her face downward. He hoped she would be able to forgive him, and just a small part of him hoped that she signed the paper anyway. Ordell shared her exhaustion. Torrent drew in his breath sharply - he'd wanted the settlement signed. Though he couldn't see Railynn directly, he suspected her smile had washed away as well. They had all decided, it seemed, that Harper ought to sign the paper. It was up to Harper now.

The man in the suit backed up. He stumbled because he was also in the process of sitting down. However, he managed to catch himself before falling to the ground completely.

Brigid's eyes popped open at Ordell's words, and in his imagination, she had the features of a hungry jaguar. He had guessed correctly. That gave him more strength.

"I can't agree to this, Harper," he continued. "It's time to do something bigger than us, and this situation may never happen again."

Harper nodded her pale face up and down in acknowledgment but made no other sign that she had heard him. The man in the suit flushed and motioned violently to the guards outside, who entered the room. One grabbed him by the neck and pulled him from his chair to the ground. Another placed a knee in his back. His lungs felt as though they were caving in under the man's weight, but as soon as the man got up, Ordell found he could breathe again. He discovered his hands had been locked together behind his back instead of in front this time. They half dragged him by his arms, while he struggled to turn his neck, but couldn't see Harper from any angle he could achieve.

"Enjoy your lunch, courtesy of Emergent Biotechnology," he heard the man growl to the group. He thought he heard Harper's voice calling after him, but there was nothing he could do. He knew they wouldn't kill him without endangering their lawsuit, yet. He hoped that they were taking him back to his room, with the Natural Order guards, but he guessed that his refusal had earned him some sort of punishment. Some punishment, he thought, that wouldn't kill him, but might make him wish he were dead.

32

Criminal Charges

Monday, October 10, 2185

Harper arrived at the apartment ahead of Torrent, having left before him to make a quick stop at Brigid's office. The door hung precariously from its hinges. Across the back wall of the living room were the words, in what looked like red spray paint, "Die Shill Lover!" Furniture was overturned and ripped, and someone had smashed the dishes they'd left out earlier. The vandalism might have been HPM, but whoever it was hadn't signed their handiwork. It could just as easily been someone from Emergent Biotechnology, disappointed by the settlement not moving forward.

Neither possibility encouraged her. Both groups had armies of lawyers and resources at their disposal. The only support Harper and Ordell had was a pro bono lawyer and the ACLU. The idea that winning might be possible was something Brigid consistently pushed and Harper could tell that Brigid was a very skillful woman. Her apprehension was not assuaged by the woman's constant encouragement, however. Only her obligation to Ordell kept her from signing.

Harper quickly picked up the furniture innards from the floor and stuffed them into a trash bag she'd procured from the kitchen. The lawsuit wasn't Torrent's battle to fight, and if she could clean the mess up before he returned, he wouldn't be too upset by it. Harper wondered what his breaking point was. At what point would he decide that enough was enough, and jettison her to save his career and reputation? He would have to do it soon, as every day found them in the newscasts more and more.

But she didn't believe that he would ever actually leave her. There wasn't a future she could imagine where Torrent would abandon her. He would ride her case to his doom, rather than leave her now. If either of them were in danger of fleeing, she was a likelier candidate.

"Harper Rawls?" a voice interrupted her cleaning meditation.

Harper turned her head to see a uniformed policeman standing, arms stiffly crossed in front of his chest. Her first thought was that he looked like a male stripper, complete with a tacky handlebar mustache and excessively trimmed eyebrows, furrowed into a frown. The firmness of his stance reminded her of her father's unforgiving harshness when he had stood near the living room mantel, gun barrel smoking. She stifled a nervous laugh from leaving her mouth.

"What do you want?"

"Please come with us," he said, as another equally ridiculous-looking policeman breached the doorway, this one with a studiously-trimmed five o'clock shadow. She turned to him and shot him what she'd hoped was a crippling glare. It seemed to work, as his speedy entry into the room slowed precipitously.

"No."

"You're under arrest for the grand theft of over $100,000 of goods from Bowie Construction. You have the right to remain silent..."

The rest of whatever the officer had to say tapered off into nothing in her ears. Harper felt suspicion growing in her heart that Emergent Biotechnology sent both the vandals and the police. How could their arrival have been a coincidence?

Stone-faces with bad haircuts stared at her, unfeeling.

The police presented her with handcuffs. She refused again and muttered some useless thing about her lawyer. The policemen fastened the cuffs around her wrist anyway. The noises blurred together, and her vision faded as thin curtains disappeared and let the full force of the sun hide everything in its brightness. The sounds stopped altogether, and her only perception was the gentle calling of whales, though she knew that wasn't right. She suffered a severe panic attack, and maybe another mental break. She grew angry with the realization of how fragile she still was.

Willing herself to her feet, Harper stumbled through the door, partially blinded and with staggered breaths. With determination, she made the trip to the car unassisted. These men wouldn't see her suffering.

After a short ride, they escorted her through the station's door as though it were just another day at the office and until someone interrupted the progress.

"Handcuffs? Seriously?"

Her vision had returned to full clarity by then, and she made out the voice's owner to be a giant looking man with white hair and a boisterous demeanor. Unlike her abducting officers in uniform, he wore a dark gray suit. A green argyle tie hung around his neck with the words "world's best dad" printed down the front in a childlike font. It dropped cleanly from a tight Windsor knot but swelled out into a curve sitting atop his belly, which caused it to stop short of his belt.

"Yes, Bob, they said she might be a flight risk."

"Who is 'they'? And get those damned things off."

"You know, the victims. Bowie."

"Listen, Calista, the clairvoyant one. Bowie doesn't get to tell us who's a flight risk and who isn't. There are a trial and all of that due process stuff, remember?"

"But..."

Even while he argued, 'Calista,' which Harper guessed wasn't the man's real name, fumbled with the key to remove the handcuffs. He seemed relieved when they finally clanged to the floor.

"You," Bob said, pointing at the other one. "Take him and leave. Please."

The two left without saying another word. Harper said nothing, unsure of what her relationship with Bob would be. She was back in reality at least, so there was that small miracle.

"Harper Pavina Rawls?"

"Yes, that's me."

"You are under arrest, but I have a feeling it won't last. You can sit over there on that bench. Want some coffee? There's some down that hall over there."

"You're just going to let me wander around in here?"

"Are you going to try to leave?"

She shook her head, no. She was way too scared to leave, even though everything in her wanted to run.

"Okay, then. Coffee is down the hall there," he pointed to her right past some people who she could tell were detectives just by the way they carried themselves. Every one possessed slightly depressed hygiene and subconscious swaggers, much like Bob himself.

"If you want some air or a cigarette or something, go right instead of left. There's a little veranda over there. Comms are that way too."

Harper didn't know what else to do, so she nodded anxiously and traversed back to the solitary bench at the front of the station where it looked like visitors frequented. She walked toward her seat and then pulled out her communicator.

"Why am I here?"

"A bit existential, don't you think," he joked, though she found it less than amusing, and her face must have portrayed that as he choked on his laughter less than a second later and cleared his throat.

"I just said you're under arrest. What else do you want to know?"

"For what?"

"Stealing a clone."

"Model," she corrected him. "But I didn't steal anything. He came to me."

"You had possession," he told her. "According to Madison's rule, the fact that you failed to turn him in means that you stole him."

"That's ridiculous."

"A little. But I don't make law, just do what the prosecutor tells me. They say arrest you, so I arrest you."

"Even if you don't agree?"

"Yep," he told her. "There are many laws with which I disagree. My job isn't to agree; it's to enforce the law. And the law says you belong here."

"I see," she told him, trying out a condescendingly disappointed mother tone with him, but it seemed to make no difference. He was only marginally more polite to her than he'd been with the Storm Troopers.

"Sit," he told her forcefully, pointing, "over there. When it's time to process you in, we'll come get you."

She sat and immediately called Brigid on her communicator.

* * *

After leaving Harper, and suffering through a lengthy, emotional afternoon working with needy potential clients, Brigid allowed herself the rest of the day off. She had just lowered herself under a protective armor of scented bubbles when her communicator buzzed.

At first, she ignored it. Once, twice, the device buzzed and flashed. When it finally projected the image of Harper Rawls across her floor, she ended the bath.

Brigid slipped out from under the clinging surface of the water. She wrapped herself in her warmed towel before plodding across the tiles to retrieve her communicator from the counter and hitting the button on the bottom to accept the call.

"Brigid Kostic," she said, careful to leave her image off.

"Brigid, it's me."

Harper's panicked voice stuttered into existence. Something had happened in the few hours that they were apart.

"Are you okay?" she asked.

"I am, I think. But I'm at the police station."

As Harper told her about the destroyed apartment and the affect-less guards seizing her and dragging her away, Brigid went livid with anger. Like Harper, Brigid didn't believe in coincidences. She had dealt long enough with corporations who felt that the law was only for poor people to follow.

"I'll come down to the station and talk to the police. They won't be able to hold you. You'll be safe with the police until I get there. They're not monsters. Be strong."

Brigid disconnected the communicator and exited the bathroom into the large master bedroom.

She hung up with Brigid. Having nothing else to do but wait, Harper soaked in her surroundings. There were no walls, just multiple attached desks, arranged in a circle against windows.

The furniture looked modern, but modern without class, almost utilitarian. A little island supported multiple cardboard boxes and something that looked like a printer, but she guessed probably wasn't. Three overhead monitors floated on the walls over her head. One showed a local news station, and on the other two rotated traffic camera images. She didn't see a single holo-monitor anywhere.

Of all of the furniture, the bench was the most disappointing. Closer inspection revealed that it was plastic supported by a metal frame, and seemed designed to maximize discomfort. Harper sat anxiously and stared at Bob, who may have suggested that she be processed, but had not meant that he would do it. He now chatted with one butt cheek on the desk of an uncomfortable looking female officer. As if she sensed her watching, the woman glanced her direction, in a way that said, 'thank you for being my way out.' She slid around him and crossed the open bay to greet Harper, pausing only to pick up a form.

"Harper?"

"Yes."

"Let's get you processed in," she said.

Processing wasn't lengthy, and nor was it as intimidating as she'd thought it would be. From the movies she'd seen, Harper had assumed the woman would lock her into a jail cell or something, but that didn't happen right away. She filled out three forms, and then they took her fingerprints with a scanner device. Her brief time so far in the police station seemed strangely docile and pleasant. But, she reminded herself, she was still under arrest.

After processing, they took her through a door and into a clean cell that smelled of lavender. The bed seemed like a real mattress, and there was a little desk that she imagined writing lonely notes to her loved ones, or her loved one. Instead of bars, there were actual walls, although Harper assumed there were probably bars in the walls. Overall, the cell was as spacious as Torrent's studio apartment.

She sat on the foot of the bed after the amiable processing woman left her to see to some other duties. Harper then folded herself up on the bunk. They'd taken her communicator and wallet. Any minute now, she expected someone to toss white scrubs to change there in front of the many cameras.

"Is anyone here?" she asked loudly.

Her cries echoed through the halls and came bounding back to her ears. If any other arrestees were lingering in similar cells nearby, nobody spoke up. It was so quiet, it reminded her of the room in her college meditation class after an intense session when everyone was so relaxed that they were afraid to break the atmosphere by speaking accidentally.

She wondered how long they could keep her in that cramped little cell. Loneliness pushed in from all sides as she waited.

Brigid flew down the stairs. She popped open the door of her car and sped out of the parking garage, very nearly hitting a gentleman in a red cap. She managed to avoid him but was closer than she'd liked, and guessing from his offensive gestures, more intimate than he would have liked either. He was probably one of those types who thought that the self-driving cars were safer. Brigid could never give control of her vehicle – it was one of the little joys she allowed herself. Besides, with all of the self-drivers, it was easier than ever to speed through traffic.

33

Accident

Monday, October 10, 2185

As he watched Ordell being escorted away, Torrent's stomach clenched and his eyebrows tightened in anger. Large enough to undoubtedly crush the guards even with cuffs, the man didn't struggle as two guards forced him sideways through the door. He could have done what it took to set Harper free. Whatever hold he had over her, Ordell could have relinquished it with an affirmation. Torrent didn't understand. When Harper glanced his direction, Torrent only looked away.

"Give me a ride back to work?" He asked Railynn, who seemed as shocked as he was.

"Yeah, okay," she responded, nodding as she fished through her purse for her keys. Railynn's transportation didn't even auto-drive, nor did it fly. In the post-lunch rush, her car would take at least a half-hour to cross town back to work. Still, he refused to go with Harper. He looked toward

279

the door in time to see her exit with the legal team. It wasn't as though she'd waited for him anyway.

The parking lot for cars like hers was on the bottom floor of the garage since the top floors were reserved for volantrae. The distance proved too far for Railynn to cross in silence.

"Why so angry?" Railynn asked.

"We need this case to be over."

"It won't be over for him, either."

"How is that my problem? I have a lab to run and I can't do it because I have reporters trying to sneak in, extremists threatening us, and I'm pretty sure there will be a criminal investigation at some point. And…"

Torrent stopped. Complaining to Railynn about Harper seemed like a betrayal to him, so instead he clenched is jaw and shoved his hands into his pockets, while he followed the rest of the way without speaking. As they left the building, he was pretty sure that his foul mood had rubbed off on Railynn. Every time he looked at her, she stared straight ahead with narrowed eyes . He sighed and turned his attention to the window just in time to see a semi truck bearing down on them. Then he felt a violent lurch and everything went black.

Tuesday, October 11, 2185

"It's funny how that works," a woman's voice bounced around in Torrent's throbbing head.

"What?" A second woman responded.

"Well, he was on the hit side, but the damage was all on the other side."

"Not so funny for them. Learn to be quiet."

A minute passed in complete silence before Torrent heard another whisper.

"Pay attention to his vitals. If he's not awake now, he will be soon."

On cue, Torrent moaned as he opened his eyes. The bright hospital light shot like razors through to the back of his skull. He closed them against the onslaught. He'd only gotten a flash of sandy-blonde hair, and for a moment, thought Railynn hovered over him.

He opened his mouth to speak, but his lips and throat were so dry that nothing came out. One of the nurses held up a glass of water, which he slurped loudly, sucking some of it into his lungs and coughing in response. When the gagging finally stopped, he swallowed again and opened his eyes to see that the woman's face above him wasn't Railynn at all.

"What happened?" He asked.

"You had an accident, Mr. Toussaint." The woman holding the water answered.

"Accident?"

"Yes. You strayed into oncoming traffic and collided with a semi-truck."

He remembered that part. Railynn slumped over across the steering wheel and pulling to the left. He recalled the oncoming semi and the smell of the tires. But he couldn't seem to remember anything else.

"Railynn?"

"Don't know. She's in critical right now."

"Critical?"

"Yeah, she took the worst of it. It's a good thing the autopilot monitored for the parking garage exit, or we wouldn't be having this conversation at all."

The words bounced around inside his throbbing head, keeping tempo with his quickening heartbeat as he struggled to focus his thoughts. The smell of chemical sanitizers assaulted his nostrils as he lay there, his energy level obscenely outpaced by the urgency he felt inside.

"Calm down, Mr. Toussaint."

He suppressed the urge to correct her and change the

prefix to 'Dr.' instead. It seemed such a trivial thing in light of the danger Railynn faced.

"Calm down, or you'll hurt yourself more. You need rest," one nurse continued. "You're both in the best hands."

He closed his eyes, only because he lacked the energy to keep them open. As he did, the image of Harper, immobile on the couch as she spent her days, with eyes puffed up with tears, forced itself to the front of his mind. Her slim brown legs curled up beneath her, in an off-white cotton robe. He hated himself for not loving her more, and for not being willing to suffer more. He hated himself for the knowledge of what he would do to her by his leaving. He began to understand what it was like to feel helpless in the face of something he couldn't control. Torrent felt ready to offer his own life for a guarantee of Railynn's safety.

Then his eyes shot open.

"Children!" It seemed like a shout in his head, though the muted reaction of the nurse implied that he hadn't been nearly as loud as he'd thought.

"You have children?"

"No," he heard himself whisper, "Railynn."

"We'll gather them, Mr. Toussaint," the nurse told him assertively, in a tone that implied it to be a mundane task upon which she regularly embarked.

"Doctor," he whispered, correcting her.

"The doctor will be back in about half an hour," she told him apologetically. "Do you feel you need him now?"

He closed his eyes and rolled his head slowly to the left and right, then relaxed as much as he could, though a dull ache now joined the pain in his head throughout his back and shoulders. He was glad she'd misunderstood when he'd wished her to change her means of address. She smiled at him and then left the room with her companion.

Torrent suffered from an underlying discomfort that

nudged his body sporadically as soon as he shut his eyes. He tried to turn onto his left side, stretching the limits of his IV. When that side pressed hard at him, he rolled over onto his back. Shortly afterward, another nudge near by his kidneys. It was as though his body had rebelled against him.

He listened to the slow drip of the intravenous tube and the whirring of machines he didn't recognize. For all of the equipment in his lab, these were mysteries to him. The fluorescent light glared through his eyelids now even when he closed them. The sandpaper sheets scratched at bruised muscles, and the smell of chemicals pressed unrelentingly against his sinuses.

He tried to listen past the chaos of patients' pacing to see if he could hear Railynn's voice, but it was futile. Torrent pressed on until eventually, sleep took him.

When he awoke the second time, a portly dark-complexioned man with thick-framed glasses stared down at him. Even with puffy, wiry hair, the little man seemed inches shorter than the two nurses had earlier. He took notes on what looked like a pinamu, occasionally stopping to gnaw at the end of his pen before continuing. The pen crackled briefly as blue sparks flew from the back, and the man jumped. Then he muttered some words in a language Torrent couldn't understand. The pen, Torrent realized, was a recorder. The man had written nothing over the lines of text displayed on the device. The pen remembered for him. He began to raise the pen to his lips again but caught himself.

The man shifted his gaze on Torrent. Thick lenses gave his eyes an over-sized presence in any conversation they were about to have. The man furrowed his black eyebrows into a look of concern that Torrent was sure would have been quite moving, except for the thick glasses blocking their full view.

"Dr. Toussaint," the man began, with a soft drawl that lingered a little and vaguely reminded Torrent of his extended family in Louisiana.

"Yes?" Torrent replied, faintly, but more forcefully than he had managed with the nurse.

"You're going to be fine," the man smiled, bringing down his eyebrows. Happy, his eyes popped out like those of an asylum inmate. The man continued.

"I'm Dr. Aguillard. Just lookin' through your chart here, and it looks excellent."

The man nodded absently, as Torrent wondered whether they made actual conversation. The man nodded again for emphasis.

"Real good."

"Can you tell me anything about Railynn, Dr. Aguillard?"

The man nodded and gave an amiable smile, but didn't answer Torrent's question. It seemed to Torrent that he was thinking deeply about something.

"What about Railynn?" he repeated.

"Did you know you are her emergency contact?"

Torrent hadn't known that. Dr. Aguillard looked around the room, pulling back the white privacy curtain with little balloons dancing across the top. They looked out of place with the graveness of his new demeanor.

"Torrent, she'll be fine after this accident. We expect her to be awake in a day or two."

"A day...or two?"

"Yes. We had to induce a coma to keep you're girlfriend's brain swelling down. Once it's under control, we'll wake her up."

"She's not my girlfriend."

"Oh, I thought..."

"No," Torrent said firmly. "Just a friend."

Almost as though he'd seen the fear that Torrent was too weak or cared too little to hide, Dr. Aguillard continued more quickly.

"I see. I'm very good at this, Dr. Toussaint. Been doing this for a long time, and Ms. Marche is textbook. That's not even a little concern. But..."

"But what?"

"Well, we gave her an MRI to look at the swelling, and...we found something unusual."

"Unusual?"

"I guess there's no good way to tell ya. A brain tumor, Dr. Toussaint, and she's dying."

The word felt like a shot from a plasma rifle. The wind sucked out of Torrent while he processed.

"Dying?"

"Dying. Maybe a month, maybe a year, but not much longer."

Torrent knew the color had washed out of his face. He felt the blood as it fled. Then he remembered and told the doctor what had happened before the crash.

"She fainted. Slumped right over before that truck hit us."

"I'm not surprised," Dr. Aguillard replied. "Given her condition. It would be best if you didn't let her drive at all, ever. And your girlfriend..."

"She's not my girlfriend," Torrent interrupted.

"Sorry. Your friend - the police picked up her children from daycare. Right now, one of the officers is taking care of them. Does she have a relative nearby?"

Torrent didn't know. He thought hard through all of the conversations he'd had with Railynn, and most, he decided, had been about him. Him complaining about his relationship with Harper usually. He realized that he knew very little about Railynn's family at all. Feeling guilty, he shook his head no.

"Then it's you, Torrent," Dr. Aguillard told him. "We haven't been able to find anyone either."

He lowered his voice to a whisper and leaned in.

"Torrent, if she can't care for them, and I will not sign anything saying she can, then someone will have to. They come home with you or go to the state orphanage. Do you understand?"

Torrent nodded slowly.

"The state orphanage has improved, but it's not a home, and it's not family who love them," Dr. Aguillar continued.

"Are you a social worker?"

"No, just a medical doctor with an opinion. Now listen. When Rachel - your nurse - gets back, tell her they're yours. I'll explain everything to Railynn when she wakes back up."

Torrent shook at the suggestion. The children would show as relatives on any modern genetic test. They might even have enough shared DNA to look like they were his. There was no way he could care for children. The enormous eyes behind the thick glasses fixated on him. The children were essential to Dr.Aguillard, and he wasn't going to accept no for an answer.

"Okay, I'll do it. Railynn and I will figure out what to do with them together."

"Good man, good man."

34

Holding Cell

Tuesday, October 11, 2185

Harper willed the white cell door to open. Her heartbeat rose with every shadow passing in front of it, and fell as the shadow faded away. She still had not changed into the thoughtfully provided white prison scrubs that she'd discovered on the foot of the otherwise bare bunk. Nor had anyone been in to ask about her.

She'd made a series of desperate calls on her communicator, first to her lawyer, then to Torrent, and Railynn in turn. Neither of the latter two had picked up, though Brigid had indicated that she would be coming to help. For the first hour after, Harper had believed her. Now, she no longer had that faith. Now, she felt scared and alone, the way she had after her parents died and it was just her and two bloodstained corpses. Only instead of being in her home, she was trapped in a cell.

When the red low-battery light appeared on her

communicator, she felt the familiar feelings of panic well up inside of her. The flashing indicator was a pulse monitor - her lifeline to the world. As much as that world seemed to have forgotten about her, watching that connection slip away was more than she thought she could bear.

Where is Brigid?

She threw her communicator against the bars and buried her head into a pillow, which smelled like nothing. She could only imagine the generic detergent they used to achieve that lack of aroma. The thought made her eyes fill and she let the tears fall into the pillow. It seemed as though she had an unending supply of them. She was no longer sure if she cried for herself, or Ordell, or for her parents. The tears must have been for all of the calamities that kept crashing into her life.

An eternity later, the door at the end of the cellblock opened, and through it walked a man in an expensive-looking gray suit. He held a briefcase and a very stern look that eventually changed into a warm smile when their eyes met. That smile was the most sincere looking fake smile she had ever seen. Harper tried to smile back, though she knew that her eyes were puffy and red, and her hair disheveled. She must have looked like a lunatic.

"Ms. Rawls?"

"Yes."

"I'm Francisco Reyes, with Walsh and Moody. Let me apologize for not being here sooner. We only just discovered that Ms. Kostic would not be able to assist you further."

"What?"

The man didn't answer.

"If you're ready to leave this cell, the police have agreed to release you to our custody."

"Francisco, where is Brigid?"

Francisco, a lean man with a thin mustache centered in an oval face, looked the same age she was. The suit hung limply from of his slim frame and gave her the impression that he would disappear into it at any moment.

He didn't respond to her question, and Harper could tell by his reaction that he was hiding something. Francisco turned his head toward the door through which he had just entered and nodded. Immediately, a harsh buzzing noise sounded, made more vicious by the prior silence in the cell block, and the door to her cell swung casually open. She shoved past Francisco and into the hallway, knocking him back against the bars opposite her. She stopped and sucked in air, noticing that somehow the air in the hallway outside of her cell door was fresher than the air inside.

Francisco collected himself, pulled himself taller, and tightened his tie. He was even less impressive now, though he did tower over her. He seemed accidental. That was the best word she could come up with to describe him. Compared to Brigid, Harper felt less safe with Francisco. He spoke the next few words as he led her out into the brightly-lit squad bay.

"I'll be representing you in the criminal case, Ms. Rawls."

"What about Brigid?"

Again, there was no answer. This time, Harper stopped just before the glass doors exiting the precinct. She noticed that he no longer smiled and hadn't since they left the cell block.

"No, Francisco. Where is Brigid?"

"Ms. Harper, I've been asked to represent you in the criminal case, free of charge. I'm aware that Ms. Kostic is representing you in the Emergent Biotechnology civil lawsuit. This is a different matter. I don't know where Brigid is."

"Why wouldn't Brigid represent me here as well?"

"That's not how it's done, Ms. Rawls. Unless you have her on retainer, which you don't, legal counsel is case-by-case. I have vastly more experience in criminal trials than she did."

There was something about the way he said 'did' that alarmed her. But she continued to follow him through the front doors and into an expensive-looking black volantrae.

"Walsh and Moody," Francisco muttered as soon as they were seated. The volantrae came on immediately and lifted up out of the parking spot. As the vehicle pulled away, the two sat on opposite sides of the roomy circular couch-like interior. She stared at him. From his age alone, there was no way Francisco had more experience than Brigid at anything life-related, including criminal trials. She wondered what else he might have been lying about, but she sank back into the weathered leather cushions, convinced that he wouldn't become any more forthcoming.

At Walsh and Moody, the pair continued on in silence. He offered no more elaboration than what he'd told her when they initially met, and she asked for none. They walked through the bright translucent doors with Walsh and Moody emblazoned on them, and she was deposited in an office.

The room in which Francisco abandoned her had one massive desk in its center, with more room behind the desk than in front. Behind her, several curved bookcases were adorned with what she assumed to be legal books, far more than she expected anyone could have read. However, Harper suspected Brigid probably was familiar with most. An aroma hung there that she couldn't quite place, somewhere between lime and chocolate. She thought of several expensive colognes it reminded her of but didn't quite fit. Even the trash can looked expensive, a finely polished wood grained container, housing on a single yellow crumpled worksheet.

Moments later a tall man, in attire worthy of the room, walked through the door. This man was large, almost the size of Ordell, and seemed fit like he probably could play football if he wanted to. He was just short enough that he didn't have to duck to get through the doorway, but another inch would have put him over. Long black dreadlocks swayed down his back in a ponytail, and lines creased the edges of his dark eyes.

"Ms. Rawls?"

It was a mixture between a statement and a question. The man was intimidating by his presence alone, but the voice emphasized her imagined danger. Being alone with him in the empty room somehow made Harper feel vulnerable and out of place. Everything about him pointed the same direction – someone to be respected. More importantly for her, though, he seemed to be a man who probably knew where Brigid was.

"Will someone tell me what happened to Brigid?"

"Gone, Ms. Rawls," he said. "Just….gone. We haven't heard from her since two this afternoon when she left to retrieve you."

Harper gasped out loud. She tried to stifle it, but it squeaked out between her fingers and hung in the air between them for a moment before the man continued.

"Your case..." he began, but then stopped. Harper noticed the broad shoulders slumping.

"You think she's been killed?"

"Maybe. We got a cryptic message from HPM earlier today claiming responsibility."

Her mind raced to the two calls she'd made earlier. Neither Torrent nor Railynn had answered their comms when she'd called, and she hadn't heard back from either. She then wondered about Ordell, all alone, "protected" now by people who would probably rather see him dead.

She sat without asking onto the microfiber down couch. The case meant nothing anymore. Here she was, in an office with someone she'd never met, alone. She was ready to give it up. At that moment, for the safety of everyone she loved, she would gladly take the settlement.

Emergent Biotechnology won.

35

Dead Man

Tuesday, October 11, 2185

The guards who marshaled Ordell back to his isolated captivity smelled like leather and hand cream. Polite, yet distanced, the experience hardly qualified as personal interaction. When they deposited him in his room, they were ritualistic about it. The first popped open the wide white door while the second rushed through, leaving dirt-covered footprints behind him as he moved room-to-room and searched for...whatever it was they sought. Ordell hadn't been able to figure it out in previous searches either. The only difference was that this time, when the guard gave the sign for 'all clear,' he held in his hand the communicator that Ordell had been allowed to use to call Harper. When Ordell tried to grab it back, the guard pushed him down to the floor.

"Sit down, Shill. This communication device is the property of Emergent Biotechnology."

He stared after the communicator as one might watch an

old friend depart for the last time. Sadness overcame him and his body felt as if it slowly turned to lead. The heavy door closed and snapped into place. Then he heard two chunky clicks, like a refrigerator door slamming shut quickly, and followed by silence. He couldn't make out the sounds of the guards walking. He listened and picked up the sound of steady feet approaching his room in a slow gait. A gentle tapping rattled on the door across the hall from his. As soon as the door creaked open, he heard two meaty thunks and felt the floor shake as something heavy fell.

He rose to his feet, careful not to make noise. Ordell knew the sound of gunshots when he heard them, and he would do no good to anyone if he was dead. He couldn't be sure that it had anything to do with him, but it would be a strange coincidence if not. He slowly drew on his running shoes and worked his way backward away from the hallway door until he found himself in the bedroom. Thankful for the accommodations, he pulled the door closed as slowly and quietly as possible. Then he heard the knuckles outside of his living area in the other room.

Ordell's room was on the second floor. He'd imagined jumping out many times. At times during the worst of his stay, the idea of jumping to his death was somehow enticing. Other times he'd wondered if he would only break a leg, possibly steal a car and leave. From as high as he was, he put his odds of survival at fifty-percent. Ordell rubbed the scar his face, reminded what even a little misstep might do.

But now, he had the motivational free of death and a fair bit of luck. Beneath his window, a delivery van waited, which lessened the drop to a little less than a story. If he hung down first, he might be able to do it.

He wrestled with the window and forced it open at the bottom. It wouldn't open wide enough, so he struck it by the brace with the palm of his hand, breaking it with a loud crack just as pounding sounded on the door to his bedroom.

He pushed himself through quickly, then swung his legs down and dropped. He was so focused on watching the door that he didn't notice the delivery van had moved. Mid-fall, he realized that he should have landed and shifted to look down, just in time to feel shooting pain as he tried to brace his fall by stiffening his left leg. He'd never had a broken bone before, but given the level of pain he experienced, he thought that must have been what it felt like. He screamed out sharply and rolled the rest of the way down as the leg gave out, scratching his elbows and knees on the pavement. He thought he was in a successful roll until his head collided with the black surface of the pavement, dazing him temporarily.

Recovering from the pain by a flood of endorphins and adrenaline, he pulled himself up on his other leg, which seemed uninjured, and staggered toward the valet stand. He reached underneath and found a set of keys stashed beneath the abandoned podium. Ordell staggered toward the valet parking lot, dragging his left leg behind him, wincing every time he had to use it. He found the car, a Sampson P3200 utility vehicle in red, and pulled away from the building.

Hoping for information, he turned on the radio as a police car passed him without slowing, heading in the opposite direction.

"...suspect is still at large and dangerous. Four people are thought injured at the shooting in the Akson Regency downtown location, all models. A spokesman from Emergent Biotechnology has indicated that the company has a long-standing contract to use the building for the on-boarding of new models. We don't know what the shooter's intention is, but more deaths are expected. Police are inbound. If you are in the hotel and listening to this, lock your door and don't let anyone in. The Police have informed us that they will announce their presence and display their badges before entering. Be safe.

"Next, Rawls v. Emergent Biotechnology and what it could mean for our nation. There are already rumors that this case will end up at the Supreme Court. The result could be the second biggest shake-up in twenty years for the cloning, er, modeling industry. Stay tuned!"

Indeed. Ordell would stay tuned. He had no idea where he was going. So far, the only place he'd been downtown was Meitner's Bistro, which was on 2nd avenue. He racked his brain for options. He could go back to Harper's house and wait, but if the hotel shooting had anything to do with him, he was sure it wasn't too long before the shooter would find his way there. Other options included trying to find Toussaint Labs since he Railynn might help him hide. But he had no idea where that was, but he thought *could* find Meitner's Bistro, and he felt like Ms. Kostic's law firm was near there.

There were four legal firms on 2nd avenue alone. Ordell parked in a nearby garage, with no intention of retrieving the vehicle. He stepped out, wincing on his leg, and began the work of finding Brigid Kostic's law firm, kicking himself mentally for not even knowing that much about his legal counsel. But he wouldn't have known, not being an actual citizen. There was nothing he would have signed or even received from them. His life or death was left to people he had only met once. Busy professionals crowded the sidewalks, mobbing to and fro, yet parting in a wave around him as he emerged from the garage. Nobody stopped him, but nobody asked if he was okay. That was more than Ordell expected anyway. He moved through the crowd pulling his left leg along behind him, heading for the first law firm he saw.

36

Jackson

Tuesday, October 11, 2185

Jackson held the communicator closer to his ear. He didn't want to miss a single word that his counterpart on the other end muttered. The news had been great so far. The Akson Regency, clones shot. It had been a tip worth making.

HPM had been looking for a way to up their profile in the city since a thwarted bombing attempt earlier that month had made them look like bumbling idiots. Jackson knew this because he had several friends in the organization. Working for Emergent Biotechnology had some benefits, like knowing where the HPM on-boarding sites were. The relationship between modeling companies and HPM was an eccentric one. Usually, Emergent had to be very careful with information about where they kept specific clones. An occasional leak had its benefits. When clones got out of control, there was always a boogeyman on standby.

The public story of a college-aged girl and her surrogate

father, taking on the pre-eminent cloning corporation in the United States had started to sway public opinion. He felt it, and his employers thought it, which was why they offered such a lucrative deal. When that fell through, the man in black still had a case to win, and one that looked more difficult with every passing day.

One communicator call, and even though the public would cry and wail about its injustice, and the case would die. Jackson was confident of one thing: without Ordell Bentley, there was no case.

Before he could celebrate, he needed to be sure, so he'd sent his own man to investigate and make sure that the HPM attack had done what Jackson wanted. The official line was to get Ordell out of harm's way if possible – but he would soon know if they had been successful.

"I'm in the room, but there's no sign of him."

"Really?"

"Yeah. The bedroom window's open – maybe he got out?"

"From the second floor?"

"I don't know. There's no blood or anything. I hope he got away. I'll see if I can find him outside."

Jackson hung up. Shills and their lovers – the lovers were almost as bad as the shills. He wouldn't miss either.

37

Reunion

Tuesday, October 11, 2185

Ordell sat in the lobby of Walsh and Moody. His left leg, now throbbing incessantly, extended out away from the chair. He'd spent the last half of a block hopping on his right leg, which ached with overuse. He'd asked for Brigid Kostic at two legal firms so far but only got a blank stare in response. He summoned the courage to ask yet again as he approached another desk, dragging his hurt leg behind him, where a young woman examined something on a translucent screen.

"Name?" she asked without looking up, which he thought was just as well since she'd probably panic seeing him in his current state. Splotches of dirt and blood decorated his lightweight, breathable workout t-shirt. On the back of his running pants, a bloodstain reached the size of a baseball. He had been afraid to pull up the pants to examine at the wound. Ordell looked anxiously around to determine whether anyone other than the receptionist seemed interested. No one did.

"Ordell," he whispered. "Ordell Bentley."

She didn't seem to recognize his name at all. Her hands flew across a flat surface, touching it gently, but rapidly. Then she re-stated his full name clearly and much too loudly for his comfort.

"Ordell Bentley."

"Yes."

"No, that was so the computer could understand, sorry. Oh. It looks like you don't have an appointment."

"I was hoping to see Brigid Kostic?"

The woman finally looked up at him, taking in his whole situation with a stifled gasp as her eyes widened.

"James Walsh, please," she said firmly, still staring at him. Then she paused.

"What's up, Kathrine?" a voice came through.

"Someone's here for Brigid."

A sigh sounded on the other side.

"Who?"

"He says he's Ordell Bentley?"

"Send him up."

The elevator ride was short and uneventful. With both legs now throbbing, Ordell changed his walking strategy to distribute his weight more evenly. The pain to his left leg was intense but tolerable. He thought he might not have broken it after all. Katherine didn't accompany him, but pushed him onto the elevator and told him when to get off. She smiled broadly as she expunged him from the lobby of the office building.

When he exited the elevator, Harper jumped onto him with a massive hug, which almost knocked him down as he shifted weight to his hurt leg. He winced, which she noticed and backed away, taking in the blood-soaked clothing he wore and how he favored his right leg.

"Mr. Bentley," a voice from behind Harper boomed. "Jim Walsh."

Harper released the hug and swung around to Ordell's left side, still gripping his hand violently, as if to tell him that he would never be allowed to leave her side again. She was careful to support his weight instead of the opposite, for which he was thankful. He stuck out his right hand to shake with Jim.

"Might as well call me Ordell," he said.

"How have you been?"

Without further invitation, Ordell filled the two in on the events at the hotel. Harper listened wide-eyed. Jim stood with patience and calm that couldn't have been natural. After Ordell finished talking, Jim expressed a look of concern.

"You may not know," Jim began his reply, ambling back to his office, "that my best legal mind is currently missing."

The door closed behind them. Jim pulled down a whiskey bottle and asked with his eyes and a nod, whether anyone else wanted some. Both nodded back, and he poured three fingers over ice in each glass before handing them out. Then Jim sat behind his desk. He motioned to them to take the couch, which Ordell obliged greedily after having walked firm-to-firm for eight blocks.

"Do you know the holovids, where the bad guys are killing off the good guys one-by-one, and eventually the good guys win anyway? That's not how this works," he told them, resigned.

"What happens is this. Without Brigid, we may continue the case, but it will delay for six months to a year."

He paused and eyed them over, then continued.

"During which time, this will continue to happen. We can hire security, but not forever. Do you understand what I'm saying?"

"To drop the case?" Harper asked.

"No. I'm saying decide what it's worth. From what I understand, there's a settlement on the table, quite a generous one. If you take it, you can move to Canada, become naturalized, and never look back. This whole thing becomes a bad memory."

"We're settling," Harper said, avoiding Ordell's gaze.

There would be no more discussing the possibility of expanding the trial scope to save the countless lives who had watched in anticipation of their freedom. Millions of models would never be free.

Ordell didn't contradict her. He had asked too much of her and this was the least he could do in return. He watched her melt into the couch. She seemed relaxed and at ease for the first time since he'd met her. Despite his desire to make her happy, a tiny seed of betrayal sprouted in his mind.

"Are you certain? Once I put in the call, there will be no going back."

Harper pulled her arms around Ordell's neck, but he shrugged her away. He felt no freer now than he did trapped in the luxury hotel.

"Yes!" she nearly shouted, as if daring Ordell to say anything different. He didn't.

Jim made the call and then sat, nursing his drink. There they left him to plan out the signing. Ordell limped in cold silence next to his soon-to-be new guardian.

"It's time to get you to a hospital."

"I don't need a hospital," he grumbled at her, hoping silently to himself that he was right.

38

Departure

Tuesday, October 11, 2185

Harper steered with one hand and held the communicator with the other. She wanted to ask Ordell to call Torrent for her, but she could tell that he was angry, though unlikely to admit to it. Having just forced him to trade his one shot at citizenship for safety, Harper couldn't blame him. She wanted to plead with him that she'd made the right choice, and it wasn't worth it to keep fighting a fight that had gotten him shot at, but she could tell from his face that it wasn't time to have that conversation yet.

She would have to be patient.

Ordell fell asleep in the passenger's seat, offering Harper no distraction from the monotonous drive. She felt the tug of exhaustion as she counted cars, then lamp-posts and finally pedestrians. Her head nodded down and she jerked it back up. At this rate, they wouldn't make it home alive. Between her throbbing feet and Ordell's snoring, she required a distraction.

"Call Torrent," she told the comm.

A click told her when he answered.

"Torrent, where are you?"

She exhaled as she finished with the question, regretting calling him already. Harper wasn't ready to talk. Her heart raced and she felt the relentless pressure of a migraine headache building. She longed for her broken stabilizer to be functional again, but willed herself to be patient and wait for his response as her mood deteriorated.

"I'm in St. Joseph's," he replied. "It's a long story. Are you okay?"

"You sound horrible, Torrent. What's the matter?"

"It's bad, Harper," his voice sounded as though he spoke through swollen lips. "There was an accident."

Harper listened as Torrent delved into the recent past, informing her of the car being totaled by a semi truck. Her first thought was about Brigid.

"Was it HPM?" she asked.

"HPM? No, not them. Railynn blacked-out behind the wheel. I didn't even know it was happening until we were in the other lane."

Harper could tell by the hesitation in his voice that he left something out.

"Torrent, what's going on?"

Torrent sighed audibly. He responded with a waiver in his voice.

"She has a brain tumor, Harper."

Nobody was safe. Nobody would ever be safe. Her entire world crumbled in slow-motion, one person at a time. Harper's lips trembled.

Don't fall apart.

Harper gathered herself, then recounted some of her story to Torrent, but left out the part about Brigid, or about the violence at the Akson Regency. His tenor told her that he neared breaking. The next destructive event would change him in some unknowable but fundamental way, the way fire warps plastic, the way that she felt herself deforming already. She skipped to the part about which he probably cared the most.

"Torrent, we settled the case."

"Really?!"

"I'm signing tomorrow."

"That sounds great, Harps."

It didn't sound great, the flat way he said it. How could anything sound great when Railynn's life hung in the balance? She thought he still kept something from her, though. If she was there, with him, she could figure it out by watching his face. Being on the communicator and driving, she would have to drag it out of him with words.

"Torrent, are you okay?"

"Just tired."

She waited a few minutes, then offered an awkward goodbye, which Torrent returned in a tinny, empty way.

Harper pulled her hand across her face to wipe away tears that she hadn't realize were falling. The sweat and tears mingled together and stung a tiny, invisible cut on her face. The pounding in her head escalated until it replaced her other senses. Her sight dimmed, and she nodded her head just long enough to swerve over into the next lane. Harper swing back between two self-driving cars, which predicted her movement and adjusted accordingly.

Railynn had a brain tumor and would probably die. She'd been so concerned about how Torrent felt that the information hadn't processed correctly. Guilt rose up inside of her, even though she couldn't possibly be the cause of a brain tumor. Unprompted thoughts congealed into her consciousness.

The pain and pressure released from the back of her mind, and she could see again. The rows of cars marched on to their destinations, full of citizens who hadn't noticed her swerving among them. It was an analogy for the march of civilization. Onward and onward, but unaware of the impact on the people involved.

She thought of herself, and Ordell, and Torrent, and Railynn. Two of the four of them were dangerously injured in the hospital. Ordell survived, but at what cost? She dared a glance over to him to see his bushy eyebrows pressed against the glass. A line of drool grotesquely from the corner of his lip to his shoulder. She knew the pain she'd brought into his life. If it hadn't been for her, Ordell would have gone back to Emergent Biotechnology, and that would have been the end of it. No reward, no useless trial, and no being shot at.

It had been all for nothing, and she wanted no more of it.

Harper found herself later at Torrent's apartment. It had been practically her home for so long that it seemed more "her" than her parent's house ever really had. She needed rest, maybe a shower or an evening of peace.

But she had forgotten the walls. As soon as she cracked the door and crossed the threshold with Ordell following groggy from his nap, she remembered the wall of graffiti.

Both she and Ordell were far too tired to care about the state of the apartment. With a forceful shove, Ordell pushed the door back into its frame and successfully locked it.

Harper motioned Ordell silently over to the bed, to let him have that since he was the one with the most injuries. He was so big that the tiny studio-apartment-sized couch wouldn't support his frame anyway. Harper, on the other hand, had room to spare among the plush cushions. She lay her head down, closed her eyes, and passed into a troubled sleep.

* * *

Wednesday, October 12, 2185

When she awoke the next morning, Ordell had again arisen before her and this time had prepared french toast for the both of them. Aside from a few piles of clothing, the apartment was clean, the walls scrubbed, and the buckets put away. She should have expected as much by now, since cleaning was Ordell's modus operandi. Emerging from her sleep cocoon, she confused Ordell with Torrent for a moment from behind. Ordell's big frame corrected that misconception as soon as she stumbled into his back.

"You're awake," he said as he turned and smiled. As he shuffled from the stove to the kitchen counter, still favoring his left leg.

"Today's the day," she said, as matter-of-factly as she could. Then she sat at the kitchen counter and stared at him. He lumbered over to her side and dropped a plate of French toast in front of her, stiffly. He seemed like he was more hurt than he was letting on.

"Ordell, do you hate me?" she asked.

"For what?"

"For settling. I know you wanted to take the court case all the way, and help people. It was selfish of me to settle, but ..."

"No, I don't. I was angry for a while," Ordell admitted, "but with the kind of money we are settling for, we can still have a big impact."

"Even if we can't challenge the Madison Rule any more?"

He nodded.

"And who says we can't? Think about this. It would have taken years, maybe as long as a decade, for that court case to make a difference. There are so many people now in need of help who wouldn't get it. It's only a question of help now, or help later. And with that kind of money, we can do a lot of good now."

She felt her eyes tearing up again and turned away. The

last time she had cried as much as she had in the previous few days was just after her parent's deaths. The tears annoyed her, but she was incapable of stopping herself. She swallowed quietly and stubbornly tried to will the tears away, but a few still escaped.

"You're a good friend, Ordell," she spoke to the wall, but he would hear. She realized that he hadn't. Torrent's flat-screen television had come on before she finished, and she heard a familiar voice echo from it.

"Shills, models, clones," Gregory Ramsey's voice echoed in the tiny apartment. "Call them what you want. The fact is, if we don't change things, there will be more of them than there are us. It's time to come together. Remember that next year, when you elect congresspeople. Who is looking out for you and yours?"

She heard the holovid click back off and breathed sigh of relief. Gregory Ramsey scared her more than HPM did, though she couldn't think of why. Something about the way he looked and always seemed so confident that his approach was the only way. Something was unsettling about someone with such myopic resolve. Unsettling and intriguing, and maybe a little beguiling if she were to admit it.

They spent the rest of the morning preparing for their trip to Emergent Biotechnology. The signing had to take place there for the settlement offer to be accepted. She guessed it was a humiliation thing, making the enemy hovel and cower before them. Given what had happened the last time that they'd tried to settle, though, Harper guessed that they might have just been being prudent. Not everyone at Emergent could be as vindictive as the opposing lawyer seemed to be.

Emergent Biotechnology emulated the motives of the ancient kings. Pillars stood in front of the building, not in the archaic Greek styles, but rectangular columns covered in glass mosaics, jagged corners pointing flamboyantly to the sky. Marble covered massive stairs that took a full stride to cover each step's width. Ordell struggled with his hurt leg over each tier but refused her offer for help. The doors were as wide that he was tall. They slid open well before she reached them, and lingered open well after the group were inside. No administration desk greeted them. Emergent Biotechnology was a place that one didn't visit without knowing where she was going.

Harper felt the intimidation leak into her bones. The only one of their party of three who didn't seem phased was Jim Walsh, there to represent them for the signing. He'd told Harper that his presence was only a precaution and that he expected nothing unusual to happen now that Emergent got what they wanted.

The signing itself was anticlimactic. In the center of a massive room that seemed as large as the entire building looked from the outside, the man in black greeted them with the heartiest smile Harper had ever seen. It was the smile of someone who had overcome adversity and achieved things. She believed, of all the smiles she had seen him wear, that this one was the most authentic.

"I'm glad to see you came to your senses."

"We didn't have much choice, did we?" she spat back at him.

Jim Walsh gave Harper a glance that said she should let him do the talking.

"Let's get to it," he said.

Jackson produced a data-coin and flipped it across the table to Jim Walsh, who stopped its slide with the index and middle fingers of his left hand. When the data-coin ceased moving, the table displayed the first of what Harper knew would be many screens. She watched him slide through each subsequent one as he scrutinized each and provided translation.

"It's very similar," Jim told her after a few minutes of looking it over.

"I don't see any changes here, except an additional line on page twelve, giving up the right to sue in the future for any damages relating to the case."

She signed the document in three places, and then they were done. Despite the intimidation, and despite that ever-widening malicious grin firmly fixed to the face man's face, relief fell on her like sunlight in winter. She felt giddy and excited, but when she looked to Ordell, he looked as though he'd just given up his kidney involuntarily.

"You're free, Ordell!"

He must have heard her, but he didn't respond. She tried to guess what he felt. Did he hear the screams of the people who clambered behind him, and who would never taste their promised freedom after all? Slowly a wry smile crept across his lips, but it seemed physically painful for the corners of his mouth to pull back.

"There's the other matter still, Harper," Jim interrupted her musings, once they were free of the oppressive building. He stopped walking on the massive steps, turned, and looked to her directly in the eye.

"Your arrest is still very much a problem."

Harper hadn't thought about her arrest at all. Until the point that Jim brought it up, she had managed to forget that there was still a criminal case pending.

"Isn't that over now?" she asked, knowing by him bringing it up it wasn't. But it seemed to her that since they'd settled, and Emergent Biotechnology was no longer upset about the incident - surely that meant no further action was necessary.

"No. We settled a civil case. The criminal case is separate. Emergent has no control over what the state does."

"That timing sure was interesting then," she shot back.

"Well, they shouldn't have any control, anyway. And I

doubt that Emergent can stop it going forward now that the prosecutor has begun in any case."

The three of them piled into the spacious back of his volantrae before he spoke again.

"We had a stay until the civil case finished. Now that it's over, we have to discuss what to do."

Waiting. Waiting was all Harper could think of, and she couldn't wait any longer. Jim continued anyway, oblivious to her discomfort, or maybe just rightly judging that the distress was a minor thing compared to the possibility of prison time.

"We can plead it down. Right now, you're in the territory of a first-degree felony. That means between five and a hundred years in prison. And all they have to prove is that you knew about the reward and didn't turn Ordell in."

"I don't understand. Emergent doesn't even want Ordell back anymore."

"It's all going to depend on the prosecutor. The case could get thrown out, especially here in League City - or they can decide to try to make an example. League City is still a part of Texas, and you know how much the rule of law governs here. We'll certainly motion to have it tossed, and the settlement may help that."

"And if not?"

"We don't have a great case. The fact is, you did know about the reward, and yet you still harbored. Doppler will testify – you can be sure of that. It's not a question of will you get prison time. It's a question of how much. I would be a shit lawyer to tell you otherwise."

When working to represent Ordell, she had appreciated Jim's bluntness. At that particular moment, she found it less appealing.

"That's it?"

"Yes, I'm afraid so. Prepare for whatever the outcome may be. Take a day, or even two, but after that, we've got to step back into the ring."

"Jim," she began, "what did happen to Brigid?"

"Attacked on her way to bail you out. Someone shot her at a stoplight as she left her parking garage."

"Is she okay?"

"She will be. Stable now, but it's been a ride."

For the first time, she saw Jim as a man and not just a lawyer. She noticed his red, sleep-deprived eyes.

Everyone around me suffers.

He dropped them back at his office so Harper could retrieve her car. Ordell asked to go back to Harper's parents' house. For some reason, this surprised her. He could have gone back to his own apartment now. But he hadn't been there in months, so maybe he just felt like her house was home. She kind of understood that.

While Ordell showered, Harper made her way into the attic and retrieved the coins that they had left stashed there. Ordell didn't need it. He could afford whatever he wanted with the settlement money - Harper didn't want any of it. She wondered if he would have the rest of his tattoo removed. His life would probably be more comfortable if he did, but would that violate some sort of personal ethic? She would have to ask him someday, maybe, if she ever saw him again.

She let herself out of the door without leaving a note.

Harper arrived at Saint Joseph's to find Torrent in the waiting room, with his head on his hands. He may have been crying, as what she could see of his face was rosy and damp. It was like the rest of his face tried to match his freckles when he was angry, but flushed out like an alcoholic's when he was sad. She ran to him and threw her arms around his shoulders. For a second, it was like it had once been, but then he shrugged her off.

"I can't do this."

Confirmation of what she feared. She backed away a few inches.

"Can't do what?"

"You, Harper. This whole thing. It's too much."

He wasn't looking at her when he said it.

"But..."

"Look at what we've been through, Harps. I'm glad you finally settled, but why did you wait so long? Look around you. We're all broken now."

He blamed her for everything. Harper had long felt the ties between them fading and had known that it was only a matter of time. There had been no time for a dramatic overture from either of them. Sometimes, she'd heard, tragedy brought people together. For her and Torrent, it reduced their relationship to a mechanical thing with no soul. What hurt was more the fact that she had seen the end coming and still hadn't moved to avoid it.

"We can try, Torrent," she muttered in a whisper. Even as she said it, it sounded weak, like the whimper of a beaten dog trying to be pet. She had been through too much to plead harder than that. The wounds had scabbed over and if he didn't want their relationship, she wouldn't fight for it either. She would have walked away then but another question kept her. After enough of a pause to signal that she wasn't going to talk him out of it, she continued.

"How's Railynn doing? Can she see anybody yet?"

"Railynn's gone."

Harper collapsed. This time, she made it to the floor, but she didn't lose consciousness. On the way down, she even watched Torrent grow and tower above her, though he made no move to catch her. She wondered why that was, which was an odd thing to wonder as she slid to the linoleum. She recovered enough presence to put her hands down and break her fall, though the way she'd done it, her wrist screamed with pain as her hand bent back unnaturally. Still, it held, and she avoided cracking her chin open.

Then she pulled herself up to her feet with as much dignity as she could muster, turned, and stormed out through the sliding glass door without looking back. Every reason for being there was gone now. Tears streamed down her face freely. Too much loss blurred her eyes and clawed at her.

Railynn, who had become her fire - extinguished like a burnt-out star. Harper wanted her pink room again, in her parent's house, and the unchanging fluffy matching blankets and boy-band posters on the walls. But that wasn't home anymore. Then she thought that normal was what she wanted, Torrent's home, with the eternally cluttered studio apartment they shared, but that wasn't home either. She had no home.

And she didn't want any of it. She slowed her gait to match her steadying heartbeat as she stepped out onto the scorched pavement and stopped her anxiety with a thought. She opened the door, climbed into her tiny, ancient car, and drove. The destination was secondary. She needed to leave, to go somewhere, anywhere different. In the distance, she heard a buzzing of the communicator through her open window. It took her a moment to realize it was hers and that she must have dropped it on the pavement. It would be Torrent, but what else did she have to say to him? The sound faded to silence as she pulled across the parking lot.

There was nothing Harper could do to bring Railynn back. Her brown eyes and warm smile, even her sly little jealous looks that Harper probably wasn't supposed to see, all of these were gone forever. Larken and Oliver? She nearly turned the car back around but stopped herself. They would find a home without Harper as easily as with her. She couldn't care for them from jail. The worst that would happen to them was the orphanage program, and no matter how

Torrent had incessantly complained, he was living proof that it couldn't have been that bad.

Harper drove herself to a local branch of Texas First Bank and pulled out all of the money she had saved. It neared ten thousand dollars. The banker stalled, giving her that much at once, but in the end, it was her money, so they handed it to her in a bag of cash-coins. She pocketed that along with the others she'd brought from the attic at home. She couldn't live forever on it, but it would make a good start. She shoved the coins into her glove box and headed north.

The steady march of driverless cars reminded her of ants, trailing in a line that grew thinner and thinner the farther away from civilization she traveled. The city faded into suburbs, then into a rural landscape, and finally just country. When the charging stations became scarce, she filled up her battery, just north of Navasota, and then she drove some more.

She left the state on old I-29 out of Amarillo. The distance between charging stations grew wider, then trees disappeared, and eventually even the grass vanished. Finally, it was her alone in dunes as high as skyscrapers towering over her on either side of a dusty, deserted asphalt trail. The sun burned away the lingering losses.

Her lips parted slightly as she breathed in hot desert air. Harper leaned forward over the steering wheel, and stared out over barren sand. She swallowed and her eyes went wide with possibilities. In Canada, a fresh start awaited.

For the first time, she felt free.

39

Funeral

Saturday, October 15, 2185

For a second, Ordell paused his walk between the two white marble pillars at the cemetery entrance. Each post was almost as large as he was, and hosted a marble angel with hollowed out eyes. He shivered on the unusually cold Saturday morning. When he pushed his cold hands down into his coat pockets, his fingertips touched something. He followed along the edges and made it out to be a piece of paper, which he then grasped with two fingers and pulled free.

Ordell recognized the half-triangle across the front. Siblings of the Natural Order used it as a representation of their ascension. The correct positioning was to have the point aiming up towards the sky like an arrow. Ordell shook his head slowly while he unfolded the parchment with care. When the settlement check cleared, he would find a way to help. He read through the handwritten document.

Dear Ordell,

I heard that there might be trouble today. Emergent Biotechnology isn't what it seems if you haven't figured that out yet. I guess neither are we.

You once helped me, and it cost you blood. A construction site, years ago, when I was younger. You warned me, I ignored you, and we both paid the price. It's been a long time since, and I hope you believe that I have grown a lot.

Models do escape, Ordell. Those stories we heard about the ones who got caught – those were not the whole truth. The Siblings of the Natural Order have moved thousands into Canada. We can help you too.

It won't surprise us if you stop the case if what we hear comes to pass, which I guess it has if you're reading this. Keep this letter, and show it to anyone in the Order, and they will help you because I said so. You wouldn't believe it if I told you what has happened since we last met.

Some day, Ordell, I hope to meet you in person again. Since you're reading this, I guess there's still a good chance for that to happen.

Sincerely and Perpetually Yours,

Phineas Lancaster

Ordell looked up from the paper and scanned the gathering crowd. He didn't see anyone who looked like Dan or Mora. Lancaster, even bigger than Ordell, would have stood out in any group - he wasn't there either. Ordell folded the letter and returned it to his pocket. He then made the mental note that he would need to reach out to Lancaster soon. But first, he had to pay his respects. He carefully made his way toward the viewing.

He had only met Railynn Marche once, but he had been impressed by her bravery. Her silhouette in the doorway of Doppler - that tiny girl facing off to three hardened bounty hunters - would have impressed anyone.

His communicator vibrated once to inform him that he had a voice mail to check. Ordell pushed away from the the crowd to find a bit of privacy by a tree before pulling it out of his pocket to answer. His heart skipped as he heard the sound of Harper's voice.

"Ordell, don't look for me. Jarro is yours if you want it <static> three years. The house too. I'm sorry I had to leave. I'm fine, and please know that this isn't as impulsive as it seems. I'm not running from you. Everyone I love has been hurt, and I can't be responsible for their pain any longer."

Then he heard a sigh and there was a brief pause before she continued.

"Anyway ... not coming back. Take care of yourself! I love you."

That was the last he heard from her. He didn't recognize the comm number, and when he called, there was no answer. He tried twice more before he gave up.

"Ordell?"

Torrent's voice interrupted his thoughts. Ordell turned toward him and casually smoothed his new black suit while placing the communicator into an inside pocket. The closest thing he'd ever worn to a suit was a work uniform.

"Have you heard from Harper?"

Ordell considered. He had so many questions of his own that he wanted to ask about what exactly had happened that day when Harper left. He and Torrent weren't close, even with the shared tragedy.

"I haven't talked to her either," he replied, which was technically correct as the voice-mail wasn't a two-way conversation.

"Do you know if she's safe?"

"She has money, and transportation. Probably?"

Torrent nodded toward two policemen standing near the open casket for the viewing.

"It looks like they don't know where she is either."

"Probably a good thing."

Ordell waved at an officer in uniform, who smiled genially and waved back at him as though they were best friends. The other only scowled. Ordell then stepped away from Torrent, in the direction of the casket. He wanted one last look at the woman who had so impacted his life and helped make possible the new journey upon which he was about to embark. As he leaned forward, Torrent hovered behind him. While Ordell glanced into the coffin at Railynn's resting body, he overheard a conversation between Torrent and a woman he didn't recognize who had brought two children with her.

"Here's your uncle Torrent, children," the woman's voice said. Ordell glanced toward the woman and the two children, who she pushed around in a double stroller. They looked just like a combination of Torrent and Railynn. It seemed that such thoughts as infidelity were out of place at the funeral, or he would have guessed that they were Torrent's illegitimate children. That would have painted a very different picture of Torrent from the one Harper had left him with – diligent, faithful, smart, and slightly obtuse. Torrent must have sensed Ordell looking because he turned his freckled face toward him, and there was no longer any point in being discrete.

"What's going to happen to them?" Ordell asked as the woman took the children away, "and who's that?"

"The nanny," Torrent added, looking thoughtfully after them, "and I don't know yet. There's a private boarding school in Washington State that I'm looking at to take them. I think maybe..."

"The Orphan Program?"

Torrent nodded as his face flushed.

"It's all I can do, Ordell. They're too much like her."

"Are they yours?"

At first, Torrent shook his head side-to-side, but then the

shaking slowed, and he paused.

"Close enough, I guess," he said, and then he turned to walk away. Ordell didn't stop him to ask what that meant. He interpreted it as a no and was glad because that meant he didn't have to be disappointed with Torrent after all they'd suffered. Maybe Torrent had a brother or something. Ordell knew nothing about the man except that he had a research lab that worked with modeling.

That evening, Ordell walked through the doors of his own house and crossed the living room in silence. Despite the darkness, the place looked surreal and bright like a brilliant sunset obscured by clouds. He crossed the living room to the back door and stepped through into the salty air. The massive rocking chair to his left was large enough to fit his oversize frame perfectly. He settled into it and felt the hardwood behind the thin cushions against the backs of his thighs. He closed his eyes and imagined Harper's tiny car crossing the border just south of Winnipeg. By the time he dozed to sleep that night, Harper would be in Canada. But then, whatever money she'd had couldn't have been much. He would have to remember to figure out how to get her the money for the house and the bar, nearly seven million dollars if he managed to close the deal. Lawyers were stalling him, but he figured most of that was her money - some of the settlement too.

That would be work for another day. For the evening, he rocked and enjoyed the warm ocean breeze as a free man. The humidity coated his skin in a disgusting oily film as it mixed with his sweat, but all he could do was smile. He could almost hear Aayushi's voice whispering to him over the waves.

THE END

40

Dear Reader,

Thank you for taking the time to read **Models and Citizens**. Part of the reason I write is so that I can share some of these ideas with others, and present some possibilities of the future. It helps me to keep writing when I get feedback and know that readers like you are enjoying the experience of reading my works of fiction! Please let me know by leaving a review, which can also help others find my work too!

Thank you so much for your time! Also, keep on reading! I've included the first chapter of the next book **Bodhi Rising**! Enjoy!

Goodbye for now,
  Andrew

41

The Dying Boy

Tuesday, June 2, 2201

Bodhi survived on the knowledge that if he died right now, his mother would be equal parts guilt-ridden and angry. He had been stupid not to bring enough extra food. The disease that ravaged his body stalked him through the halls of a thick-walled mansion just outside of Winnipeg, Canada. He scowled realizing that he could no longer recall how to navigate the monstrosity of a home.

His supporting hand slipped against the white marble walls, struggling to keep his body upright, and thin shoulders slackened as he neared a potential exit. He slowed to listen for voices, hoping that it led to freedom, confused and directionless in his weakened state. Bodhi lifted his head and strained to distinguish among the sounds emanating through the pale ivory door. He distinguished the high, rich tone of his mother's voice and Aiden's deeper masculine vocalizations as they drifted in from the garden outside. The sound of a United States newscast lay beneath. He pushed against the cold metal, swinging the door outward and revealing four overgrown stairs descending toward a garden as anemic of vegetation as his body was of iron. Any discussion ceased when he crossed over the threshold. Bodhi stiffened his back and let out his breath slowly.

They had been talking about him again.

That probably meant another course of treatments that wouldn't work.

Bodhi's mother swept dark black hair away from her hazel eyes and smiled up at him from where she'd been pulling weeds.

"Hey, Bodhi, how are you?"

A different question hid beneath that veneer of simple greeting. She wanted a rundown of his physiological condition to determine how anxious she should be for the day. His head began to swim as the temporary effects of his back-up chocolate bar faded faster. If he didn't get more food soon or a session with the damned erythropoietin pump to boost his failing kidneys, he would collapse.

He refused to give her the ammunition to lock herself into a downward emotional spiral.

Bodhi pushed his lips up at the corners to reassure, but his knees failed him. He repositioned his feet to stable himself. Bodhi's shoes found no purchase and he tumbled forward headlong toward the dry, rocky dirt. His mother screamed. Aiden rose to lunge toward him, but the man was too far away and too slow. The last thing Bodhi saw was the ground advancing toward his head.

Awake.

A fire burned between his eyes.

The world brightened before him with natural sunlight and warmth as the flash-blindness waned.

He closed his eyes against the repetitive thud of pain in his forehead, diminishing as the grogginess dripped from his mind. Re-opening them, he looked to his left, where his haptic gear lay, an invitation to escape from reality. The nearby erythropoietin pump caught his attention next. This resembled a swag light hanging overhead, issuing forth vibrations that, on some level, told his body to produce more blood cells. His cheeks flushed and he grit his teeth. Weeks of effort to gain more autonomy over his life evaporated due to an inept sense of direction. Collapsing before his overprotective mother would siphon away what was left of his freedom.

He rolled over toward his haptic rig.

"Don't even think about it, Bodhi," came his mother's voice from the opposite direction. Startled at not having seen her, he turned back over and tried to gauge how angry she was. Her eyebrows furrowed over her eyes, set against her sandstone-brown skin. Her fixed jaw usually meant that nothing he told her would matter. He gulped and tried anyway.

"Mom, I just got lost. That's all."

Embarrassment flashed through him, and his cheeks grew hot. Anger flashed in his mind at what he knew was coming. He'd made yet another mistake.

"You got - lost?"

"I went exploring and took a wrong turn. That's all that happened."

She sighed, and her jaw loosened slightly.

"Would it hurt you to be more careful?"

He had been, but he couldn't tell her about the two back-up chocolate bars that had lasted less than thirty minutes between them. Nor could he share that even when they did work to give him energy, the mental clarity was hit or miss. In Aiden's half-underground mansion, the walls all looked the same when his mind went fuzzy. To tell her that would mean that his condition deteriorated, and he wouldn't do that to her.

But now, she had to know.

The best and worst thing about living with Aiden was that he could afford to have a doctor on site at all times. Every time Bodhi's illness flared, his doctor appeared on the scene almost immediately. The routine check-ups and interviews that happened nearly weekly remained tedious, but worse were the visits when Bodhi hurt himself. The doctor didn't even knock, but barged into Bodhi's room with his mother in tow. Despite the doctor's ongoing feud with his mother over formalities, Bodhi liked the man. His crooked teeth beneath a coal-black bowl cut of could be off-putting when he wasn't expected though.

"Ms. Periam," the doctor addressed his mother, and Bodhi felt her reaction before it erupted from her mouth.

"Rawls," she corrected. He always made the same mistake, as though he insisted that the Aiden and his mother be married. He ignored her and engaged in an examination which involved a lot of wand-waving around Bodhi's body and questions about his exhaustion.

"Your son can't keep his blood count up."

"We knew that already." She scowled at him now.

"It's gotten worse, Ms. Periam."

"Rawls, doctor. It's Ms. Rawls. Aiden and I are still not married." Again he gave her no response.

"Can I speak to you in private?"

Bodhi started up from his bed to leave the room and make his way to the virtual reality jump point down the hall. He was still sore from the previous day's fall, but he could use some escape time. Before he reached the door, his mother grabbed him by the arm and pulled him back.

"No. You stay. You're fifteen - you need to know what's

happening with your body. Go on, Doctor."

The doctor shifted his weight and stammered as he began.

"Very well. Even the erythropoietin pump isn't keeping up. Its effects seem to be wearing off. His body -"

The man stopped for a moment then turned to Bodhi directly.

"Your body is shutting down. The increasing shakes and seizures are signs of advanced degenerative muscle and nerve disease. The lack of oxygen is starving it. Life expectancy is lower than it says in your chart because of all the recent changes. They're escalating."

Bodhi's heart skipped, and he leaned forward.

"To what?" Bodhi whispered.

The doctor pulled his lips into a tight line.

"One year, maybe less."

Bodhi's mother's hand shot up to cover a gasp. She drew her head backward and stared at Bodhi with glassy eyes.

His expected life span had just been sliced in half.

"Mom, it's okay," he tried to reassure her, the words falling empty from his mouth as he processed. She only shook her head at his attempts.

"Don't do that," she said. "Nothing about this is okay. It's shit."

For Bodhi, the moment was fuzzy and distant. The idea that he, a fifteen-year-old, could be dead before his sixteenth birthday, seemed ludicrous. Many assumptions about how his future would be crashed down around him. Part of him had expected to meet someone and fall in love. A family he would never have evaporated before his eyes. Somewhere in the back of his mind, a voice told him to be upset and to rage. But it was small and hidden and easy to ignore as all feeling drained out of him.

Bodhi stared up at the ceiling and imagined that he was free of his body, flying around over the trees. He longed for that type of freedom, with the sky stretching before him and the warmth of the sun on his back.

Bodhi tried another coping technique from his endless supply. He imagined running through the forest, in a body that never tired. He dove into a lake in his mind, feeling the cool rush of water as he slid through it. The dirt beneath his healthy feet gripped as he walked, clawing him to the earth. Thick, muscular legs carried his broad shoulders. He jumped and soared up into the sky, landing a few meters away, and it took no more energy than to blink.

But when his eyes drifted back down and landed on his mother, her tears were still there, and his life was still over.